KILLED IN ESCROW

KILLED IN ESCROW

Jennifer L. Jordan

Clover Valley Press, LLC
Duluth, Minnesota

Clover Valley Press, LLC
6286 Homestead Rd.
Duluth, MN 55804-9621
USA

Cover design by Stacie Whaley, i.e. design

Author photo by Ginny Rutherford Photography

Printed in the United States of America on acid-free paper. Sustainable Forestry Initiative® (SFI®) Certified Sourcing.

Library of Congress Control Number: 2014946254

ISBN: 978-0-9846570-8-7

Books by Jennifer L. Jordan

Lauren Vellequette Mystery Series

Killed in Escrow

Kristin Ashe Mystery Series

If No One's Looking

Selective Memory

Disorderly Attachments

Unbearable Losses

Commitment to Die

Existing Solutions

A Safe Place to Sleep

Author's Note

I wrote this book in 2004, but then didn't get around to having it published until ten years later.

Little did I know in 2004 (although I had my suspicions) that the real estate landscape I was documenting would lead to the greatest financial crisis of our lifetimes.

Maybe I should have been writing to Alan Greenspan instead of writing mysteries!

At any rate, this book would have remained a manuscript if it weren't for Charlene Brown of Clover Valley Press. I owe her a debt of gratitude for everything she's done, but most of all, for bringing a part of me to life again.

CHAPTER 1

"I have a confession to make: I hate real estate agents. I know, I am one. But I hate them anyway, and all the other scammers in this shady business. The title companies that steal a thousand bucks every time you refinance, the mortgage brokers who encourage you to take out a new loan three times a year, the appraisers who inflate a property's value, the home inspectors who won't touch roofs, attics, or crawl spaces . . . don't get me started.

"Let me tell you why I'm different. For starters, I don't wear suits. Neither would you if you'd seen the places I've been. I don't drive a luxury car. Why broadcast that I make fat commissions I rarely deserve? I don't advertise using a twenty-year-old photo of myself. Prom was fine once, but no need to repeat it. I don't tell people their houses will sell for more than I know they will. Nor do I tell buyers they can afford a house I know they can't. I don't belong to any chambers or business groups. They're a waste of time and make me feel like a whore."

Ignoring the giggles, gasps, and gapes, I continued.

"I make my living helping people buy and sell homes, but don't go thinking my day is full of deep thoughts about architecture and interior design. The houses—I barely see them anymore. All I see are the clients and their anxieties as they prepare to close one of the biggest deals of their lives. They count on me to take care of the details: the easements, liens, and assessments; the twenty-page contracts and five nitpicky addendums; the financing, point spreads, and prepayment penalties; the brain-draining closings.

"I help sellers who are moving for no good reason and buyers who are clueless about what they value. I negotiate past people's fears and personalities to get deals done, and I do them with dignity and respect. If that appeals to you, and you have a burning desire to be on call every hour of the day, every day of the year, every year of your life, by all means, choose real estate as a career."

Silence followed.

At the back of the room, the ashen-faced teacher took a second to regain her composure. She put her hands together, as if praying, and called out in an unnaturally bright voice, "That was a unique introduction for career day, Ms. Vellequette."

"Please, call me Lauren."

"Thank you, Ms. Vellequette." Ms. Tripp produced a fleeting, insincere smile, before gesturing with her hand, palm upward, to the stranger next to me. "Mr. Rayburn, could you tell us something about yourself?"

The stiff tore his eyes away from the side of my neck, cleared his throat (a big Toastmaster no-no), and gave a five-minute, nasally monologue.

For the first three minutes, the stares didn't subside, and they were all directed at me. I affixed a benign half-smile to my face and did nothing to suppress a sequence of deep yawns. Soon the juniors in the first-period Life Skills class at Central High School yawned in unison.

Eventually Rayburn took the clue and cut short his speech, a fact I noted when he pulled up at six pages, folded the other three handwritten yellow sheets, and meticulously placed them in the inside pocket of his pin-striped blazer. He wiped a thin bead of sweat from his upper lip and reflexively brushed back hair that had vanished.

Another awkward silence ensued while Ms. Tripp struggled to determine if Rayburn had intended to end in the middle of a thought.

When the sounds of fidgeting, shuffling, and whispering threatened her tight reign, she made a decision and clapped her hands. "Time for questions. One at a time, understood?"

Or none at a time. Not a single hand moved toward the ceiling. Not even a digit.

Rayburn and I sat still, in straight-back chairs, like mannequins in a store window. I would have liked a table or desk in front of us, for protection, but we had none.

Apparently accustomed to apathy, the teacher wasted no time before improvising. "Very well. I'll start. Mr. Rayburn, please tell us what qualities someone should possess before deciding to become a real estate agent."

While the other sucker who had been roped into this gig droned on about honesty, attention to detail, and the desire to work hard, I counted the stains on the acoustic ceiling tiles.

That accomplished, I moved on to contemplating what these teenagers saw when they looked forward: a forty-something woman with hair that was somewhere between burgundy and orange, a side effect of the seventh hairdresser in as many months; the ever-so-slight paunch that no amount of hiking, Pilates, or starvation could seem to eliminate; the flat chest I'd acquired, not from nature or choice; the blue eyes that shone a little less brightly each year; the permanent indent in my brow that used to disappear when I wasn't frowning; the dazzling smile, thanks to countless dental appointments, separated only by less exciting times; and the gold Rolex that symbolized the emptiness of my achievements.

A perky girl in the front row crashed my musings, with what sounded like an accusation. "You don't ever get dressed up?"

She hadn't specified me as the target, but I made a safe assumption, based on my outfit of Capri pants, cotton sleeveless shirt, and open-toed flats versus Rayburn's choice of suit, tie, and polished loafers.

"Not anymore."

"Why?" she pressed, without the courtesy of a raised hand.

"Because I don't want to ruin a perfectly good pair of panty hose when I have to get down on the floor to sniff for dog pee," I said sweetly, citing a true example from a house tour earlier in the week.

I looked at her shoe choice and said pointedly, "High heels cause bunions. No need to encourage medical troubles. Plenty will come uninvited."

Sensing a dangerous veer off topic, Ms. Tripp prodded a tall, lanky boy in the back row until he reluctantly opened his mouth, displaying a well-spent investment in silver. "Did you always want to be a real estate agent?" he asked, in a lifeless tone.

Rayburn barged in exuberantly. "My father and uncle were—"

A boy from the side interrupted. "What about her?"

"Me? Did I imagine I'd grow up to be a broker? No," I said quietly. "I wanted to be a private investigator."

A girl in the third row, with blue hair, pounced. "Then why don't you do that?"

"I am, I have been, I will," I said, fumbling. "I've worked for two agencies. At the beginning of the year, I started taking my own cases."

"What kind of cases?" the girl asked, and for a moment, our eyes locked.

Before I could respond, Ms. Tripp broke in. "Sasha, that's not relevant. Today, we're talking about real estate as a career choice."

A collective groan rose, followed by a chorus of questions from all parts of the room. "Have you shot anyone . . . how much do you get paid . . . what kind of equipment do you use . . . do you know any murderers?"

Ms. Tripp had to squelch the cacophony with a sharp whistle, one more suitable for a dog park than a classroom. "The next student who asks a question not related to real estate will be writing an essay on current trends in the housing market, understood?"

It must have been, because there were no more outbursts.

Too bad.

I could have benefited from a fresh perspective on what the future held.

• • •

On my way back to the office, I thought about what I hadn't said to the roomful of adolescents.

I'd made money hand over fist in the past twenty years, a span in which housing prices had tripled in most neighborhoods in the Denver metro area, with my commissions expanding accordingly.

As the market heated up, everyone in the industry acted as if there were no end in sight to the appreciation. Of course, that couldn't hold true, not forever. In recent years, the market had slowed, only incrementally, but enough to make some agents panic.

Not me.

Something had slowed in me long before the market turned.

For some time, the work had felt like a grind. Check the Multiple Listing Service (MLS) ten times each day. Look for new listings from other brokers or edit my own. Pound in "For Sale" signs. Pull them out. Drop off lock boxes. Pick up earnest money. Send and receive contracts. Collect signatures.

Escort buyers from out-of-state on Saturdays. Hold open houses on Sundays.

I needed more stimulation—something to kick me out of the stupor that had begun to settle in at forty and showed no signs of ebbing as I crept toward forty-three.

I'd stopped caring about things that mattered, like finding a soul mate or doing a good deed every day, and started obsessing about everything that didn't, like what time the trash would get picked up or when the screeching bird next door would die.

That's when I realized it was time for therapy or a career change. With no interest in forced introspection or pharmaceuticals, I opted for the latter.

Something new and challenging.

Why private investigation?

Because I figured I could wallow in other people's problems instead of my own. In my twisted thinking, I reasoned there would be something refreshing about feeling pain again, someone else's, when I'd been dead for so long.

I wasted no time pursuing my new path with vigor.

I took a twelve-week course through an adult learning institute, after which I apprenticed with the SOB instructor for six months. In the beginning, I spent most of my time working for free—in Dumpsters digging through the archives of people's lives and in out-of-the-way dives tracking down scumbags. From there, I advanced to minimum wage and inside investigations, which promptly brought on symptoms of carpal tunnel. The SOB had me sitting in front of a computer all day, working on background checks, asset location, and credit histories.

I longed to help the boss with more exciting cases, or at least to have access to high-speed Internet, but he kept all the good stuff to himself and was too cheap to upgrade.

I gleaned every morsel I could from his pea brain, as I dreamed about eventually making a full-time living as a private investigator.

The chances for that increased when I hooked up with a bail bondswoman, an all-but-certain source of referrals, but I chose bed over business. The relationship didn't last, and soon I had neither sex nor leads.

With that promising avenue closed off, I knew I had to keep priming the real estate pump, if for no other reason than to pay for my addiction to the tools of my new trade.

I poured through *P.I. Magazine* the day it arrived in my mailbox and never failed to find a gadget I couldn't live without. I'd spent close to $20,000, with no end in sight. I had my eye on a $600 pair of night-vision binoculars and a $2,000 miniature video camera.

Always something!

As I drove, I was glad I hadn't mentioned any of this in the classroom.

Let the Central High students discover that life was as much about sacrifice as gain, always a maddening negotiation between what you loved and what you could bear.

Let them learn that gradually, at a less soul-crushing pace.

• • •

"I need $500," I said to Bev Stankowski the next morning.

"A witness came forward?"

"Yes, a woman who was following the car that hit Jessica."

"With credible information?" she asked, straightening up.

This was a noticeable change from our meeting two weeks earlier, when she'd sat in a rigid slump on the couch next to my desk.

Today, she looked almost lively. Her blue jeans and purple sweatshirt, with an embroidered wildlife scene, fit less loosely—only two sizes too big, not three. Her round face had more color to it, the dark circles under her eyes had faded, and her cheeks looked less sunken. Her hair, a natural brown with only a few strands of white protruding from the sides, was freshly permed, and her red lipstick had been applied meticulously.

Best of all, she hadn't shed a tear . . . yet.

In our first session, which had lasted more than half a day, she'd cried incessantly. Between sobs, she'd asked why. Above her wails, I'd gathered the gist of her queries.

Why had her daughter gone jogging that day, on that street, at that time? Why had she hit the sidewalk headfirst? Why hadn't the driver stopped to offer assistance? Why couldn't Jessica have lived long enough for her mother to hold her one more time?

Why, why, why?

I'd learned to stop asking that question a hundred heartbreaks ago.

However, as my SOB instructor/employer had reminded me repeatedly, we couldn't cash our private investigation paychecks without paying homage to the three-letter bastard.

In this case, though, the most useful question seemed to be: Who? Who veered onto the bike lane of Highlands Ranch Parkway on Friday, January 30, in the minutes before dawn? Who rammed Jessica Stankowski with such force that her body traveled thirty feet before landing on the adjacent sidewalk?

In my initial meeting with Bev Stankowski, I'd suggested offering a reward to help prompt identification of the driver. Witnesses wouldn't need to testify, and any and all information would be appreciated.

The idea of a cash offering had appalled her. "How can that help? Why wouldn't witnesses have come forward by now?"

"Usually they don't want to get involved."

"Until money spurs them to do the right thing," she'd said, with disgust.

"Sometimes. Also, people don't always know someone's looking for information. Maybe they did see something but assume someone else stepped forward. Maybe they can't be bothered. Maybe they believe the police have all the information they need. A reward campaign disabuses them of all those notions."

I'd seen the uncertainty in her puffy, red eyes, but the concept of five hundred posters, with a photo of her daughter and details of the accident, had intrigued her. How could it not, flyers everywhere, tacked up and passed out, blanketing a one-mile radius from the point of death?

Between sniffs, Bev had asked, "How will you know if someone's telling the truth?"

"By interviewing them and independently verifying parts of their story."

"Can it work?"

"There's a chance."

According to the SOB, a good chance. He swore by the tactic, believing it could overcome indifference, laziness, and reluctance. He'd also warned that it could attract crackpots.

He was accurate on both counts.

After persuading Bev Stankowski to give the campaign a chance, I'd endured a busy fourteen days.

I'd hired three homeless men to blitz the neighborhood with flyers, and the phone had started ringing almost immediately. Oddball tipsters and perverted pranksters, they'd all swarmed to the "up to $10,000" bonanza. With the help of an answering service, I'd sorted through more than a hundred tips so far.

A teenager had called in her twin sister, spitefully claiming she'd caused five accidents in six months. The girl had legitimate concerns, but none that related to my case. I urged her to share her observations with her parents.

A woman with a sultry voice had phoned to report that a man and a woman on her cul-de-sac were having an affair. As if a neighborly fling had anything to do with a hit-and-run accident.

Three psychics had extended their services. Making an executive decision on behalf of the family, I'd politely declined.

A handful of people of all ages had rung up with guesses, as if I were hosting a radio game show, with backstage passes to tonight's concert as the prize.

It wasn't until I heard the soft voice on the other end of the line that I knew I'd found a legitimate witness. By her frightened and tentative nature, she seemed like someone who might have seen death.

I tore myself back to the present, returning my attention to my client, and replied, "I believe the witness, Jackie Cooper, has facts that could help us find the driver."

"At last, a blessing! What does she know?"

"I have to caution you, what she told me may mean nothing to the police."

"I don't care about the law or justice anymore," Bev said bitterly. "Those wheels have turned too slowly for my daughter. I want to look one person in the eye and ask how he can live with himself, how he could have left my baby to die."

"The driver might have been a woman," I said mildly.

"Is that what the witness said?"

"Jackie claims she didn't notice the driver, only the car, an older model burgundy Camry or Maxima. She said drivers always speed on that road, as if they're carrying water to a fire. Those were her exact words."

"Why didn't she come forward sooner?"

"She thought someone behind her stopped."

"What about my pleas through the media?"

"She doesn't watch the news or read the morning papers. They dishearten her," I said, again using the witness's exact phrasing.

"Is she reliable?"

Now that was a good question.

On the plus side, Jackie Cooper had stability in her favor. She'd lived in the same house, about two miles from the site of the accident, for twelve years. She'd managed the same dental practice for thirty years. She'd driven the same route, from her house to the office, at the same time, five days a week, since the road was constructed. She'd often noticed Jessica's early morning jogging and had given her wide berth.

On the less positive side, Jackie lived with her ninety-eight-year-old mother, Pearl, and may have craved excitement. She'd seen the poster the first day it was plastered on utility boxes but had to consult her pastor before stepping forward. Most alarmingly, she'd confided to me that she let her mother win at gin rummy. Not out of benevolence, but because she knew it would shorten the game.

That level of deceit concerned me.

"I hope she's reliable," I answered belatedly.

"Is she doing it for the money?"

Again, I hesitated.

Jackie Cooper wasn't exactly rolling in dough. She drove a 1988 light blue Monte Carlo, her home was in desperate need of rescue from its 1980s décor, and she sold handmade bird feeders to patients at the dental office. Despite all that, though, she hadn't seemed overly concerned about money.

"I don't think so. She dismissed the reward the first time I brought it up, but I convinced her the money rightfully belongs to her. If she accepts it, she plans to donate the funds to her church. I'm not sure I should tell you this—"

"Tell me!" Bev interrupted frantically.

"I'm certain Jackie knows more than she's saying. I'd like to give her the money, with the promise of more."

"What might she know?"

"A description of the driver. A partial plate number. Something."

Bev shot me a look of pure contempt. "Do I have to dole out money for every word that leads to my daughter's killer?"

"Not at all," I said hurriedly. "I just can't get an accurate reading on this witness. If she's holding back, it's out of fear, not greed. I need to get her to trust me, and that takes time. The money would be a nice incentive. People say they don't care, but they do."

"I'll have to trust your judgment," Bev said, with no enthusiasm. "This is good news, I suppose. The first step toward closure."

"It is," I said cautiously, "but I have to brace you for some bad news."

Bev Stankowski eyed me warily. "What?"

"This wasn't an accident."

Her face lost all color. "What are you saying?"

"Jackie Cooper is positive the driver intentionally hit Jessica."

"You can't be telling me . . . "

I finished the treacherous thought for her. "Your daughter was murdered."

CHAPTER 2

"No," Bev Stankowski screamed, a sound that filled the room and cut off my breath.

I spoke slowly, in a soothing voice. "The witness described the action as a hard pull on the steering wheel, not a gradual straying."

"She could have been wrong," Bev said, her voice shaking.

"Possibly. But Jackie Cooper swears she saw the car speed up, swerve, hit your daughter, and continue on without slowing."

"No," she kept repeating, in an anguished whisper.

I took a deep breath. "Do you want me to turn this over to Sergeant Miller?"

Bev shook her head vehemently. "He made it clear five months ago that I should stop calling him, that he'd update me at the appropriate time."

"Are you sure?"

She nodded, at the same frenzied pace. "This doesn't concern him. When we have something specific, I'll call his superiors, not him. I didn't appreciate Sergeant Miller's attitude. He acted as if Jessica's death didn't matter. That's why I hired you."

To make it matter.

From reading the accident report, it appeared as if the officer assigned to the case, Sgt. Joe Miller of the Douglas County Sheriff's Department, had done his job. The bare minimum anyway. This unglamorous category of crime—failure to render assistance—wasn't high on law enforcement's list of priorities, including Miller's, but he'd followed protocol. He'd determined that Jessica Stankowski was running about three to five feet off the side of the road when she was hit. He'd admitted to her mother that, in all likelihood, her daughter had died instantly, although Jessica's time of death was fixed at 6:50 a.m. at Denver Health Medical Center, where paramedics had rushed her.

Miller had measured skid marks, sorted out debris, and issued an alert for a burgundy vehicle with minor damage to the front grill and hood, with possible paint chipping and a cracked windshield. Officers had recovered a burgundy paint sample from the scene but had no way to verify that the color belonged to the hit-and-run incident. The sergeant assured Mrs. Stankowski that the driver would be prosecuted to the full extent of the law, once he or she was apprehended. Those charges could range from leaving the scene of an accident involving death to vehicular homicide.

Then, in so many words, Miller told Bev Stankowski to stop bothering him with her grief.

Easy to understand why she had hired me. The only surprise? That she had waited as long as she had, which didn't make my job any easier. The fact that anyone had called the tip line with credible information represented a small miracle. Typically, memories fade in seconds and never gain acuity in months.

Bev broke into my thoughts. "Do you still feel it would be helpful to retrace Jessica's movements the last week of her life?"

"It could be, but you were concerned about the expense." At our first appointment, she'd explained that her husband didn't support the idea of an investigation and would be furious with her at the cost.

"I don't care about money anymore. If my daughter was murdered, I want you to find her killer. I'll work out the finances. If I have to, I'll take money out of my 401(k) and explain it to my husband next April."

I matched her thin smile. "Let's get started."

With that, we spent the next two hours talking about the last days of Jessica Stankowski's life.

• • •

Later that afternoon, the girl from the third row of the Life Skills class at Central High hovered over my desk. She'd added yellow streaks to her blue hair. An interesting touch.

She wore a lime green skirt that left a foot of thigh showing, a yellow halter top, and purple T-strap sandals.

She dropped her backpack on the floor and checked out the surroundings. When her eyes reached me, they made a rapid scan but didn't rest. She seemed more intent on touching the items on my desk. The bottle of water. The stapler. The desk calendar stuck in the middle of May, which she flipped until she came to the correct date in early June.

"This looks different than I thought," she said absentmindedly.

"How so?"

"Neater. And no cats."

What the hell did that mean? I chose not to pursue it. "Can I help you with something?"

"I've come to work for you."

I gave her a bland look. "I'm not hiring."

"As an intern or apprentice or something," she said, with forced cheer. "It'll look good on my college application. You know, community service shit."

"Aren't you supposed to do that for a nonprofit?"

"Probably, but I'll like this better."

I looked at her skeptically. "You're fascinated by real estate?"

"Yuck, not that. I want to learn how to investigate people."

"If you worked here, you'd have to support me in what I do, which is a lot of real estate and a little detection."

Her disappointment was apparent in the pout. "I could deal, I guess."

"What about school?"

"Prison's out next week. I'll be free until August 23."

"I'll consider it." I tried to match her laser stare, but it unnerved me, and I had to drop my eyes. "Come back Monday afternoon for an interview."

"Can't we do it now?"

"I don't have anything prepared," I said, letting out a breath I'd held since she'd entered the room.

"Can't you make up something?"

"All right," I said tersely. "I'll improvise. What's your name, and what do you—"

She plopped onto the folding chair opposite my desk and cut me off.

"Sasha, and don't ask anything about my scar."

"What scar?"

Sasha pointed to her left leg, where the skin was mashed and twisted. The angry damage extended from her knee to the tips of her toes. "As if you didn't notice."

"I didn't," I lied.

"Usually it's all people see. Anyway, what do you want to know?"

"Here goes . . . you either answer the question or give an opinion, the first thought that comes to mind. Fair enough?"

She pushed air out her lips and dropped further into her slouch. "If I have to."

"Abortion, for or against?"

She shot me a surprised look, but answered instantly. "I don't want one, but women should have a choice. An unwanted baby would have a horrible life."

"Mother Theresa, saint or fraud?"

Sasha giggled and covered her mouth.

"Never mind." I blasted forward. "Sex before marriage?"

"Been there, done that," she said defiantly.

"Sex during marriage?"

She straightened up. "Are you for real?"

I tried to hide my smile. "Sex after marriage?"

She shook her head solemnly. "No sex with an ex."

"Homeschooling?"

"Lame."

"Why?"

"No parent should have that much power."

"The death penalty?"

"Maybe not," she said, after a moment's hesitation. "But the really bad criminals should be chained up and locked away forever. I don't want them coming to get me." She released her two pigtails, which had stuck out from the sides of her head, and held the squiggly hair ties in her mouth. She pulled in unruly strands from all directions and secured them in a loose ponytail. "Are these questions legal in a job interview?"

"I don't know or care."

"Don't you want to know anything about my computer skills?"

"Not particularly," I said, only because I didn't know what to ask. "Can you drive?"

"Yes, and I know PowerPoint."

I managed a faint nod. "Okay."

"That's for presentations. And Excel, for spreadsheets. And Dreamweaver, for websites. And a little bit of Photoshop. I learned that in seventh grade. I make awesome flyers. Do you need flyers?"

"I pay a graphic designer to create all my marketing materials. Back to my questions. Gay marriage?"

"Sure. I might need it myself someday."

I raised an eyebrow. "Really?"

Sasha shrugged, her shoulders almost touching her ears. "Right now, I'm into boys, but last year, it was girls."

"Nuclear war—if or when?"

"When."

"Interest rates, up or down?"

"Up."

"Why?"

"People borrow too much, and it's bad for them. Maybe they'll stop doing it if it costs more."

"Well thought out. Moving on, the Internet?"

Sasha leaned forward, animated. "Millions of windows into the brightest and darkest sides of people's lives. Very cool."

I studied her with open admiration. "That was poetic."

"Thanks. I wrote a paper on it last semester. That was my best line."

"Life after death?"

"Definitely. I'm there. How about you?"

"I'm counting on it," I said quietly. I had to clear my throat before I could speak again. "Big box stores?"

"Third-world rape."

I smiled. "We'll get along just fine."

I stood, signaling the end of our interview.

Sasha didn't budge. Avoiding eye contact, she said loudly, "I have a question."

"Ask it," I said, guessing her query would relate to parking, opportunities for advancement, or hours of operation.

In a stage whisper, she said, "Suicide?"

"The last death," I replied, startling myself.

When Sasha met my steadfast gaze, I could tell she knew what I meant, because our eyes held the same amount of pain.

Neither of us spoke for a few seconds, until she said softly, "Would you be disappointed in a person who did it?"

"Not at all."

"I'll come in Monday," she said, and left.

• • •

For a long time after Sasha's exit, I thought about her suicide question and wondered if I should have answered it differently.

But how could I have?

Three years earlier, I'd had to deal with all degrees of contemplation on death and dying. Not theoretical scenarios—practical, insistent ones.

In the same week, my parents were diagnosed with cancer. Colon cancer for my mother, stage one. Prostate cancer for my father, stage three.

Both were expected to make full recoveries. The experts in white coats practically guaranteed cures. My mother and father scheduled chemo together, one more chance for quality time to bicker.

Within a year, they were dead.

And in that miserable 365-day span, my brother and I had taken turns doing jobs no one should ever have to do.

I told my mother she had to have a colostomy. He told my father he couldn't drive anymore. I cleaned up shit and vomit. He cleaned out our childhood home using day laborers. I contacted my parents' friends and managed to get a fraction to stop by for visits. He contacted a lawyer and drew up wills and medical directives.

We divided up the jobs, but not equally.

My brother lived in Salt Lake City, while my parents and I were in Denver. He had three kids, a wife who didn't work, and a job that didn't pay much. The youngest kid wanted to be an Olympic gymnast, the middle had learning disabilities, and the oldest was constantly threatening to drop out of high school.

It was a bad time for my brother to travel, always a bad time. Something had come up or was coming up or would come up.

Urgent. Unavoidable. So sorry, Lauren. Maybe next time.

I said I understood, but I didn't.

He stayed a state away, and I closed out savings accounts and opened medical supply accounts. I moved my parents to an assisted living facility, to a nursing home, and finally, to a hospice. I supervised doctors, nurses, therapists, and social workers. I bought diapers and wheelchairs and funeral services.

I filled prescriptions, sorted thousands of pills, and fought with Medicare for reimbursement. I interpreted X-rays and blood work and asked for translations from people who knew everything about the human body and nothing about human beings.

I held my mother's hand—our most outward display of affection since my childhood—and trimmed my father's toenails—a familiarity that made us both shrivel.

I chose the clothes my parents would be burned in and paged a priest four times before he would come administer last rites to my mother. I didn't bother calling him for my father.

As I watched their worlds contract, I shrank with them.

I stopped breathing fully in order to block out the smells of death. I stopped calling friends who couldn't understand my reluctance to plan ahead. I stopped sleeping well, hyperalert for the call in the middle of the night. I stopped dating, unable to fathom intimacy.

And I stopped caring.

About almost everything.

Through those wretched times, only one thing had kept me going.

The thought of suicide.

• • •

I couldn't take much more of this crying.

The next morning, in our first hour together at Starbucks, Holly Stamos had dampened my entire stash of tissues. In the second hour, she'd shredded a small stack of napkins. By now, she'd resorted to wiping her eyes and nose with the sleeve of her black, form-fitting workout top.

In the overstuffed chair, where she sat cross-legged, her tiny skeleton looked dwarfed. She wore pink velour sweatpants and black flip-flops and had inserted designer sunglasses in her straight, shoulder-length black hair. Without jewelry or makeup, she could have passed for a teenage cheerleader. She had the perfect visage for the role—heart-shaped face, swollen lips, languid eyes, and porcelain skin. When she wasn't fiddling with her hair, she twisted the band of her runner's watch.

I had repeatedly tried to turn her attention to the weeks immediately preceding her best friend's death, but she continued to digress.

I heard about her elementary school days with Jessica Stankowski, when they played tricks on a babysitter and found a litter of kittens in a field. I heard about middle school adventures, when they ditched school and fought over a boy named Kevin. I heard about teen years, when they worked at a gift shop in Park Meadows Mall and attended every Littleton High School football game. I heard about college escapades at the University of Northern Colorado, when they discovered shots and wrote award-winning poetry. I heard about post-University times, when they looked for jobs and dated twins.

They'd enjoyed a twenty-five-year friendship, and with each recollection came a fresh stream of tears.

I steered the conversation to the more immediate past. "In the weeks before Jessica died, does anything stand out in your mind?"

"I didn't see much of her." Holly sniffled. "She was getting ready to leave for Costa Rica. I was supposed to go with her. We were going to teach microenterprise in a small village, but I was offered a marketing position with a Fortune-100 company in San Diego. I couldn't turn that down, and Jess understood. Now I don't have Jess or the job."

"What happened to the position?"

Holly shrugged listlessly. "I couldn't do it, not after Jess died. It felt wrong to leave Denver."

"Something will come up," I said encouragingly.

"I don't even care anymore. I wish I'd spent more time with Jess. We were supposed to go to lunch the day she died . . ." Holly's voice trailed off helplessly.

"Jessica was working a temp job in Highlands Ranch?"

Holly nodded. "She started last fall."

"She was jogging before work, near the office, when the car hit her?" I said, checking the facts Bev Stankowski had related.

"Yes. She would dress in gym clothes and drive to work early to avoid traffic. After she finished her run through Highlands Ranch, she would come back to the office and put on her work clothes and makeup."

"Jessica was living with her parents in Littleton at the time of the accident?"

Holly nodded. "I had moved back home, too. That was weird, but what else were we supposed to do? Our houses sold so quickly. Jess needed a place to stay before she left for Costa Rica, and I hadn't found an apartment in San Diego."

"A quick sale is actually a good thing," I pointed out.

"That's what our real estate agents said, that we were really lucky because of the time of year. We put our houses on the market in November, and Jess had an offer right away. She had to move before Christmas, and I had to be out in January."

"Where were your houses?"

"In Washington Park, two blocks from each other. I lived on Elizabeth Street, and Jess lived on Josephine. We loved those houses. Sometimes I still drive by them." Holly lowered her voice and leaned toward me, before adding, "I go in Jess's house, to try to feel her again. I can't stop missing her. I don't want to."

"You go in the house on Josephine?"

She released a slight, guilty nod. "I have the key."

That raised my eyebrows. "What about the new owner?"

"She hasn't moved in, not into Jess's house or mine."

"What do you mean?"

"The same woman bought both of our houses."

"An investor?"

"Some woman who uses two names," Holly said dully.

Goose bumps blanketed my arms. "Two names?"

"Deidre Johnston bought Jessica's house. Dee Jackson bought my house, but she was the same woman."

"How do you know?"

"Jess recognized her. She met her at her own closing. Two weeks later, she bumped into her at my closing, but the woman acted like they'd never met."

"Jessica was certain she was the same woman?"

Holly nodded. "After my closing, Jess only spent a minute with her, but when she went to shake her hand, the woman freaked out."

"Why was Jessica at your closing?"

"She wasn't. I went to my closing with my agent, and Dee Jackson was there with her agent. After we signed the papers, the four of us took the elevator down. Jess was in the lobby, waiting for me so we could go out and celebrate."

"Fascinating," I said, chewing on the end of my pencil. "Could I take a look at your closing documents?"

"What are those?"

"The packet of papers they gave you at the closing. They were in a long folder, with the title company's name on them."

"Oh, those," she said, indifferent.

"Do you still have them?" I prodded.

"Somewhere, but what does Dee Jackson buying two houses have to do with Jess's death?"

"I'm not sure, but it's worth pursuing," I said levelly.

I had a feeling about this. A few, in fact. A bad feeling about a woman with two names. A good feeling about the possibility of another lead in the case.

CHAPTER 3

We parted with Holly Stamos agreeing to drop off the paperwork from her closing at her nearest convenience, but we couldn't come to terms on what that meant.

I tried to press her to do it in the next few days, but she waffled when she remembered the duty would require a trip to her storage locker.

As my last task of the day, I called Bev Stankowski and asked if she could locate the papers her daughter Jessica had received at her closing. Bev said she'd check in the safe box, where Jessica stored all her important documents.

I gave myself the remainder of Saturday off.

I figured I needed my rest if a teenager was going to join my one-woman team on Monday.

• • •

Sunday, I performed my meaningless monthly ritual of holding an open house for a property at Eighteenth and Lafayette in central Denver. Meaningless, because no more units in this fourplex would sell. Not in my lifetime. Not at this price. Maybe not at any price.

By some small miracle, before I'd arrived on the scene, the developer had persuaded a friend of his to buy one of the middle units, thus beginning and ending sales momentum. Fortunately, the buyer was a consultant for Oracle who traveled frequently. A small mercy for me, given his allergies. Every time he sneezed, I could hear the violent sound through the thin walls.

To have paid good money for a unit in this building, the guy must have been sick.

Eons ago, I'd written up a contract for the south end unit, but that had come from a real estate agent notorious for submitting offers from out-of-town buyers who never set eyes on the property. As soon as the prospective buyers traipsed through, the offer fell.

Since then, the three units had remained vacant, and for good reason.

The three-story monstrosity was so out of proportion it looked like it might topple over in a big windstorm. Each unit was at least five times as long as it was wide, and a handful of tiny windows on the end units did nothing to mitigate vast expanses of gray stucco and concrete.

I'd held the listing for eighteen months and had extracted four minuscule price decreases out of the developer. Still no action. At my suggestion, he'd landscaped the parkway, but that was no help. The tiered boxes held little more than sickly saplings and mulch, because he'd run out of money for a sprinkler system.

A series of poor decisions in the design and build-out had led to the catastrophe I'd inherited, and no amount of marketing could correct the inherent flaws.

I'd reworded the flyers three times, scrambling the order of the features.

What difference did it make? None.

Pretend for a second that I could find buyers who would tolerate the hideous exterior design and impractical room layout. How could I get them to overlook the graffiti on the telephone pole, utility box, retaining wall, garage door, and sidewalk? Taggers in this particular section of the city had even hit a few trees, an insult that paled in comparison to the trash on the block. Remnants from the shelves of the nearby 7-Eleven were scattered everywhere, with used condoms and syringes thrown in the mix. Forget about the noise at all hours from the auto repair shop on the corner and the smell of grease and garlic from the Chinese restaurant two blocks away—I had greater concerns.

When single women asked if the neighborhood was safe, how could I explain away the electric meter someone had stolen from the back of the building? An act of thievery the customer service rep at Xcel Energy had never heard of in thirty-two years of answering phones, how could I whitewash that?

Assuming buyers could see past all the negatives and still had an interest, would they choose one of the interior units with no natural light and two party walls or opt for one of the end units? How about the end unit that butted up against a thirty-space parking lot with eight-foot-tall weeds on the perimeter? Or why not take the one next to the pit bull that lived next door and raced up and down the chain-link fence, only inches from the property line?

Understandably, I didn't expect any traffic that Sunday afternoon, and I wasn't disappointed.

At my suggestion, the owner had rented contemporary furniture and furnishings for one of the units the first year. Now, in month eighteen, I sat on plastic lawn furniture purchased, by me, at Wal-Mart. I stayed inside, because the street scared me too much, and there wasn't a backyard, courtyard, or balcony anywhere on the creepy property.

Curious neighbors with no money or genuine interest had toured the units six seasons ago. Qualified buyers, attached to savvy brokers, could tell the property was overpriced and stale and hadn't bothered to stop by in months, preferring to visit one of the 27,529 other properties for sale in the Denver metro area.

Why had I taken on this albatross? In the hope of getting my hands on an exclusive listing for the developer's next project, a conversion of a long-stay hotel in the Tech Center into one- and two-bedroom condos. Take 120 units, multiply them by an average sales price of $150,000, times my negotiated two percent commission, and that explained my suffering.

There were a hell of a lot better things to do on a gorgeous June day, with blue sky and eighty-degree weather. Anything but this.

Sacrifice today for gain tomorrow, the story of my life.

I was wondering how I could endure another summer of Sundays at this miserable townhome when I had an epiphany.

I couldn't.

Two hours shy of four o'clock, my advertised quitting time, I pulled up the open house signs and left.

• • •

On the drive back to my apartment, I phoned the seller, George Engleton, who never bothered with chitchat.

"How'd it go?"

"Not well."

"Not much traffic?"

"Zero."

"Maybe next month. The market's supposed to be heating up."

An inferno wouldn't help this property. "We need to talk, George."

"Shoot."

"You need to lower the price."

"Again?"

"Again. There's been no traffic and no interest, almost since we completed the punch lists. I can't sell units if no one will look at them. You want to get the money out of this project in order to transfer it to your hotel conversion deal, right?"

"Correct," he said warily. "How much do we need to knock off?"

"One hundred thousand on the end units and one twenty-five on the middle unit."

"You can't be serious," he said, the frustration in his voice morphing to anger.

Thank God videophones hadn't caught on with the masses.

Nonetheless, I had a vivid picture of George Engleton at that moment.

I could see him pulling at the edges of his gray mustache with both stocky hands, the vein on the side of his head bulging. His green eyes would look as if they were about to explode, and his pockmarked face would be red with exertion. His chest was heaving with the weight of an extra fifty pounds, and right about now, he was reaching for the pipe and malt at his fingertips.

"The project has significant flaws," I said calmly.

"Such as?"

In a cathartic barrage, I listed them.

When I ran out of breath, he responded in a cold tone. "Why didn't you tell me this eighteen months ago?"

"I did, and every month since," I said lightly.

"Not as bluntly," he retorted.

"I was trying to spare your feelings. I know you've put a lot into it."

"Damn right," he said, his baritone deepening. "Try seven months of my life and $1.1 million. Now you want me to give it away!"

I took a deep breath and exhaled quietly before speaking. "I want you to sell each unit for the highest amount a buyer will pay."

"You think that's now $395,000 on the two ends and $365,000 on the other?"

"At best."

"But the unit that sold was appraised at $505,000. How can you come up with these numbers? They'll whittle my margin to nothing."

"When did the $505,000 appraisal come in?" I asked, knowing full well the answer.

"When I sold it."

A year and a half ago. An eternity in real estate. "By an independent appraiser?"

"A friend of mine."

"I see," I said quietly.

"There was nothing fishy about it. My guy pulled a dozen comps to justify that price."

"Appraisals mean nothing. Buyers set prices, not sellers."

"Before I wipe out every dime of profit, I need to get a second opinion."

"Feel free," I said, without emotion. "Bring in another agent, or two, or ten. Show them the marketing I've done and the price adjustments we've made. Have them pull current comps of the immediate area, not Cherry Creek North or LoDo. Spend some time down there yourself," I said pointedly.

I happened to know that the seven months of his life that George claimed he'd devoted to the fourplex project had consisted of one-hour meetings once a week, most held off-site, as he applied his general contracting skills to at least a dozen other projects.

"You're sure we're this far off on the price point?"

"I'm positive. Do some research on your own, interview a few agents, and let me know what you decide."

After the conversation ended, I felt like celebrating.

For the first time in my real estate career, I could have cared less what a seller decided.

• • •

"You have a girl with blue and yellow hair sitting in your reception area," Rollie Austin said, in a loud whisper on Wednesday afternoon.

"I know. Shut the door."

Rollie entered, gently closed the door, and bent over my desk. "What's the story?"

"She's my new intern, Sasha," I said, in a low voice. "She's working for free to learn the ropes."

"Of the real estate game?"

"Of the private investigation business."

Rollie peered at me through rose-colored lenses. "Do you believe that's wise? Are you sure she's good for your image?"

"I'll keep an eye on her, and who cares about image?" I said crossly. "No one comes into this office. I drive fifty thousand miles a year, meeting clients at their convenience."

"What made you choose her?"

"She walked through my door and asked."

"Ah."

Sensing Rollie's judgment, I promptly tacked on, "Sasha has phenomenal computer skills, web and database. She's ten times as fast as I am at research, and she's compiling and cross-referencing every scrap of information I've ever come across."

"I suppose she can't get in too much trouble here in the office, under your direct supervision. But the nose ring and clubfoot boots are a bit off-putting."

"The what?"

"The black boots with the four-inch platforms, the ones she has laced up to her knees."

"I didn't notice."

"Sugar, we've got to work on your observation skills."

"Maybe," I said vaguely, not bothering to inform her that I'd taken in other details of Sasha's appearance. The skull and crossbone earrings and serpentine barrette. The black nail polish and lipstick. The ghostlike color of her skin and pierced tongue. The blue eye shadow and half-jar of mascara.

Rollie hadn't seen anything I hadn't seen. She simply had a different perception of it.

And she was one to talk.

If Mary Kay and Tammy Faye could have conceived, this woman would have resembled their offspring.

Everything about Rollie Austin was oversized: big hair, big nose, big glasses, big teeth, big eyes, big forehead, big bones.

She was three inches taller than I, all in her legs, and she never missed an opportunity to cross and uncross them in every manner. Furiously, sternly, blithely, coyly, suggestively, brusquely—she had a calf and thigh move for every emotion.

She claimed to be forty, but I was certain she'd celebrated that birthday at least twenty-five times.

Rollie bought a new car every year, outright purchase, never a lease. This year's choice was a convertible Nissan 350Z, and she'd had it pimped-out in Los Angeles. Only there could she find the right brand of spinning gold rims and the proper shade of mint-green paint to match her favorite nail polish.

She had the annoying habit of naming cars, and I'd told her "Sassy" was a carjacking waiting to happen. Pity the poor sap who tried to take the family member away from Rollie Austin. She carried an antique derringer in her purse and a nine millimeter semiautomatic handgun in her glove box.

We'd met four months earlier when she came through one of my open houses without broker representation and asked if I would serve as her buyer's agent. At the time, she'd assured me that she wanted to move out of her luxury apartment, on the seventeenth floor of a Cherry Creek high-rise, into a luxury condo in downtown Denver, Capitol Hill, or Cheesman Park.

By now, we both knew that wasn't true.

I'd shown her close to a hundred units, some with outstanding features.

After every outing, she lamented that she hadn't found "it" yet. Maybe the next one . . .

I tolerated the fiction and the monumental waste of time because Rollie Austin happened to own one of the largest private investigation firms in Colorado.

Or so she claimed, but I'd learned over time that most of her boasts were large, sometimes supersized.

Did Austin Investigations employ fifty full-time employees and generate millions in revenues? Probably not, but Rollie had taken me under her wing and sent me contract work, and that's all I cared about.

"Bring me up to speed on the Hesselbach investigation," Rollie said, referring to a cream puff case, with guaranteed billable hours, that she'd turned over to me a month earlier.

The scenario: Kelly Hesselbach, the owner of Kitchen and Bath Remodels, suspected one or more of his employees of stealing from him. A countertop, a toilet, a pedestal sink, a bank of cabinets, and other assorted items had disappeared. Not debilitating losses for a multimillion dollar company, but an insult to an honest man who expected the same from his workers.

Foul-ups were to be expected in an operation that included three warehouses, hundreds of full-time employees, and a computer system that hadn't been updated since the early 1990s. Could the losses have come from inventory mix-ups?

They could have, but they hadn't.

"I've narrowed it down to the Brighton warehouse, to a foreman named Mike Schmidt."

"How'd you get to him?"

"By studying two years of records."

"Next move?"

"I'm going to try to buy some of the stolen goods from him."

Rollie cracked a sly smile. "Tell me more!"

"I spent some time at the Longbranch Bar, which is across the street from the warehouse. Apparently Mike has a side business, offering handyman services at nights and on weekends. I took one of his business cards off the bar's bulletin board. I'm planning to call him and ask him to bid on a kitchen remodel for me."

Rollie nodded. "What type?"

"One that includes a granite countertop that's missing from the inventory at Kitchen and Bath Remodels."

"You go, girl," Rollie said, breaking into a broad grin.

CHAPTER 4

Soon after Rollie departed, as I started to comb the Internet for faux kitchen remodeling inspiration, Sasha entered my office, stumbling across the threshold.

She slouched against the wall. "When do I get my own case?"

"You've been here three days," I said reasonably.

"I know, but I'm bored."

I turned my eyes away from the screen but then had to work to rip my attention from her clothing choices.

The wrap-over brown pants looked like they were on backwards. The sweatshirt that began below her shoulders looked like a remnant from a strapless gown. The black sports bra should have been worn below the top, not above it. And the boots Rollie had noticed were a bit intimidating.

I tried to pretend I was in a normal office environment with a normal coworker. "Did you complete all the filing I gave you?"

"In thirty minutes."

"The database entry?"

"After I upgraded your software," she huffed.

"Cleaned the bathroom?"

"Duh. You were just in there. Why do I have to clean a bathroom down the hall that everyone uses? Doesn't a janitor or something come in at night?"

"Yes, but he doesn't do a very good job, does he?"

"He doesn't do any job. Except maybe empty the trash."

"My point exactly." I scratched my head. "You're completing work faster than I can create it. Maybe you should skip a day."

Sasha looked stricken. "I can't do that."

"Why?"

"I just can't," she muttered.

"Well, I can't conjure up work every day. Why don't you bring something with you tomorrow, something to keep you busy."

She raised her head and looked pleased. "Like my beads?"

"Sure," I said, having no clue what that entailed, but any distraction had to be an improvement over her breathing on me.

"I'll make you a necklace, like mine," she said, gesturing to the strand on her neck, a riot of colorful glass beads.

"Super," I said, relieved to hear beads didn't involve chanting or casting spells.

"I'll need money for supplies."

I rubbed my eyes. "How much?"

"Thirty dollars. Fifty if you want something sweet, with a matching bracelet."

I didn't. I handed her a twenty and a ten from the petty cash stash in my top desk drawer.

"Can I go now? The shop closes at five, and I need time to pick out the right combination to match your eyes and skin tone."

I glanced at my watch. Four hours? Oh well, I supposed that art couldn't be rushed.

"I'll see you tomorrow."

Sasha came around my desk and shocked me with a virtual strangulation. "You have a skinny neck," she said, matter-of-factly.

"Thanks," I replied, a bit uncertainly. I'd never fielded that exact compliment.

"Do you want a choker, a mid-length, or a full-length?"

"Surprise me," I said weakly.

As she scampered out the door, I took a deep breath and tried to release the tension that had started in my toes and climaxed in my shoulder blades.

My God, why hadn't anyone told me teenagers were this high-maintenance?

• • •

Every time I pulled up to my residence, I smiled.

After my parents died, when I realized the toll it took to sort, disperse, and discard a lifetime of possessions, I'd decided to take on the task before I stopped breathing. Better I should throw away love letters, high school annuals, and outdated magazines than leave the burden to someone else.

Especially my brother or his wife.

I'd spent three months moving out of a 3,200-square-foot, four-bedroom townhome in Cherry Creek North into an 800-square-foot, one-bedroom apartment in West Washington Park, and I'd never felt more at home.

I had southern exposure, hardwood floors, and eclectic neighbors, none of whom knew that I owned the building. On the first of the month, like all the other tenants, I slid my check under the apartment manager's door. She forwarded the receipts to my accountant, who deposited them in my corporate account, and we all lived happily ever after.

Especially me.

I loved to look at the replica of the see-through giant pocket watch that stood sentinel in the front of the building or to glance up at the neon *WatchTower* nameplate, complete with timepiece logo.

The three-story glass entryway welcomed visitors with its deep rust and pale olive walls. On two walls, surrounding the rows of metal mailboxes, hundreds of wristwatches hung behind shatter-proof glass. From vintage to modern, the watches created their own museum of timekeeping. Some ticked, others chimed, and a few buzzed. To further the theme of time, black and white photos of watchmakers hung in silver frames, suspended from the ceiling, lit by an eight-bulb fixture that resembled the eyeglass used in the trade. A grandfather clock from the early 1800s stood in the corner, away from the door. Even the pattern in the tile on the floor, random accents of circles, squares, and lines, brought forth images of hourglasses.

I bought the building after an acquaintance of mine had gotten in over his head. In the past ten years, he'd snatched up every Class B and Class C apartment building he could find in central Denver. Most of the buildings he'd acquired were similar to mine: blonde brick, built in the 1950s or 1960s, three stories, flat roofs, limited parking. Nothing wrong with them, but nothing right, either.

The acquaintance had started each project by attaching unique architectural features to the outside walls to break up the building's monolithic appearance. Moving inside, he'd remodeled the kitchens and baths, hired interior designers to pick out striking paint and carpet combinations, and added laundry facilities and workout rooms.

He had done everything right, except accurately measure his ambition against available cash.

When he ran low on funds midway through the renovation of one of his buildings, he had to liquidate something, and pronto.

I'd picked up the building for the distressed rate of $1.05 million and beamed every month when I saw the statements from my accountant. After eighteen renters' checks were deposited and all the bills were paid, a healthy amount of cash remained.

Did I feel bad for my acquaintance or guilty that I'd taken advantage of his crisis? Not for a moment. Developers who tried to make their fortunes on the velocity of money lived and died by their own greed.

Plus, who was I to begrudge myself a real estate maneuver now and again?

• • •

The next morning, Bev Jankowski stopped by my office.

"I thought you might like this," she said, handing me a small electronic device. "It belonged to Jessica. It may be of some use, if you can figure out how to turn it on. My husband and I haven't had the energy."

"Thanks," I said, turning the black gadget over in my hands.

"Do you know how it works?"

"I'll take care of it," I said, unwilling to admit my ignorance.

"Let me know what you find. Also, here are the papers you wanted, from the closings. Jessica's and Holly's. Holly needed a little nudging, so I went with her to her storage locker. We made a day of it, with lunch and a nice walk around Columbine Lake."

"Thanks for doing that. I've been anxious to review these."

"You believe the woman who bought the girls' houses may be involved in Jessica's death?"

"It's too soon to tell, but I'll follow up immediately."

"Why would someone want two houses?"

Good question, but I'd given the matter a bit of thought.

Assuming the buyer was the same woman, more than likely she was an investor, eager to cash in on the money to be made in that neighborhood.

The Washington Park neighborhood, where Jessica and Holly had purchased homes, was one of the hottest neighborhoods in Denver. Centrally located, it was comprised of bungalows and Tudors that dated to the early 1930s. Little by little over the previous decade, many of the small houses had been fixed up or scraped off, making an untouched house a find.

It made sense that an investor would be attracted to the area, and not particularly surprising that someone would buy two properties. According to Holly, neither her house nor Jessica's had undergone any type of significant remodeling, making them prime targets for a part-time fixer-upper.

The venture had appeal. Serve as your own general contractor, hire a core group of reliable subs, and if everything went well, you could pull $30,000 to $40,000 profit out of each house, for six months of work and minimal risk.

As I presented my theories to Bev Stankowski, she listened attentively. She agreed with most of my conjecture, but posed a key question. "If it's the same woman, why would she buy the houses using different names?"

"I don't know, but I'll start with the information in these packets. I'll contact the agents, the title companies, the mortgage brokers. I'll get to the bottom of it, trust me."

"I do," she said briefly. "What was the other matter you wished to discuss?"

"This may be premature," I started cautiously, "but another witness called in response to our flyer. Keelie Dunham. She's in a soccer camp for the next few days, but I've arranged to meet with her next Tuesday."

"That's wonderful!" Bev said, cheeks flush with expectation.

"I don't want to get your hopes up—"

"It's too late for that."

"I'm fairly certain she's telling the truth."

"But?" she said, reacting to my uncertainty.

"She's young."

"How young?"

"Fifth grade."

"Splendid," Bev Stankowski said, unfazed. "That's when children are the most observant."

CHAPTER 5

"How would you like your own case?" I said nonchalantly, as Sasha settled in at her desk on Friday morning.

Her face lit up. "For real?"

"For real."

"What is it? Murder?"

I took a seat next to her. "Not exactly."

"Kidnapping?"

I shook my head and smiled faintly.

"Burglary or missing persons?" She squirmed in her chair. "Tell me!"

"Try fraud."

"Fraud," she said, elated. "Where do I go? What do I do?"

"Our client is the Vista Hills Golf Course, up north, off 120th and Monaco. You'll talk to the head pro, Kip Livingston."

"Did someone steal something? Is an employee working under an assumed name?"

"Slow down," I said, amused at Sasha's nervousness. "I want to go over interviewing techniques with you first, before we get into the details of Kip's problem."

Her face fell. "That's no fun."

"I want you to concentrate. What I'm about to teach, you can apply to any case. Are you ready?"

"In a minute." She rummaged through her backpack and pulled out a cell phone, an iPod, sunglasses, tangerine jelly beans, and a photo of whales before retrieving a bottle of nail polish. She started in on her toenails.

I looked at her, stunned. "Aren't you going to take notes?"

She stopped midbrushstroke, unabashed. "Do you think I should?"

"Yes," I said, barely checking my temper.

Sasha dove into the pack and came up with a device about the size of a deck of playing cards. I waited for a pen and paper to emerge, but they never did.

After an awkward pause, she said in a snippy tone, "Speak."

"What's that, a tape recorder?"

"A PDA." In response to my blank look, she added, "A personal digital assistant. A Palm Pilot. Everyone has one. Except you."

I had to bite my tongue to rise above the sarcasm. "What can you do with it?"

"Everything. Notes. Address book. Daily planner. To-do list. Calendar. Memos. Budgets. Lists."

"You use it for all that?"

She cracked a guilty smile. "Mostly I play games and listen to music. Sometimes I download e-mail."

"A client gave me something that looks like that, one that belonged to her dead daughter. How long would it take for you to print out her calendar and address book and any other relevant information?"

"About two seconds. All you have to do is put the PDA in a cradle and sync it with—"

I put up my hands. "No details."

"It's easy," she assured me. "I'll do it tomorrow when I come in."

"That soon?" Somehow, I didn't feel ready to turn over such an important project.

"I'd do it now, but I need a USB port cable, Microsoft Outlook, and a synchronization utility—"

"I'm in no hurry," I said hastily. "How do you know all this?"

"I taught myself by reading the directions. May I start taking notes now?" she said, her voice dripping with condescension.

"Anytime," I said irritably.

Something about feeling as if I had been born into the wrong generation—electronically—miffed me. The generations before me could avoid the revolution, and the ones behind me had been trained on computers since elementary school. Where did that leave people my age? Pissed off in the middle.

Sasha pulled out a pen-like stylus, tapped on the screen a few times, and began to glide the instrument across the screen.

"What did you just write?"

"Interviewing techniques."

"Okay," I said, more calmly. "All investigations should begin with a visit to the site of the incident."

"Did my incident take place at the golf course?"

"Yes, but I'm talking in general terms here. Could you forget about Vista Hills for a minute?"

"If you say so."

"Next, you need to understand the issues of the investigation, what's in dispute and what's at stake. Whenever possible, you'll conduct interviews in person, not by phone or e-mail."

"That's a waste of time."

"Not at all. You can pick up clues from body language and from people's surroundings. You need to get them to like you. That's easier to do face-to-face. Be relaxed, and you'll put witnesses at ease. Start by handing them a business card, make small talk, break the ice."

"I don't have business cards."

"You can order a set at Office Depot this afternoon."

"Can't I have nice ones, with lots of pretty colors? There's a company online that'll send you—"

"No," I said sharply. "Take one of mine and match it. We're investigators, not interior decorators."

"You're in a bad mood today."

"I wasn't before this conversation," I said, not quite truthfully. I'd been in a funky mood since I'd woken up, one that hadn't improved with three scoops of ice cream for breakfast. "Before the interview, decide on your five most critical questions and write them down. After you've established rapport, ask your key questions as soon as you can. Get your subjects' full legal names, and don't refer to them as witnesses. That scares them."

"What if people won't answer my questions?"

"We'll threaten them with a subpoena."

"What's that?"

"A court order compelling them to show up at a deposition, hearing, or trial."

"Doesn't that scare them?"

"Hopefully, because subpoenas are a pain to get. That's why you use them as a last resort."

She nodded knowingly. "I get it."

"Here are some good general questions. Where were you at the time you saw what you saw? Were there any obstructions? Was anyone with you? Did you have anything to drink at the time?"

Sasha frowned in concentration. "Slow down!"

"As you delve further, stop and dissect every answer, splitting it into more questions. To obtain specific answers, you have to ask specific questions."

"What if people lie?"

"They will. You can count on it, but lies reveal as much as the truth."

"How am I supposed to know if they're lying?"

"You get a feel for it by watching their mannerisms and comparing their responses to the ones you receive from other witnesses. Typically, you'll catch them in a lie because someone or something will contradict their version of events."

Sasha's eyes were glued to the PDA screen. "I never knew all this."

I hadn't either, not before I'd sat through the SOB instructor's course. He claimed to have conducted 10,000 interviews. I was behind him by about 9,950, but I added a few tips from my own experience. "Watch where you sit in the room. Never get boxed in."

Panic spread across Sasha's face. "Could something happen to me?"

"It won't. Not with this golf case. Just be careful. That's a good rule of thumb, whatever the circumstances."

"Are you sure?"

"Please! This is a country club. But I'll go with you, if you'd like."

"Maybe," she said, her cockiness in remission.

"Whenever someone offers you food or drink, accept, regardless of whether you feel hungry or thirsty."

"What if I'm allergic to it, like shellfish?"

"I swear to God—" I started, before adopting a more patient tone.

"Not that, but everything else. Refreshments help you bond."

"What about the calories?"

"Take small sips—" I began, before matching her impish smile. "Could you try to focus?"

"I fooled Lauren!" she said, with way too much satisfaction.

I ignored her thigh-slapping display. "At some point in the interview, ask if the subject is on any type of medication or under the influence of alcohol or drugs."

"Isn't that an invasion of privacy?"

"Everything we do is an invasion, Sasha. You get used to it after a while."

"Do you solve all your cases?"

"I'm not sure *solve* is the accurate term," I said, after a moment's consideration. "I usually obtain the information the client is seeking. I build facts until I've exhausted all avenues, which requires patience and problem solving. Do you think you're ready for this?"

"I was born ready," she said, full confidence restored.

"Here's your first test. Describe the man down the hall, the one you said leers at you."

"He's fat and bald," Sasha said, without hesitation.

"And?"

"Old."

"And?"

"And . . . I don't know. I try not to look at him. He makes me feel slimy."

"What color's the carpet in his office?"

"Brown or tan. Or gray," she said, agitated. "Faded. Why are you doing this to me?"

"Now you know what witnesses go through. They don't pay attention, and we come along and ask for details they never absorbed or can't remember. They often become frustrated. You'll need to gently probe for accurate facts. With people, write this down, we need—"

"I'm writing as fast as I can."

"Good. With people, we're looking for specifics of sex, race, age, height, weight, and build."

"Slower!"

"Hair—color, length, and style. Eyes—color, size, and shape. Facial hair.

Glasses. Jewelry. Clothes. Distinctive speech patterns. Tattoos or piercings. Scars or blemishes. Did you get all that?"

"Enough."

"Are you ready to hear about your case now?"

Sasha looked at me expectantly and bounced up and down in her seat.

I spoke solemnly. "Two weeks ago, a golfer hit a hole in one on the seventh hole of Vista Hills Golf Course. Kip Livingston, the head pro, is hiring us to independently verify that the player, Bud Cauldron, is telling the truth."

Her eyes widened. "That's it?"

Not exactly the reaction I'd expected. "Is there a problem?"

"This sucks!"

CHAPTER 6

I overlooked the poor reception and added a pertinent detail to the case. "The seventh hole is 520 yards long."

"So?"

Sasha had perfected the sullen look, I had to give her that. "It's a par-five, which means it takes talented golfers five strokes."

"So?"

"Bud Cauldron did it in one," I said, my tone conveying the remote likelihood.

"Good for him," she said lifelessly.

"Pros on the golf tour can't hit a ball that far. No one hits it 1,520 feet with one swing, much less accurately enough to roll the ball into a four-inch cup."

Sasha studied her fingernails. "Someone must have."

"Do you know what the odds are?"

"Do I care?" she said, under her breath.

"On any given hole, six thousand to one for a club pro, three thousand to one for a PGA tour pro."

"Big deal."

"If this is true, Bud Cauldron will set a record."

"Who cares? Golf is such a stupid sport."

I'd had about enough lip for one session. "Not to our client, it's not. Not the longest hole in one in American history. You can have an immediate attitude adjustment, or you can pass on this case," I said, my voice rising.

"Pass," she replied instantly. "Totally."

My reply came in the form of an ominous whisper. "Then you're fired."

That roused her out of a slouch. "You can't do that."

"I just did. You can still do office work, but I'm not wasting any more time training you on fieldwork."

"This was my first case," she said, employing her patented little girl voice. Most five-year-olds had more developed vocal chords.

"And your last."

"That's not fair. Can't I have another chance?"

After a long pause, I said, "One, but you need to take this seriously."

She straightened up. "I will. I promise."

"Clients pay us good money to care about their concerns, regardless of whether they interest us."

"Does that mean you don't like golf?"

"I hate it," I said fiercely. "Why do you think I'm assigning you the case?"

With that, we both laughed, she more nervously than I.

The merriment ended with her next whine. "How am I supposed to get to the golf course on my Vespa?"

"Where's your car?"

"I don't have a car."

"Borrow one from your parents."

The pained look returned. "I don't have parents."

"Very funny."

"It's true," she said offhandedly. "I live with a foster family."

"Why?"

Sasha chewed her lower lip. "Because."

I chose not to engage. "Can't you borrow a car from your foster parents?"

"Not until I get my license. They're anal about that."

"You don't have a license?" I screeched.

"I have my learner's permit."

"In your job interview, I explicitly asked about driving," I said, trying to hold on to what little of my composure remained. "Do you remember answering in the affirmative?"

Sasha shrugged. "You asked if I could drive. I can drive. I took stupid Driver's Ed for one whole semester. I had to give up a commercial art class for it. I almost fell asleep every afternoon, but my instructor said I rock at parallel parking."

"Why haven't you taken the driver's test?"

"Because if I do, the witch will make me run her errands."

"The witch?"

"My foster mom."

"Do you want to learn how to be a full-fledged private investigator?"

Sasha nodded.

"Do you want your own case?"

"Yes."

"How badly?"

She turned it on with a pleading expression and the return of the squeaky voice. "Pretty please."

I rolled my eyes. "Oh, for Christ's sake! Take the bus to your first appointment with Kip Livingston, and schedule a time for your driver's exam."

She looked horrified. "The bus? I've never ridden the bus. I don't know how."

"You stand at a bus stop. When the bus comes, you step on and put $1.75 in the holder. When you're ready to get off, you pull a cord. After the bus comes to a complete stop, you stand and walk off."

"Which bus?"

"Look online for the bus schedule, and figure out how to get to 120th and Monaco. You'll probably have to transfer."

"I can't ride the bus," she wailed. "Poor people ride the bus."

"How do you know who rides the bus, if you've never done it?"

Sasha scowled. "I see them waiting at bus stops. They look dirty."

"All kinds of people ride the bus, including people who have jobs but no licenses," I said meaningfully.

"Do I have to?"

I didn't budge. "That's the deal."

"If I find a ride to the golf course, will you take me to get my license?"

"You can't ask your foster mother for a ride to the DMV?"

"No, don't make me," she whimpered.

"You're that afraid of her?"

"You would be, too, if you met the witch."

"All right," I said reluctantly. "But you should stand up for yourself. Tell her you're her daughter, not her personal servant."

"Foster daughter," Sasha corrected reflexively. "You want me to say that to her?"

"Yes, you deserve to be treated with respect."

"Did you talk to your parents like that, when you were my age?"

"No," I admitted, unable to add that I'd barely managed it when I was forty.

• • •

I enjoyed a relaxing weekend free of Sasha, open houses, real estate showings, and private investigation work.

I slept in both days, read the newspaper cover to cover, watched two movies, exercised three times, and devoured gourmet meals—all without ever leaving the comfort of my air-conditioned apartment.

Monday morning, bright and early, I returned to the real world of responsibility.

At half past six, a huge inconvenience for me, I was at the office, preparing for the arrival of Dan Reed, the real estate agent who had sold Jessica Stankowski's house in Washington Park.

On Thursday, I'd retrieved his business card from the closing papers Jessica's mother had dropped off. When I'd called to schedule the appointment, he'd chosen the hour—tucked between a morning workout at the Glendale Bally's and a mandatory staff meeting at his Cherry Creek office.

I put on a pot of coffee, reviewed my notes, and tried to adapt to the preternaturally early start to my day. My body felt as if it were in a different time zone than my mind, and it didn't help matters when Dan Reed showed up, high on exercise endorphins.

For the first five minutes, he stood across from my desk, legs spread wide, hands in his pockets. He couldn't have been older than twenty-five, and he had broad shoulders, a small head, and close-cropped, reddish-brown, wavy hair. He wore black pants, a white ribbed muscle shirt, and a tawny suede jacket.

He must have suffered from the delusion that he'd called the meeting, because after I convinced him to sit down, he spent the next twenty minutes outlining his far-flung career plans.

He intended to set up a real estate private equity fund, and he was certain he could achieve an annual rate of return of 14 to 29 percent for his investors. Numbers he'd derived from punching fiction and fantasy into an Excel spreadsheet.

What qualified him to set up and manage this fund? One year of selling the Kraft food line to gas stations across Wyoming, six months as a real estate agent, an annual income of $23,000, and a net worth of negative $30,000.

When he finally sat, he squirmed restlessly and pressed his thumb into the indent in his chin as he offered to let me in on the ground floor as one of his founding investors.

I politely declined, before wrestling the topic of conversation to one that interested me. "I need to ask you a few questions about the Jessica Stankowski deal."

"Bummer she died, isn't it?" he said, with about as much regret as if he'd found out there was a ten-minute wait at Chili's.

"How well did you know her?"

"Not very. We met at church."

"Let me guess, you canvas the services for potential clients," I said, only partially kidding.

He looked at me, as if I were Miss Cleo's mentor. "How'd you know? Every week, I go to the Saturday night mass and two Sunday services. I met Jessica last fall, through the young singles group. I could tell she dug me. I asked her out, but she turned me down because of the mission to Costa Rica."

"Oh sure," I thought, but said aloud, "Was she your first client?"

"Second. My mom was my first."

"Was there anything unusual about the deal?"

Dan thought for a moment. "No, not really."

"The buyer, Deidre Johnston, what can you tell me about her?"

He flashed a wicked smile. "She paid full price."

"And . . ."

"That's all I cared about."

"That's all you remember?" I said, beyond aggravated.

He shrugged.

I kept my voice under control and continued prodding, but he told me nothing else.

He couldn't remember what Deidre Johnston looked like, how she acted, or what she said.

Before he wasted any more of my day, I marshaled him to the door.

At the threshold, he said, almost as an afterthought, "As a more experienced agent, do you have any advice for me?"

"Get out while you can," I said, not smiling.

His grin never faded. "Come on!"

"I'm serious."

"I listened to 168 hours of lectures to get my real estate license, and everyone in my office is a millionaire. Why would I quit?"

I decided to humor him. "You really want to know how to be successful?"

Dan nodded earnestly.

"Find a niche of services, the more narrow the better, and market on a consistent basis."

He frowned. "Why would I limit myself?"

"Every person in Denver knows at least one real estate agent, and usually more. You need to separate yourself from the other brokers competing for the same listings and buyers. Specialize."

"I don't understand."

Had Dan Reed paid someone to pass the Colorado Broker Licensing Exam or flunked it the first fourteen times?

"First-time home buyers," I said, way past patient. "Or empty nesters. Go after corporate relocations or foreclosed properties. Choose an area of Denver and become the neighborhood pro. Do something to distinguish yourself."

He raised his eyebrows. "That's all I have to do?"

"No," I said, my last nerve jangled. "You have to put together a marketing plan and stick with it."

"What's wrong with word of mouth?"

"Nothing, if you want to starve. If you prefer to eat, you have to do something to promote word of mouth."

"What do you do?"

"I give out expensive gifts and send a quarterly newsletter," I said, divulging my most effective forms of marketing.

He guffawed. "The IRS only allows you to deduct $25 for gifts, and no one reads junk mail."

Obviously, my finer points were lost on this dunce. Maybe it was a guy thing, maybe it was an IQ thing.

In frustration, I brushed back my hair and stared at him hard, debating whether to expound on the secrets to my fat paychecks.

When I came to a closing, I always arrived armed with gifts, starting with candies, cookies, or pastries. The sugar-laden treats helped counter the numbing effects of signing paper after paper, and if a few treats were left over, I made the sacrifice and ate them on my way home.

I also brought bouquets of flowers and $100 American Express gift certificates for buyers and sellers. No other agents did this. Most of my colleagues stuck to the paltry $25 IRS limit and distributed presents only to the parties they represented.

Foolish move.

With the size checks we real estate agents took home these days, twenty-five bucks was an insult. A few agents with marketing savvy exceeded the tax-deductible restraint, but I'd never met one who lavished gifts on everyone involved, a practice I'd begun with my first deal.

The gifts had proven their value over the years, leading to copious amounts of repeat business.

As for Dan Reed's reference to junk mail, well, I resented that.

My quarterly newsletters were full of interesting tips and articles appropriate to the season. The upcoming one would include ideas for staging a home for a quick sale, water conservation suggestions, a list of Colorado weekend getaways, and a recipe for bing cherry smoothies.

Granted, I'd grown weary of folding twelve hundred newsletters, stuffing and licking envelopes, and attaching mailing labels and stamps, but my past, present, and future clients seemed to enjoy the content. After every issue, I received compliments and new listings.

Last year, with a marketing plan that only included the gifts and newsletters, I'd closed twenty-seven deals and cleared $243,000 in commissions.

Did I tell Dan Reed, future uber-mogul, any of this?

Nope.

I patted him on the arm, thanked him for stopping by, and wished him well with his real estate career.

• • •

The next day, around lunchtime, I took a trip to Highlands Ranch, to visit the ten-year-old who might have witnessed the hit-and-run accident that had killed Jessica Stankowski.

Pulling up to the home where Keelie Dunham lived, I was reminded of everything that I disliked about Highlands Ranch: lots too small, houses too close together, two- and three-car garages overwhelming the architecture, shoddy construction, and bland paint colors dictated by home owners' associations.

I parked my car on the street, and as I walked up the driveway, I observed a young girl on the front porch. She sat with her back to me, legs crossed, bent over.

When I neared, she turned her head slightly but didn't divert her attention from the flip phone she held in both hands.

"Hi, there," I said cheerily. "I'm Lauren Vellequette."

"I know. I just told Morgan you're here."

"Morgan?"

"She's my stupid nanny," the girl said, raising her voice to accentuate "stupid."

"Are you Keelie Dunham?"

"Yes," she said with a pained sigh, spinning around in a smooth motion.

She was dressed in a black-and-white plaid skirt, teal shirt with Yosemite National Park graphics, and no shoes. Her shoulder-length blonde hair was parted in the middle, held down by a headdress that looked as if it had been made from pink party streamers. Her freckled face was sunburned, and her nose was peeling.

"Is your mom or dad home?"

"No," she said, waving the phone at me as if it were a magic wand. "Just Morgan."

"Can you ask her to come out here?"

"I just did. She's busy."

"With?"

"Talking to her stupid boyfriend. But she says it's okay to talk to you." Keelie turned the phone around, and I read the text: *u can talk*.

I hesitated. "Where are your mom and dad?"

"At work," she said impatiently. "That's why stupid Morgan's here. I hate her," she said, not bothering to lower her voice.

I sat on the porch step, a few feet away from her. "Why don't you like her?"

"Because all she ever does is talk on the phone to her stupid boyfriend."

"Mmm," I said sympathetically.

"Because she makes sweet potato fries in our oven, and she ruined one of our cookie sheets."

"That's annoying."

"Because she makes me go with her on her stupid errands. Why can't she do them some other time?"

"How long has she been your nanny?"

"Since last year. She's so stupid, and she doesn't like to do the things I like to do."

"Like what?"

"Like soccer. And running. And dance. I love dance!"

"Speaking of running," I said slowly, watching for a reaction that didn't come. Her attention was back on the phone, her thumbs moving at a rapid pace, controlling objects in a game. "Your mom told me that you might have seen someone hurt while you were jogging. Back in January. Is that true?"

She nodded solemnly.

"Did you tell anyone about the accident, when it happened?"

She shook her head and raised the phone closer to her eyes.

"Why not?"

"I didn't want to talk about it."

"Why?"

She lowered her head, until it was almost touching her knees. "It was stupid. And it made me sad."

"But you want to talk now?"

"Maybe," Keelie mumbled.

"Because of the reward money?" I said, without judgment. "You saw the flyer?"

She looked at me out of the corner of her eye, never raising her head. "Maybe. Is that bad?"

"Not at all. I'm glad you want to help. And I'll give you a hundred dollars as a thank you."

Her head snapped up, and she looked at me shrewdly. "The flyer said $10,000."

"Up to $10,000," I corrected quickly. "Depending on the circumstances and how many witnesses come forward."

"Did someone else see the accident?"

"Yes."

"What did they see?"

"I can't tell you that."

"Because it's a secret?"

"No, because I don't want it to influence what you remember."

"Do they get money?"

"Yes."

"How much?"

"The same as you," I lied, feeling a twinge of guilt.

"And I only get a hundred?"

I nodded, guilt gone, unwilling to give in to a tween shakedown.

She scrunched up one cheek and, after a long silence, said, "Okay, I guess."

I extracted a small notebook from my purse. "Would it be okay if I take some notes?"

Keelie nodded and watched with interest as I wrote her name and the current date on the top of the page.

"So you saw the accident?"

"Parts of it?" she said, her nose, once again, buried in the phone.

"How did you see it?"

"I was jogging with the lady."

"With her?" I said, surprised.

"Well, behind," Keelie admitted, in a quiet voice. "That's how we liked to run. With each other, but a little apart."

"Really?" I said, careful to reveal nothing with my tone. "Did your mom or dad know you were jogging with someone?"

"No. I'm supposed to stay away from strangers."

"But you don't like jogging alone?"

She shook her head vigorously. "It's more fun to run with someone, but all of my friends think running is stupid. And they don't like to get up early."

"Me neither," I said with feeling, which made her smile slightly. "How long had you and the lady been jogging together?"

"I don't know. Awhile."

"Did the lady jogger ever talk to you?"

"No," she said, pulling the phone closer to her face. "We never met each other, but I liked her. She had shiny hair and long legs. She would have liked me, but I could never run fast enough."

"How far behind were you when the car hit her."

"A long ways," she said softly. "I didn't see it really. I heard it."

"What did it sound like?"

"A big smack," she said earnestly.

I made a note, which drew her attention. "Did you hear a squealing sound before the smack?"

"No."

"Are you sure?"

Keelie looked confused. "Why? Am I in trouble?"

"Not at all," I said. "You're helping a lot. What did you do after you heard the sound?"

"I turned around and ran home as fast as I could. I knew something bad happened."

"Do you remember any cars that might have passed right before the lady was hit?"

She scrunched up her face and scratched her nose. "A light blue one."

I wrote that down, which seemed to please her.

"And a reddish-purple one," she added, which delighted me.

My heart raced, but I willed it to slow down.

Not an easy feat when I had my first big break.

Corroborating evidence.

My young witness had just described the color of Jackie Cooper's

Monte Carlo and the color of the car that Jackie believed had intentionally hit Jessica Stankowski.

CHAPTER 7

I wanted to crush Keelie Dunham in a bear hug, but I continued casually. "Do you mean the car was burgundy?"

"What?"

"A color like wine," I said helpfully.

When that didn't register, I pulled out a page I'd printed from an auto trader site on the Internet. I showed her a burgundy Camry. "Like that?"

"Yes," she said confidently, "but not that shape."

I shuffled through papers until I came across another sheet, this time a white Maxima, the only color I could find on the site. "Like this?"

"Yes, yes, yes," Keelie said, jabbing at it with her finger. "That shape."

"With the other color?" I verified.

She pulled the pages from me and squished them together. "This is the car the man drove."

"How do you know it was a man? Did you see him?"

"No, but I know a man who drives a car like that."

I did a double take. "You do?"

She nodded in slow motion. "The mean man who buys stupid beer every day. Me and my friends see him at the store next to the arcade."

I kept my tone calm. "Why do you think he might have hit the lady?"

"Because he has a new truck. Before that, he had a van. Before that, he had this car. Maybe he hid it. I'll bet he did," she said emphatically.

I felt butterflies in my stomach. "He's driven three different vehicles, since when?"

Keelie furrowed her brow. "Since it snowed."

"Why is he mean? Has he said or done something to you?"

She flipped her phone closed. "He just looks mean."

• • •

I didn't waste any time acting on Keelie Dunham's information.

I paid her the hundred-dollar reward in twenties and raced back to the office to clear out an afternoon's worth of work in two hours.

By five o'clock sharp, I was parked outside the HR Liquor Store. I'd chosen a spot in front of the arcade, out of view of the clerk working the counter, and I didn't have to wait long.

The mean man was punctual.

Keelie had told me he came to the liquor store every weekday between 5:00 p.m. and 5:30 p.m., and at 5:18, there he was.

My heart skipped a beat when I saw the man Keelie had described pull up in a blood-red Chevy S-10 pickup. As he entered the store, I assembled the tricks of my trade, trick being the operative word. From the backseat, I retrieved a clipboard and pen.

When he came out, with his twelve-pack of Coors, I was ready.

I approached him from the side, with a friendly smile and flirtatious cock of my head, and asked him to sign my petition. His initial recoil turned to cooperation when he heard my cause—legislation to make drunk-driving laws more lenient.

As if Colorado didn't have enough trouble with this issue. *Men's Health* magazine recently had declared Denver "The Most Drunken Big City in America." My birthplace had earned this moniker based on two irrefutable stats: the drunk-driving arrests per capita when compared to other major U.S. cities and the alcohol-related car accident fatalities per capita.

The frightening designation made me want to park my car on Friday and Saturday nights, and every morning, afternoon, and evening the rest of the week.

Apparently, the mean man didn't feel the same. He fell for my ruse, confirming my long-held theory that people believe what they want to believe. As he filled out the required information, we chatted about the gestapo-like state we lived in and lamented people's obsession with sobriety.

He drove away with a small wave and a big grin, which I returned.

I had reason to smile.

Ramon Garcia had just saved me two hours of tailing and surveillance by providing me with his full name, address, and Colorado driver's license number.

I killed time in the suburbs with a trip to the Container Store and a light dinner at the Cheesecake Factory.

After dark, I drove by Ramon's home on Blackberry Lane, where my luck ran out.

I saw his truck parked in the driveway, but no Maxima.

It was time to let my fingers do the walking.

I drove back to the office and fired up the computer.

By midnight, I knew how Ramon Garcia had spent the last nineteen years of his life, and I wished I'd never touched him. As details of his latest infraction appeared on my computer screen, I could still smell his aftershave on my hand, and the sickly sweet scent added to my growing nausea.

Two months earlier, in the middle of a Saturday afternoon, traveling eastbound on Dartmouth, at speeds in excess of seventy miles per hour, he'd hit a Volvo, which had been stopped at the light on Colorado Boulevard. The posted speed limit in the residential area was thirty miles per hour. In a smaller car without airbags, the Volvo's occupant would have been killed by Garcia's van. As it was, the sixty-three-year-old woman was airlifted to Denver Health Medical Center with internal bleeding and head injuries.

Garcia escaped without a scratch. When police arrived on the scene, they found him staggering in the street. On the Breathalyzer test, he blew a .215, almost triple the legal limit in Colorado. For his height and weight, which I'd extracted from his license, at five feet five inches and 150 pounds, that meant he'd consumed between eight and twelve beers, glasses of wine, or cocktails.

In an hour!

Booked on suspicion of reckless driving, vehicular assault, and driving under the influence, Garcia was in a world of trouble, but presumably nothing he couldn't dodge, given his track record.

The Dartmouth accident represented his sixth DUI arrest in Colorado.

The first two, documented almost two decades earlier, hadn't inconvenienced him at all. It wasn't until he'd been arrested for his third DUI that he had his license suspended, and that was only because Colorado law calls for anyone convicted of a third DUI or DWAI (driving while ability impaired) to endure a one-year suspension.

The fourth violation earned Ramon 200 days in jail, 170 of which were suspended. He served 30 days under work release, no major blow to his lifestyle. By conviction five, he was sentenced to 15 days in jail, all of which he avoided when he agreed to undergo alcohol counseling.

Apparently, the counseling hadn't made much difference, because I was staring at the mug shot from arrest number six.

In it, he wore a Hawaiian shirt, barely buttoned, revealing a hairless, light-colored chest below a darker, wrinkled neck. His puckered lips were too small for his broad face, and his black, wavy hair stopped at the top of enormous ears. His bulbous nose implied years of alcohol poisoning, as did three layers of bags below his eyes. Dark and out of alignment, the eyes looked dead, as if absolutely nothing registered in them.

After several minutes, I tore myself away from Ramon Garcia's photo and felt the onset of outrage when I recognized a pattern in the timeline of his convictions. In Colorado, any driver found guilty of three alcohol-related offenses in a seven-year period loses driving privileges for five years. That would have put a serious cramp in Ramon's ability to work or socialize. Interestingly, while he hadn't had the discipline to quit drinking and driving entirely, the lout seemed to have had enough willpower to time his habit to ensure minimum punishment.

How many days and nights had Ramon Garcia made a conscious decision to drink and drive? How many times had he weaved down the road after a binge? Hundreds, maybe thousands.

Had one of those times included an early morning jaunt down Highlands Ranch Parkway, as Jessica Stankowski was taking her last run?

To know that answer, I had to find his burgundy Maxima.

• • •

The next day, as I was contemplating the fact that a driver's license could be a weapon, Sasha came running up to my car, waving her brand new one.

"Let me see," I said, after she clambered in and buckled up.

She cupped it in her hands. "I hate the picture."

I turned on the engine. "Everyone does."

"They do?"

Pulling out of the parking lot at the Department of Motor Vehicles, I inclined my head toward the backseat, where I'd tossed my purse. "Check out mine."

Sasha retrieved my license from my billfold and laughed until she snorted. "Why did you have an afro?"

"I didn't," I said blandly. "That was a bad wave."

"Whatever. It looks weird. Can I have tomorrow off?"

I shot her a look. "You need a day off already?"

"I'm getting a car from my grandma."

"Your foster grandma?"

"My real grandma. She still loves me. She told me I could have her car if I passed my test on the first try."

"What kind of car?"

"A regular one, with four doors."

I rolled my eyes. "What color?"

"White or tan, I can't remember."

I nodded approval. "Nondescript. Perfect for the business."

Sasha smiled, leaned back in her seat, turned on her iPod, and closed her eyes.

• • •

In the silence, during the drive back to the office, I had a chance to mull over another angle in the Stankowski case.

Because of budget cuts at the Department of Motor Vehicles, Sasha had spent three hours waiting in linc to take the written exam and street test.

I'd put that time to good use by poring over the stacks of papers Jessica Stankowski and Holly Stamos had received at their respective closings.

With a triple-shot caramel macchiato to sustain me, I'd reviewed listing terms, sales contracts, addendums, property disclosure sheets, and bills of sale for personal property. I'd read mold, lead paint, and square footage disclosures. I'd examined settlement sheets, warranty deeds, and closing instructions. I'd breezed through tax assessments, water and sewer agreements, affidavits, and indemnity statements. I'd glanced at Colorado Department of Revenue and IRS forms.

Was it any surprise that no one ever read these papers, before, during, or after a closing? The very act was enough to trigger a coma. One time, in my twenty-year career, a guy had tried. After four hours, he'd started skimming, or we'd still be there.

In comparing the two real estate deals, I couldn't find any common denominators that would explain the same woman buying the properties under different names.

The listing agents were different: Jessica had used Dan Reed of Urban Properties, the former Kraft food salesman; Holly had chosen Rebecca Bishop of Bishop Properties, one of her sister's friends.

The buyer's agents were different: Freddie Taylor of Fine Homes brought Deidre Johnston to purchase Jessica's house on Josephine Street on December 11. Jack Barton of Colorado Homes represented Dee Jackson in her purchase of Holly's house on Elizabeth Street on January 22.

Prior to my appointment with Dan Reed, I hadn't met any of the four agents, but that wasn't unusual. Thousands of us in the Denver metro area try to earn a living in this occupation.

From the settlement sheets, I'd ascertained that Jessica's buyer had used Prime Service Lending for her financing, while Holly's had secured a mortgage through Capital Quest.

Front Range Appraisal had confirmed Jessica's home was worth the $289,500 selling price. Maxwell and Associates had vouched for Holly's $273,000.

The only link I had found was Guaranty Title, the company that had issued policies on both houses, but that meant nothing. As the largest title insurer in the nation, they underwrote more than half of the residential deals in Colorado. I used them exclusively because they had eight metro area branches and were fast, efficient, and accurate.

In a stroke of good fortune for me, both Jessica Stankowski's and Holly Stamos's closings had been conducted at the Cherry Creek branch, my personal favorite because it occupied the tenth floor of a high-rise across from a French bakery.

Whenever I attended a closing in Cherry Creek, I made a point of picking up pastries. Whether it was the desserts or my personality, I'd made a few friends at Guaranty Title, including Mary Jo Channing. She'd started as a closer and worked her way up to "Supervisor of Operations."

If there was a scam in progress, MJ would be the one to detect it. She was one of the few people I'd told about my career conversion, and she loved a good mystery.

In the first hour of my wait for Sasha, I'd placed a call and left a message on Mary Jo's voice mail.

Five minutes later, she'd called back, I'd briefed her, and she'd assured me that she would initiate an internal investigation.

Knowing her pit-bull personality, I wouldn't have to wait long for an answer.

• • •

Thursday, the office felt empty without Sasha.

I moped around, not accomplishing much, until three o'clock when I left for afternoon tea at the Brown Palace.

Built in 1892 and designed in the Italian Renaissance style, the luxury hotel was one of the most distinctive and elegant structures in Denver. Crafted with Colorado red granite and Arizona sandstone, the curved, triangular-shaped building faced Broadway, Tremont, and Seventeenth Street. Anchoring the financial and cultural districts of downtown, the four-star hotel had hosted presidents, royalty, movie stars, and cardinals.

For generations, mothers and daughters had enjoyed tea in the historic lobby. I'd heard about the tradition but had never experienced it.

Apparently, I was in the minority.

Freddie Taylor of Fine Homes, the agent who had represented the woman who bought Jessica Stankowski's home, chose our meeting spot. When I'd called to set up an appointment, Freddie insisted that no woman's life could be considered complete without at least one afternoon tea at the Brown, an indulgence she allowed herself several times a month.

I hated to admit it, but the prissy ritual lived up to its billing in every respect.

The atrium lobby was opulent, with marble floors, rich carpets, and red leather sofas. From the entrance, all eight floors of the hotel were visible, with iron railings and ornate grillwork distinguishing one level from another.

Freddie and I companionably shared melt-in-your-mouth scones with Devonshire cream and preserves, curry egg salad sandwiches, multilayer petit four cakes, mini éclairs, and hand-dipped chocolates. We plucked from a three-tiered serving dish as we listened to the soft sounds of classical harp music.

When we fought—in a ladylike manner—over nut-bread sandwiches with cream-cheese frosting and kiwi slices, the server, who recognized Freddie as a regular, brought a backup plate.

We'd even discovered that we had a mutual acquaintance, Valerie Edbrooke, someone I once considered a close friend, and that had accelerated our chumminess.

After general chitchat and specific real estate gossip, Freddie came to the point before I could. "Something's wrong with the Deidre Johnston closing on Josephine. Tell me what."

"Not necessarily," I said, evasively.

She shot me a chastising look. "I could hear it in your voice on the phone. You may as well spill the beans. I've been in the real estate business long enough to know that not every deal is aboveboard."

"Honestly, I don't know what's going on."

"Do you suspect something?"

I let out a sigh. "Deidre Johnston never moved into Jessica Stankowski's house."

That caught Freddie off guard. "Is it still vacant?"

I nodded. "Do you remember if she purchased it as an owner-occupied property?"

"That's the impression she gave me and Jim Nalen, the mortgage broker, but she wouldn't be the first to bend the truth in order to receive more favorable financing."

"True," I said, all too familiar with the practice.

Amateur investors who intended to fix and flip properties or rent them out frequently posed as residential buyers. If the amateurs pretended that they intended to use the condo or house as their primary residence, they benefited from a smaller down payment and a lower interest rate.

Freddie pursed her lips. "Is that your only concern?"

"There's more. Six weeks later, Deidre Johnston bought another house a few blocks away, using the name Dee Jackson. She hasn't touched that one either."

The gap between Freddie Taylor's precision-plucked eyebrows narrowed, aging her. From a distance, she could have passed for thirty. She wore a lavender silk jacket and skirt, a double-strand necklace made from marble-sized black stones, and diamond stud earrings. Her brown hair was pinned in the back, with strands of bangs hanging loosely at the sides. Her makeup was impeccable, and only the lines on her neck disclosed her entry into the sixth decade.

I continued. "I'm involved because Jessica recognized Deidre at the second closing. By coincidence, the house belonged to a friend of hers, Holly Stamos. Jessica confronted Deidre, who denied having met her. Eight days after Holly's closing, a hit-and-run driver killed Jessica on Highlands Ranch Parkway."

"Oh, that poor girl," Freddie said, her eyes flickering with what seemed like genuine concern. "You believe the closings and her death are connected?"

"Possibly."

"What can I do to help?"

"Do you have current contact information for Deidre Johnston?"

Freddie shook her head. "About a month ago, I tried to reach her. I met a personal injury lawyer in one of my leads groups and thought he might be able to help Deidre. She'd injured her back on the job, and her employer didn't have coverage. My intent was to connect the two of them, but all the phone numbers I had for Deidre were disconnected."

"How about an address?"

Freddie closed her eyes for a second, displaying impressive eyelashes. "That's a dead end, too. The day of the closing, I sent her a thank-you card, and it came back as a bad address."

"Where did you meet Deidre?"

"At an Investors International meeting in Aurora."

I looked at Freddie in surprise, and she threw up her hands sheepishly.

There were dozens of investor groups in the metro area. For a time, I'd belonged to one. People from all aspects of real estate—part-time investors, property managers, real estate agents, mortgage brokers—met to listen to speakers, to network, and to participate in roundtable discussions. Some of the groups had excellent reputations and served a valuable purpose.

Not Investors International.

I'd barely lasted through one meeting five years ago and had vowed never to return. The evening began with an assault of flyers on my chair, forty-seven in all, and went downhill from there.

My recollections were of a group of slick men and women, all schemer-scammers, who had gathered to bullshit with each other. Long ago, I'd reached the conclusion that the more people talked about how much they used to make, how much they were making, or how much they would make, the less money they had.

All of the people at this gathering had talked about nothing but money.

The room had been filled with wannabes, poseurs, and shady characters. What had begun as a vibe of not-so-quiet desperation, with most participants on the lookout for "other people's money," had soon approached a cult-like frenzy.

At the break, I didn't walk out.

I ran.

I sprinted past the lettering peeling away from the windows in the former bingo hall, through the weed-infested, cracked asphalt, and to my car, one of the few late models in sight. With everything promised inside, the parking lot should have been crammed with Mercedes and BMWs. Instead, there was a sea of rundown American cars—rusted-out, dented, high-mileage jalopies. The only other place I'd seen such a cluster of clunkers was in Blackhawk, the gambling town thirty miles west of Denver.

I did nothing to hide my judgment from Freddie Taylor. "You go to Investors International meetings?"

"From time to time," she said, with a thin smile.

"How do you stand it?"

Her smile grew. "Two antacid tablets before and a glass of sherry after."

"Do you meet clients?"

"Now and again, but I attend for an entirely different reason. I need to stay one step ahead of the latest swindle."

"Did you approach Deidre Johnston, or did she approach you?"

"She came up to me. My usual MO is to hide in the back of the room and observe."

"Was there anything unusual about the transaction with Jessica Stankowski?"

"Other than Dan Reed, the puffed-up buffoon?"

I grinned sympathetically. "I met him the other day. Is he as incompetent as he seems?"

"He's terrible with details, and I had to draft every addendum, his and mine. That boy needs to find a new occupation."

"Don't worry," I said mildly. "This is just a stepping stone for Dan."

"What's next, pray tell?"

"He's going to form his own real estate private equity fund."

We shared a laugh, before Freddie said, in a serious tone, "I do remember worrying the deal might collapse if we couldn't find the right financing."

"What did you need?"

"Deidre insisted on a no-money-down loan. I should say Richard, her boyfriend, insisted on it. I put her in touch with Jim Nalen at Prime Service Lending. He picked up the closing costs in exchange for a higher interest rate. Jessica agreed to add the down payment to the price of the house and credit it back at closing. It was a neat deal, but of course I had to step young Dan through it."

I felt a ring of alarm. "Deidre's boyfriend was involved in the purchase?"

"He was quite domineering throughout the process. She seemed afraid to make a move without him. At the slightest confusion or glitch, she'd call to find out what she should do. Never mind that I have twenty-six years of experience, she felt more comfortable seeking direction from him."

"Did you meet Richard?"

Freddie shook her head. "Early on, I suggested he come with us to the showings, as he seemed to be the decision maker, but he declined. Frankly, I breathed a sigh of relief when it was all over. At several points, I was certain he was about to call it off, which would have been a shame. That was a cute house, on a great block."

"How many houses did you look at before Deidre chose Jessica's?"

"Only one, in the same area, but it went under contract before we could make an offer."

"Was this her first home purchase?"

"Deidre said as much, but she seemed to be more savvy than your average first-home buyer. I'm surprised she waited. She's in her late thirties, and with that dream profile, she should have owned something before now."

"Dream profile?"

Freddie smiled slyly. "High income and perfect credit."

"Perfect?"

"One of the highest credit scores I've seen."

CHAPTER 8

Friday morning, Sasha scampered into the office, out of breath. Jumping up and down, arms flailing, she grabbed me by the hand and tried to drag me from behind my desk. "Lauren, come see, come see!"

I pulled back. "Come see what?"

"It's a surprise," she shouted.

With that, she turned and sprinted out of the office, through the hallway, down three flights of stairs, and out the side door.

I had no choice but to follow. In the parking lot, gasping for air, I almost lost it when I saw the surprise. "What happened to white or tan?"

"White or tan?"

"The color of the car," I shrieked.

"Oh, that," Sasha said easily. "My friend and I painted it. Isn't it the coolest?"

I rubbed my forehead, trying to dissolve the headache that had appeared instantly. "Is bubble gum your favorite kind of ice cream?"

She looked at me with amazement and joy. "How did you know?"

"Because this looks like that."

"You're right," she said, admiring her work. She'd taken a Ford Tempo with no body damage and painted it sky blue, then added dinner-plate-sized polka dots in all colors.

I groped for words. "Do you remember when I said a nondescript car would be perfect for private eye work?"

"Maybe," she hesitated. "But I didn't know what the word meant."

"It means unremarkable," I practically shouted. "Nothing unusual. Why do you think I drive a white car, when I wanted the deep sapphire model? How are you going to tail someone in this car?"

"Tail someone? You'd let me do that?" she exclaimed, balling both hands into fists and pumping them in the air. "Sweet!"

"Not in this."

Sasha flashed a pleading smile. "I could borrow your car."

"I don't think so," I said, unwilling to hand over my Subaru Outback yearling.

Sasha looked crushed. "Do I have to paint my car again? It's so pretty this way."

I sighed. "Not yet. But if you drive to appointments, park down the street. You don't want to lose credibility in this gum-ball dispenser."

"I like that," she said, stroking the front hood. "I'll tell my friend. She said it looked like a sky with colored clouds, but I like gum-ball machine better."

I didn't get much work out of Sasha the rest of the day.

First, we had to take a spin in the car, a remarkable experience as people laughed, pointed, and hollered at us. Stoplights were the worst. I tried to look straight ahead; otherwise drivers to the side would roll down their windows and begin conversations.

After a few blocks, I had Sasha drop me back at the office. She went to run an errand, to buy stamps at the post office. No sooner had she returned than she declared we needed Kleenex, and she headed to the grocery store. She came back, unloaded those, and darted out for office supplies. Once she'd stocked the shelves, she dashed to the computer store for a cable. She picked up donuts, lunch, and Slurpees, all in separate trips.

So it went, but I couldn't fault her.

She'd have her first car on its first day only once.

Office work, well that would last a lifetime.

• • •

The weekend passed uneventfully—with no open houses, thank God!

When Monday rolled around, I completed another item on the to-do list for my hit-and-run case—a meeting with Rebecca Bishop, the agent Holly Stamos had hired to sell her house.

After our meeting, if you could call it that, on my drive back to the office, I munched on a red-white-and-blue ribbon of hard candy and replayed what I'd learned from Rebecca.

Not much.

Rebecca carved out a real estate career while raising and homeschooling four boys, which meant she probably sold three properties per year, if that. She was good friends with Holly's older sister, which was how she'd landed the listing. She'd attended Holly's closing and met Dee Jackson, the buyer, and Jack Barton, the buyer's agent, but she'd shoehorned it in between a karate lesson and a swim meet. She hadn't retained many details.

In Rebecca's recall, Dee Jackson had seemed "scattered" and "not excited about the house." She wasn't talkative, and she'd called her boyfriend several times during the closing, with questions the title agent, Rebecca, or Jack could have easily answered.

Jack Barton had brought a full-price offer with the first contract but insisted on no-money-down financing. He'd come to the closing late, seeming "aloof" and "sinister." Why sinister? Because he chewed tobacco. Certainly grounds for cutting short a blind date but hardly reason to put a man in the frame for murder.

In total, Rebecca Bishop had added little to my understanding of the scam I was sure Deidre Johnston/Dee Jackson had pulled off, primarily confirming facts Freddie Taylor had shared with me over tea at the Brown Palace.

However, the outing hadn't been a complete waste of time.

I'd met Rebecca and her four sons at Hammond's, a candy factory in an industrial section of north Denver. Known worldwide for its candy canes, the company had opened for business in 1920 and offered free tours six days a week.

After the tour, I could appreciate the benefits of homeschooling. My public education hadn't included field trips to candy factories, and I viewed this as a significant shortcoming.

There was something magical about watching workers as they lovingly crafted chocolates, creamy caramels, barber poles, ribbons, brittles, lollipops, and candy canes.

I considered the trip educational, too.

Take the candy canes, for instance. Math problems flowed naturally from the recipes. Division and fractions were needed to calculate proper amounts of sugar, corn syrup, and water. Science fit in nicely with cooking in the copper kettle at three hundred degrees, cooling, separating, blocking colors, pulling, and shaping, all of which had to be accomplished in less than a minute before the candy hardened. English lessons were inherent in the descriptions of the sweets—"toffee dipped in rich chocolate and hand-rolled in almonds"—and could be tested for accuracy. A social studies lesson rested in the study of candy throughout history and cultures, beginning with contemporary samples.

If enthusiasm and delight translated to heightened learning, the Bishop boys, ages six to ten, were scholars on the subject of candy.

I'd become enchanted, too.

In the Sweet Shoppe, I bought each of the boys a multicolored, twist lollipop, and threw in loads of candy for myself, enough to tide me through to the conclusion of the Stankowski case, hopefully.

All in all, I couldn't complain about the $167 charge to my credit card or the time spent.

If nothing else, between the vats and the rolling stations, Rebecca Bishop had confirmed one valuable piece of information.

Jessica had been accurate in her identification of Dee Jackson; they'd met before, when Dee had posed as Deidre Johnston at Jessica's closing.

Rebecca Bishop swore to this point, citing the "look of fright" on Dee's face when Jessica approached.

• • •

Back at the office, before I could offer Sasha candy from my stash, she stopped me in my tracks with a shrill, "I need a raise."

"But I'm not paying you anything," I said reasonably, helping myself to a cup of water from the dispenser next to her desk.

"See what I mean?"

I took a big gulp. "No, not really."

"Do you think you could pay me?"

I winced. "That wasn't part of our deal."

"Lots of large companies pay interns, at least a stipend."

I waved my arms, sending water flying. "Does this look like a large company to you?"

"No, but I'm helping you make money, aren't I?"

I crushed the paper cup and tossed it into the wastebasket. "Not yet."

"I need money," she pouted, "and I can't work at the mall. Retail is politically incorrect."

"Selling Cinnabons violates your principles?"

"They're okay, I guess, if people choose to poison themselves with fat and sugar. I'm talking about the stores. Practically everything comes from a sweatshop in a developing country. I need money, but not that badly."

"For what?"

"For things," she mumbled.

I turned toward my office. "I'll think about it."

"Can't you make a decision now?"

I threw up my hands. "Before I'd even consider paying you, we'd have to straighten out a few things."

The slouch set in. "Here comes the lecture."

I pushed aside papers and perched on the edge of her desk. "I thought you were putting in a full day today."

"I am."

"School's out, right?"

She wouldn't look at me. "So?"

"Why weren't you here earlier?"

"Earlier than what?" she said, nonplussed.

"Than one o'clock," I said, bringing notice to the time when I'd called from the road and reached voice mail.

"I had to get ready."

"What time did you wake up?"

"Eleven," she said, not bothering to disguise the attitude.

"If I paid you, do you think you could manage to arrive a little earlier?"

She said eventually, "Not really."

"Why?"

"I'm too tired," came the feeble reply.

"How did you make it to school by eight?"

"I didn't have a choice."

"Consider you have no choice here either."

Her shoulders slumped a few more inches, and she said woodenly, "But it's summer."

My voice rose. "Do you want this job or not?"

"Yes, but why can't I do my work in the afternoon or evening?" she wheedled. "The phone never rings anyway. You take all the good calls on your cell phone."

"Because those aren't my hours. For us to overlap and coordinate projects, you need to get in earlier."

Sasha scrunched up her face. "How early?"

"By eight," I said, starting low. If Sasha ever rose that early, she'd arrive to discover a darkened office.

She batted her eyes. "Noon."

"Ten," I said firmly. "Not one minute later."

"But I'll have to go to bed by midnight. And then, what if—"

"Cope," I said, using her favorite expression. I softened and added, "I'll pay you eight dollars per hour, but only for the hours you're really working."

"Thanks, Lauren," she said, with a contagious smile.

I smiled back. "And you need to dress more professionally."

Her face fell. "Why?"

"The truth?"

She dropped her gaze. "Not if it's mean."

"You need more material," I said, measuring my words. "Shoes, not flip-flops. A real shirt, not a halter top with spaghetti straps. Jeans that don't show your crack."

She sniffed. "I don't always wear stuff like that."

"True," I said, remembering her poncho-like tops, the full-length black denim skirt with the oversized safety pins, and the leg warmers in the middle of summer. "You tend to go to extremes, and some of your clothes aren't appropriate for a work environment."

"Like what?"

"Like the cropped Playboy T-shirt that showed your stomach and navel ring. And your 'One Night Stand' tank top. I'm afraid they might be sending the wrong message," I said delicately.

She dismissed my comments with a snort. "You're too old-fashioned. You used the word billfold twice the other day. No one calls it that anymore. What do you know about clothes? Only someone who was visiting Hansel and Gretel would wear shoes like those."

It took every ounce of willpower I had not to look down at the comfy shoes on my feet.

I'd scoured far and wide for my beloved Brazilian shoes with the slender swoop of strap from the open side to the contoured quarter. I loved the feel of the black suede in my updated Mary Janes. I'd worn versions of these classics since my first pair in high school.

"Listen," I retorted. "I don't want people who come into this office getting the wrong idea about you and your availability."

When I saw the hurt look in Sasha's eyes and realized that she'd never considered her choices in such a light, I quickly tacked on humorously, "They should be focused on me."

"Oh, I get it," she said, brightening and nodding furiously. "I've read about older women who lose their youthful beauty and mourn the loss. It makes them jealous of pretty girls. Especially if they've never had a husband."

"That's it exactly," I said, without a trace of sarcasm, which took effort. "And for your information, I've been married three times."

Sasha stared at me with open surprise and laughed rudely. "You have not!"

"I have been," I said quietly, more than a little insulted by her reaction. "Or I would have been, if marriage between two women were legal in Colorado."

Sasha's eyes widened. "You never talk about partners or girlfriends or anything."

"Let's change the subject," I said forcefully.

An awkward pause followed, before she ventured, "Is my makeup okay?"

"What makeup?" I said, unable to face another battle. Or maybe I'd become accustomed to the layers of blue eye shadow and the star pattern of black eyeliner that cascaded from the corner of each eye.

"If you like it," she began gingerly, "I could teach you how to be more creative with yours."

"Maybe someday," I said vaguely, opening my purse.

From my wallet, I pulled out $200, which I handed her. "Consider this a thank you for all the hard work you've put in so far."

Her eyes bulged. "Sweet!"

"Buy a few outfits. Something appropriate."

"Can I leave now?" she said, exultant. "They're having a sale at Forever 21."

"Go!"

My smile faded when Sasha left the room.

Good Lord, how much more of this could I take?

• • •

Thanks to Sasha's remarks, I thought about my first serious romance off and on for the rest of the day.

Partner #1: We'd known each other for all of two weeks before we announced our undying love to ourselves and our families.

I met her at a weekend rodeo in Greeley, an agricultural community sixty miles away from Denver, a galaxy away from Boulder where I spent my freshman year of college.

What was I thinking when I agreed to move in with her? I wasn't. I was electrified by her touch, and that seemed like enough.

The partnership—at least the part in which we lived under the same roof—lasted less than a month. Recovering from the fallout took significantly longer.

My father had reacted to my coming out with his customary denial and silence.

My mother, on the other hand, had spared no words of outrage and disapproval—of my lifestyle "choice" and my taste in women.

After the relationship ended, and in the decades that followed, I never did tell my mother that she had been right about my crush, that it had been juvenile and unfounded, and about my poor choice in women, that the one I'd selected hadn't suited me.

Forget that my first partner drank, and I didn't. That she thought she was charming when she was drunk, and I didn't. That she preferred the company of her friends over mine, and I didn't. That she wanted me to skip my sophomore year to follow her on the pro rodeo circuit, and I didn't.

My mother probably had foreseen all those incompatibilities. But what she didn't know, and what I would never tell her or anyone else, was that my first partner used violence as her primary form of communication, and I didn't.

In separating, we hadn't parted friends. We'd simply parted.

By then, I felt sufficiently embarrassed to make a return to the University of Colorado impossible. I felt like I'd aged ten years in one summer, and I couldn't bear to face the sorority sisters who might have suspected that I was gay and talked behind my back, but had never confronted me.

I dropped out of school, leaving behind aspirations of a business degree, and went to work as a secretary at a real estate firm.

Today, that position would enjoy the more glamorous title of administrative assistant, but with the same shitwork. Make coffee and copies. Type and file. Clean up after slobs who thought they deserved round-the-clock housewife services.

Fortunately, not long after I joined the firm, one of the managing brokers—a married mother of six—had taken a liking to me and encouraged me to study for and pass the Colorado Real Estate Exam.

Yes, that liking had included sex, but I learned a lot. Both from her tender ministrations and from watching her close deal after deal.

In a roundabout way, I suppose, everything happens for a reason, everything works out for the best, when one door closes another opens, and all that crap.

But there had to be an easier way.

I made a note to myself to have a talk with Sasha.

If I had anything to say in the matter, she'd follow a more sensible path than I had.

• • •

The next morning, by seven o'clock, I'd been awake for two hours, quite an accomplishment for me. Probably only the third time I'd managed it in my life.

I had good reason for the early wake-up call: Ramon Garcia, the serial DUI offender.

After rising in the dark and driving to his neighborhood in Highlands Ranch, I'd followed him to work in the hope of getting a lead on the burgundy Maxima, the one that may have sent Jessica Stankowski hurtling to her death.

When Ramon pulled into an office campus in Inverness Business Park, he drove to the back of one of the lots and parked next to the only car in that immediate vicinity.

I let out a cry of joy when I saw the car was a burgundy Maxima. The "For Sale" sign in the window, a $2,500 or best offer request, could be seen from the nearby busy boulevard.

As soon as Ramon entered the mid-rise, I jumped out of my car to take a closer look. In a cursory exam, I couldn't see any body damage, but that didn't mean anything. He'd had almost five months to perform the necessary repairs to cover up his crime.

I whipped out my cell phone and dialed Rollie. "I need a favor," I said, my breath coming in short bursts.

"Ask it."

"Could I borrow Carla for an hour?"

"She's yours," she said immediately, adding with a randy snigger, "As long as you two don't do anything I wouldn't."

I was in no mood to rise to the bait. "I need her to look at a car that may have been in an accident."

"She's on her way."

After I gave Rollie the address, my heartbeat returned to a more normal rate, and that's when my thoughts circled back to Bev and Hank Stankowski.

In raising their daughter Jessica, they'd done everything right, only to have it turn out wrong.

Meanwhile, this scum, Ramon Garcia, had done everything wrong, only to have it turn out right.

I couldn't wait to nail him.

What was taking Carla Mancinelli so long?

I'd met her at Austin Investigations and was impressed by her no-nonsense demeanor. A large woman, tall and stout, she chained her wallet to a leather belt studded with turquoise and silver, but opened it to anyone in need. Year-round, she wore a uniform of pressed blue jeans, white undershirt, plaid flannel shirt, and cowboy boots. She'd told me once, with obvious pride, that a cobbler had re-soled the faded boots seven times. She had light brown hair, worn in a braid that stretched to her middle back. Before joining Rollie's team as an auto insurance fraud specialist, she'd owned a body shop.

If anyone could spot evidence of repair, Carla could, but I wished she'd hurry up.

Every minute of delay meant another minute of freedom for a man who had no right to be free.

CHAPTER 9

"You have to keep at it," Rollie Austin said kindly, impervious to my foul mood.

"I can't believe there was no front end damage on Ramon Garcia's Maxima," I said, with the same dark look I'd held for the past four hours. At this rate, I risked a permanent etching in my forehead, but I didn't care.

Rollie had dropped by the office to bring lunch and bolster my spirits, but I hadn't touched the sushi or clawed my way out of the dumps.

"None, eh?" she said thoughtfully, as if she hadn't heard the fact a dozen times.

"None whatsoever, and no new windshield," I responded furiously. "Carla could tell by the glue in the seal that the glass had been in for a few years, at least. The paint job wasn't original, but it was more than six months old. She determined that from the chipping and fading. She said the car was in excellent shape for the miles. She wanted to call Ramon Garcia and offer him $1,500."

"Carla wouldn't dare!"

"Not after I told her about Garcia's six drunk-driving arrests."

"That woman better have some principles, or I'll kick her fanny."

"Carla does," I said, gloomily. "She let the air out of his tires. A minor inconvenience in the scheme of things, but something."

"Do you have any leads other than the car?"

I brightened slightly. "One. Jessica Stankowski and her friend Holly Stamos sold their houses in Washington Park to the same woman, who bought them under two different names."

"Around the time of the accident?"

I nodded. "Jessica sold her house on December 11 to a Deidre Johnston. Holly sold hers on January 22 to a Dee Jackson. When Jessica met up with Holly after her closing, she bumped in to Holly's buyer. Jessica swore it was the same woman who bought her house, but the woman denied it and hurried off. Eight days later, Jessica was run over by a car."

"What do you make of that?"

"I'm not sure. Both houses are still vacant, so rent-skimming is out," I said, mentioning a once-popular form of fraud whereby an investor purchased a home for little or no money down, moved in tenants and collected rents, but never sent any of the proceeds to the mortgage company.

"What else could it be?"

"The woman might be a legitimate investor. Maybe she hasn't touched the houses because she plans to demolish them. Scrape-offs are pretty common in that neighborhood. Developers will pay $300,000 for the house and lot, demolish the old house, build a contemporary one from scratch, and sell it for $800,000 to $1,000,000."

"That sounds aboveboard."

"Completely. Or the buyer could be planning on updating, remodeling, or adding square footage to the houses, and she's waiting for financing to come through. Maybe an architect's drawing up plans. She might have chosen a general contractor, and she's waiting for a break in the contractor's schedule. Any of these scenarios could explain the purchase of two houses and the vacancies."

Rollie responded to the look of concern on my face. "But not two names."

"Or the woman's suspicious behavior when Jessica recognized her at Holly's closing."

Rollie rubbed her hands together. "You're onto something. I can feel it. What's next?"

"I'll have Sasha tackle Jessica's PDA. Do you know what that is?"

Rollie laughed heartily. "Honey, welcome to this century."

"You have one?"

"I'm on my third. I couldn't live without it. I love Tetris, more than I should. I can't help myself. If you don't watch out, that intern of yours will be addicted to it, too."

"As if I don't have enough trouble already."

"How's she working out?"

"Really well," I said stretching the truth, before reducing it to actual size. "Some hours."

"Did you have the talk with her about her personal appearance?"

"Several times."

"That's a whopper of a scar on her leg. How did she come by it?"

"She hasn't said."

"She could dress in a way that didn't attract as much attention. Maybe you'd better have another heart-to-heart."

A guffaw escaped from me. This, coming from a woman who had been known to wear a tiara. Out in public. When she hadn't earned it!

"I not only spoke to Sasha yesterday, I gave her two hundred bucks to go shopping. She came back with one pair of jeans. And she's not even wearing those, obviously," I said, referencing Sasha's outfit of the day. Despite the heat and humidity—both destined to set records for that day in June—Sasha had come to work in seven layers of black, tent-like material, bare-legged.

Rollie shook with laughter. "What did you expect?"

"Change. And a few more garments."

"You didn't give her guidelines?" Rollie gathered bits of rice that had fallen from her sushi and landed on her short red leather skirt. She removed the cloth napkin she'd brought from home, and stood. After a few more brushes across her clingy, scoop-neck top and black hose, she kicked off her red pumps and sat again.

"Obviously."

"You can't send a seventeen-year-old girl to the mall with cash and no supervision. What were you thinking?"

"I wasn't," I said, annoyed. "I was reacting."

"It's time to be proactive. I tell you what, I'll hook her up with a friend of mine, an image consultant. They'll shop together."

I looked at Rollie with suspicion. "What will this cost me?"

"Nothing for the advisor. My friend Becky, she owes me a favor. I'll get her to waive her usual fee of eighty-five an hour. You foot the bill for the kid's clothes and a nice lunch or dinner for the two of them. How does that sound?"

"Is this really necessary, a personal shopper?" I said resentfully.

"Would you prefer to do it yourself? Are you prepared to spend a day at the mall, hovering outside dressing rooms, checking for plunging necklines? Do you know how to spot trends that will complement Sasha's body type? Do you care to make an enemy with every veto?"

"No, no, no, and no."

"Are you dying to keep looking at her bare midriff or the black outfits with metal spikes?"

"Of course not," I muttered.

"Leave it to an expert. In case you hadn't noticed, the trend is toward trashy. Becky helps reverse that by teaching the girls a new standard. Give her a $350 budget, and she'll help Sasha pick out skirts, jackets, tops, and pants that won't make you blush. Becky's an expert at mixing and matching. She'll make twenty to thirty lovely combinations out of those selections. She just helped one of my newbies, Greta. Did I tell you about her?"

"Not yet."

"She's one sharp cookie, but a terrible dresser. Enough about fashion, though, fill me in on the Hesselbach investigation. What's the latest?"

"I got ahold of the foreman, Mike Schmidt, the one I think is stealing inventory from Kitchen and Bath Remodels. I requested a granite countertop for a kitchen island. We're meeting next week, but on the phone, he tried to steer me toward a Black Galaxy slab. It might be the same one that went missing from Kelly's warehouse sixty days ago."

"That's my girl!" Rollie said, swelling with pride. "You've got him!"

"Almost."

"You let me know when you nail that sucker! I'll treat you to an afternoon at the spa."

When I winced, she amended the offer. "Or a juicy steak dinner at Elway's. You're a natural at this private investigation work."

"I wish I felt that way," I said distractedly. "Back to my hit-and-run case for a minute, if you don't mind."

"That's what I'm here for."

"Should I be doing something differently?"

"No, siree. You have a rhythm going. Keep at it, one lead at a time, and trust your gut. The buyer might be the key to the crime. If you can pin down a recent address for this Deidre or Dee, or whatever her name is, get over there and rattle her cage."

"Anything else?"

"Lean on the lady who saw the accident. What's her name?"

"Jackie Cooper."

"Run the inquiries simultaneously, give them equal priority. Something will pop."

• • •

Unfortunately, I couldn't deal with any hit-and-run case inquires at the moment because I had to put out another fire.

Soon after Rollie departed, my client with the fourplex that wouldn't sell, George Engleton, phoned to request a face-to-face meeting, and he didn't sound pleased.

Join the club.

As I hurried out of the office, I waved a quick good-bye to Sasha, who was on the phone.

In the parking lot, before I could unlock my car, she startled me by rushing up, out of breath.

"Lauren, stop! Check this out!"

Sasha handed me an e-mail from the Denver Real Estate Board. I glanced at the all-caps headline and photo, wadded up the piece of paper, and threw it in my backseat.

"I've got to run."

"What are we going to do?" she said, referring to the words at the top of the page. "Warning! Be on Alert."

"Nothing," I said, unperturbed. "We don't have any open houses scheduled for the next few weeks. By then, she'll be caught."

"How do you know?"

"Because they always are," I shouted as I drove off.

Open house burglars.

Every few years, the problem resurfaced, and the Denver Real Estate Board circulated a photo or sketch of the latest suspect to all its members.

The illicit pattern rarely varied. As soon as an agent was preoccupied with other buyers, a thief would tour the house and skim from the owner's personal items. Usually jewelry, sometimes keepsakes, in recent times, prescription drugs.

We agents could only blame ourselves for the problem. We may as well have sent up signal flares to would-be thieves. Wait, come to think of it, we did.

We placed online and print ads, posted signs and arrows on busy streets and boulevards, tied streamers and balloons to porches and handrails, and flung open the doors.

Come on in! Anyone and everyone! From two to four on Sunday, browse at your leisure. Take something now, or case the joint and pick up objects later. We'll greet you as you enter, with forced smiles plastered on our faces, and encourage you to peek in every nook and cranny. We don't want to crowd or rush you, feel free to explore at will, take your time.

Why did it come as a shock to us when some people couldn't resist temptation?

I swear the crime wave had surged when agents began hiring laypeople to sit in their open houses for ten bucks per hour. Undoubtedly, this latest dispatch from the board would set off another panic, and agents and brokers would respond by hosting open houses in pairs. As if one live body per site wasn't a big enough waste of time.

Years ago, I'd devised my own two-pronged solution to the potential problem: the tip sheet and the alarm system.

In the tip sheet, I tried to convey to sellers that hiding all valuables made sense. Even honest folks sometimes stray, if presented with a ripe enough opportunity. To prevent undue nervousness, I surrounded my hints with other useful morsels.

Pick up clutter. Thoroughly clean. Wash windows inside and out. Put away toys, especially ones on or near nightstands. Remove all over-the-counter and prescription medications from medicine cabinets and drawers. Limit the number of personal photos on display. Tidy up basements, attics, sheds, and garages. Hide mail, checkbooks, and bill-paying information. Take an inventory after each open house or showing, and immediately report missing items to the agent and police. Check that all windows, doors, and gates are securely fastened after visitors leave.

While paranoid types found my tip sheet intimidating, most people understood the advice was intended to prevent, not predict, crimes.

The alarm system in my gut was my other line of defense. Whenever it went off, I escorted the alleged buyers through the house on a guided tour, never letting them out of sight. If the shadowing raised their ire, I blamed the protocol on the owner's insistence. If they resisted or became rude, I politely invited them to leave.

Knock on wood, my plans had worked to perfection.

I'd held hundreds of open houses over the years, without incident.

I stand corrected, with only one incident.

That drama had occurred on account of a friend I'd hired at the last minute one Sunday afternoon when my mother was taken to the hospital by ambulance. As soon as I determined that the nursing home had instigated the trip as a precaution, I rushed to my listing in Greenwood Village to relieve my friend. After a nerve-wracking search of the five-thousand-square-foot faux chateaux, I found her in the wine cellar. Nude. With a man on top of her. Before I could shoot him with pepper spray, my friend stopped moaning long enough to introduce me to her boyfriend.

We haven't spoken since.

Just one more reason to hate open houses.

• • •

Forty-five minutes later, in a meeting downtown that lasted less than three minutes, I found out that I would no longer be obliged to hold any more open houses at George Engleton's hideous fourplex at Eighteenth and Lafayette.

He had fired me.

This was news that hurt less than it once would have, but what really pissed me off was that he'd replaced me with a real estate agent from Evergreen who was advising him to lower the prices by $100,000 per unit.

As if I hadn't given him the same advice.

I wished him luck—all of it bad—and left his high-rise office with a strange feeling.

Something that felt, oddly, like optimism.

• • •

My cell phone rang as I was cutting across the Sixteenth Street Mall, and I glanced at the screen. Guaranty Title. This had to be Mary Jo Channing, my connection at the Cherry Creek office.

"Hi, MJ."

"Greetings. Are you sitting down?"

"Soon. I'm on my way to my car."

"Call me when you're in it."

"Will do," I agreed, and we disconnected.

Five minutes later, after I'd settled a ten-dollar parking lot tab and cursed George Engleton one last time, I hit redial. "What's up?"

A strangled sound escaped from Mary Jo's throat. "I've spent the better part of the day looking through paperwork on the Stankowski and Stamos closings. There's nothing unusual in either of them. These were straightforward escrows. No clouds on the titles, no lender delays, no snags with the contracts, no holdups with disbursement of funds. I should be so lucky to have all our closings go this smoothly."

"That's the bad news, that it leads to a dead end?"

"I wish, because that would make my job easier. We're going through a rat's nest of turmoil here at Guaranty. There's talk of merging our branch with the downtown office. If that happens, they'll eliminate positions. Corporate wants to consolidate, eliminating a layer of middle-level managers. I'll be promoted or terminated. How's that for stress?"

"Mary Jo—" I cut in, aiming to avoid her usual circuitous method of storytelling.

"Two kids in college; a first, second, and third mortgage on the house; credit card debt I don't even want to think about. And a husband who's begging to retire because he thinks his job gave him a heart attack. Now this!"

"This what?" I barked.

"I need to hire you, Lauren. I can't pay much, really nothing, but I'm desperate. This isn't my fault, but my boss will find a way to blame me. That's his specialty, dodging trouble. He'll have my ass, but how was I supposed to anticipate something like this? Tell me that. We could have prevented it, we almost did."

"What?" I bellowed, and not because of bad cell phone reception. "How?"

"My closer on the Stankowski property was Dawn Bakke. She's a competent gal, but she's prickly. She was scheduled to close the Stamos deal, too, when Dee Jackson's real estate agent called at the last minute to request a different closer."

My pulse quickened. "Why?"

"According to my scheduler, Joan, Jack Barton didn't give a reason, and she didn't ask. Joan and Dawn are as close as sisters, and I'm sure she didn't want to get her in trouble. Unfortunately, Joan didn't think anything of the request, because she receives a handful every week. Now she tells me this! I could wring her neck. Dawn's going through a messy patch—ugly divorce, female problems, hair falling out. I've been aware that her personality wasn't a hit with some real estate agents and brokers, but I had no idea the problem ran this deep."

Because Mary Jo showed no sign of letting up, I rolled down the window and reclined my seat.

"I had a heart-to-heart with Dawn this morning and put her on probation. I don't mind telling you, we both shed a few tears, but I'm sure she'll pull herself together. This was a giant wake-up call, for all of us. I need your help."

"With what?" I said, leaning into the sun.

"Get to the bottom of this Deidre Johnston/Dee Jackson mess. Find that woman, and I'll deal with her."

I opened my eyes, fully alert again. "She *is* the same person?"

"Yes and no. Two entities exist with different legal names, addresses, and employment, credit, and financial histories, but the Colorado drivers' licenses gave her away. At every closing, my gals make a photocopy of the licenses of all involved parties, but you know that."

"And Deidre and Dee had the same license?"

"Different numbers and dates of issue, but—"

I interrupted excitedly, "The same photo?"

Mary Jo made a popping sound. "Identical, down to the mole on the left cheek."

I sat up straight. "This is bad."

"You're telling me. Fortunately for us, I have friends in high places. My sister-in-law, Verneeda, works for the Department of Motor Vehicles. She told me the other day that the Five Points branch is in the middle of a grand jury investigation. I wonder if this is related."

"Would Verneeda talk to me?"

"All she does is talk," Mary Jo said affectionately. "I'll have her call you. Lauren, you have to get to the bottom of this, and soon, or I'll be out on the streets in four-inch stilettos. At my age and weight, that would not be a beautiful thing."

I smiled faintly. "I'll hop right on it."

"How soon can you get back to me?"

"I have no idea. This isn't like real estate, with deadlines that we set and meet regularly," I cautioned. "I follow up leads, hoping for another lead. Eventually, they point to a solution, but not always."

"What will you do next, other than talk to Verneeda?"

"I'm not sure. Of the four agents involved in the two transactions, I only have one left to interview, Jack Barton. I've left three messages for him, but he hasn't returned my call. After that, I'm at a dead end. Do you have any suggestions?"

"You didn't hear this from me . . . " Mary Jo hesitated.

"Never."

"Or the powers-that-be would have a legitimate reason to send me packing, but if I were you, I'd call a certain company whose initials are CCC."

"Why would you do that, hypothetically speaking?"

"Because that company may have provided the credit scores for both Deidre Johnston and Dee Jackson."

"Is that unusual?"

"It could be."

"How would I find this certain company?"

"It might be listed in the phone book under Colorado Credit Company."

I jotted the name on the back of a filet-o'-fish wrapper I pulled from the floor of my car. "I owe you one, Mary Jo."

"Make this your first priority, and we'll be even."

"I already have."

"Good," she said tersely, "My continued employment might depend on it."

• • •

Back at the office, Sasha greeted me with, "I need to leave early today."

My smile vanished. "Again?"

She directed her attention back at the computer screen. "This time, it's your fault."

"How do you figure?"

"I have to go to the mall to buy the clothes you're making me wear."

I could barely contain my joy. "You made an appointment with Becky, the personal shopper Rollie recommended?"

"Yes," Sasha said, with a martyred sigh, fingers flying across the keyboard.

"Fantastic, but before you go, I need you to fill out a form."

I darted into my office and came back with her W-4.

Sasha looked at the piece of paper and refused to take possession of it. "I did."

I set it on her desk. "Completely."

She batted her eyelashes, a strenuous undertaking given the amount of mascara she'd caked on them. "I did."

"Sasha, you left the space for your last name blank."

"I told you," she said crazily, "I renounce that name."

"I understand," I said, counting to ten in my head. "But the Internal Revenue Service won't. As an unpaid intern, no problem, the matter was between you and me. If you want to get paid, you have to use your full name. Government agencies are picky that way."

She mouthed, "Sasha."

I exhaled loudly in frustration. "That's what's on your birth certificate? Sasha, nothing more?"

She picked at her pinky with her thumbnail, tearing at the cuticle. "No."

"Have you legally changed your name?"

She warmed up. "You can do that? How?"

"If you haven't, I need the name you were born with. All of it. First, middle, last."

She flicked something to the side of her desk. "Will you show me how to change my name. Forever?"

I glanced at the floor, but I couldn't see a flap of skin. "If you'll use your actual name until the change goes through. Now what is it?"

"Sasha Fuller," she said, after a sharp intake of breath. "I don't have a middle name."

"See," I said gladly. "That wasn't so hard."

She made a face. "Not for you, maybe. I never want to hear the name again."

"You'll have to get over that sentiment every Friday, long enough to cash your paychecks."

"It's not funny."

"I wasn't kidding," I said seriously, before softening my tone. "I'm sorry this is hard on you, Sasha, that your parents gave you up."

"They didn't give me up," she said, in her trademark monotone. "They're dead."

CHAPTER 10

I asked Sasha for details about how and when her parents had died, but she was done talking, a maddening power play I had to accept.

She left soon after, giving us both a much-needed break.

Fortunately, by the next morning, she'd lost the surly attitude and was sporting a new look: cropped navy blue sweatpants, tangerine cotton top, and green and orange Converse sneakers.

"Nice outfit," I said pleasantly. "How did the shopping go with Becky?"

"Pretty good. She's cool."

"Did she offer useful tips?"

"I guess."

"Like what?"

Sasha recited, in a mocking voice, "No trash or flash. No T-shirts with writing. Only properly fitting clothes, not too tight or too loose. Wear a jacket over a sleeveless blouse. Clothes can be clingy, but no tits or belly showing."

"Becky said that?"

"She called it cleavage and midriff, same thing. Hemlines can't go higher than this, the fingertips." Sasha demonstrated with her arm at her side, outstretched to its full length. "That's not fair. I have long arms."

"I'm sure you do," I said agreeably. "Maybe you could subtract an inch."

She nodded vigorously. "I'm not giving up my T-shirts with writing either, no matter what anyone says, and I won't lace up my high-tops."

"That would defeat the purpose. You have to keep some individuality."

Sasha nodded. "But I promise not to wear the T-shirts to the office anymore, and I'm trying less makeup. Did you notice?"

"I did," I said, with a slight smile.

"Becky told me all the glitz was hiding my pretty eyes. It feels weird, all these changes, but she says I'll get used to it."

"You look great."

Sasha lowered her head shyly. "Thanks, and thanks for the money and everything."

"You're welcome."

While she was still feeling grateful, I handed her a two-page spread from the Saturday *Denver Post.* On it was a list of recent real estate transactions for Adams, Arapahoe, Boulder, Broomfield, Denver, Douglas, and Jefferson counties. Every week, as a public service, the newspaper, in four-point type, printed the names of the buyers and sellers, the addresses, and the prices of the properties. Most weeks, between 3,000 and 5,000 properties changed hands.

"I have a project for you."

"Yuck, this is real estate. I told you I hate real estate projects."

"And I responded that you have to do them anyway. You're good at it. You made a nice flyer for our last listing."

"Yeah, but you wouldn't let me use the words quaint or storybook."

"Not until you're older," I said, confident she'd outgrow the desire.

"Can't I help you with a case?" she whined.

"This is a case. I need you to go through this list, carefully," I stressed, knowing her fondness for shortcuts. "Every time you see a buyer with the initials DJ, highlight the transaction."

Sasha's eyes bulged. "That'll take forever."

"Do you have something better to do?" I remarked genially.

"No, but what if I get eyestrain?"

"Use a magnifying glass. There's one on the top shelf in the office supply closet. If it's any consolation, you only have to search the listings for Denver County."

Sasha's shoulders rose and fell with her sigh. "All right. But you don't pay me enough."

"True," I agreed, grinning. "Especially when this is one week's worth, and I want you to go back to the beginning of the year."

"Six months!" she shrieked, "That's like twenty of these. Where am I supposed to get them?"

"Twenty-five," I said sweetly. "They're on the floor in the closet, in the corner, next to the filing cabinet."

She looked poised for a fight but instead said, "Can I have overtime?"

"It won't take you that long. A couple of hours, at the most, and I need you to do it this morning."

"This sucks."

"Yes, it does, but it's private investigation work."

"I don't believe you. You're making me your real estate slave."

"No, Sasha, I'm not. As much as this might come as a surprise, the world doesn't revolve around you. Jessica Stankowski is lying in Fairmount Cemetery, and it might be because she accidentally bumped into the same woman at two closings, a woman who was buying two different properties under two different names. Eight days later, Jessica was killed. Does that sound like real estate?"

"No," Sasha said softly, avoiding my unyielding gaze.

"I know this is shitty work, but that's how it is in any job, in any career. You have to do boring, repetitive tasks. The woman Jessica met used the names Deidre Johnston and Dee Jackson. I have a hunch she chose those names and fake identities because they were easy to remember and close to her real name. She bought two houses that I know of, but hasn't moved in to them or fixed them up. I want you to pore through these real estate transaction records to see if she bought any other properties. Do you think you could manage that—one simple project—without throwing a fit?"

"Yes," she said, her lower lip trembling in response to my sharp tone.

I eased up a bit. "I'd appreciate it. I'll give you two fun tasks to go with it, if you'll stop pouting."

She raised her head. "What?"

I pulled Jessica's PDA out of the side drawer of my desk. "Remember when I asked if you could retrieve information from this?"

"It's about time," she said, suddenly attentive. "I brought in my equipment days ago."

"Good. This belonged to our hit-and-run victim. I want to know what's on it, especially in the weeks leading up to her death. Print a copy of her calendar or jot down the important stuff manually, okay?"

"Sure, boss!" Sasha said, grabbing for the PDA.

"Not so fast. I want you to do some fieldwork. When you finish the report on the DJ transactions, you'll be in charge of the follow-through. You'll need to drive by the properties and let me know which, if any, are vacant. How's that sound?"

"Cool." She tossed the PDA from hand to hand. "Don't forget, I get mileage."

"I haven't."

"And lunch money," she said, all smiles.

I raised one eyebrow. "We never discussed that."

"I need to eat."

I shook my head in defeat.

• • •

A short time later, I was performing my daily penance of reviewing current and past MLS listings, when my eyes almost popped out of their sockets.

Before I could decide what to do about what I'd just seen, Sasha transferred a call.

Rollie Austin must have heard the distress in my voice. "What's eating at you?"

"You know those units in that awful fourplex I've been trying to sell, the one on Lafayette?"

"Who could forget?"

"One went under contract yesterday."

"Most people would consider that good news, sweet pea," she said equably.

"Except I'm no longer the listing agent. I told the client he had to lower the price, and he fired me. He hired an agent from Evergreen, as if she knows anything about downtown Denver real estate. What did she do? Lowered the price by $100,000 and got a contract in four hours. After I spent eighteen months of my life with that albatross."

"The client or the building?"

"Both. That bastard wouldn't listen to me, and now some chick who works one day will be taking home my $11,850 commission. God, this is a sleazy profession. I don't know why I bother."

"Honey," Rollie said soothingly, "you're just having a bad real estate day."

"Try year," I said distractedly, unable to tear my eyes away from the computer screen, away from the money George Engleton had stolen from me.

• • •

To take my mind off fantasies of throwing George Engleton off the roof of his fourplex, over the side next to the pit bull, I turned my attention toward the murder I needed to solve, not the one I felt like committing.

I hopped in the car and drove to Colorado Credit Company, the business that had provided the credit reports for Deidre Johnston and Dee Jackson.

I handed the receptionist one of Mary Jo Channing's business cards.

At our last lunch, I'd filched it, my motives innocent at the time. I'd liked the way the graphic designer had arranged three phone numbers and two e-mail addresses, and I planned to use a similar layout the next time I ordered cards.

That I could now pose as an employee of Guaranty Title, that was simply fortuitous.

Mary Jo's card landed me a quick audience with Gina Hernandez, the office manager. I told her that during a routine audit at Guaranty Title, we'd uncovered certain discrepancies with a number of credit reports, including two furnished by Colorado Credit Company.

Gina disappeared from her cubicle and returned twenty minutes later, asserting there must be some mix-up.

Reports on Deidre Johnston and Dee Jackson had never been tasked to any employee of Colorado Credit Company, and no record of either woman could be found in their computer database. Producing a merged report from multiple credit repositories would have required the formation of a permanent file. In fifteen years of providing customized mortgage reports to originators, credit unions, banks, and private investors, CCC had never experienced a significant customer service glitch. Their speed, reliability, and accuracy never came into question.

Perhaps I was confusing Colorado Credit Company with Credit Data of Colorado, a frequent, understandable error.

I agreed that was probably the case, thanked Gina Hernandez profusely, and left without pressing further. I was convinced she'd told me the truth, or at least as much of it as she knew.

However, I couldn't help noticing that while Gina and I were crouched over her desk, an information technology guy had been eavesdropping on our conversation. He'd disguised his interloping by crossing back and forth with modems and servers, monitors and cables, but the frequency of his passes and the intensity of his disinterest gave him away.

From experience, I knew he'd been listening to us.

I did it all the time myself, in coffee shops and grocery lines, on sidewalks and jogging paths. Not for professional reasons, but from an extreme curiosity I'd had since I was a kid.

The secret desire to encroach on other people's lives—I was betting the computer guy felt its pull, too.

Enough to know everything that went on in the office?

I could only hope.

• • •

Shortly after two o'clock, the IT guy came out the front door of the Colorado Credit Company building.

I followed him to a Chipotle restaurant, and as he passed through the line of lunchtime diners, I sat at a table in the back and studied him.

On his small frame, more petite than most women's, he carried no extra weight. I guessed him to be in his mid-twenties, despite black hair that was cut short and falling out. He'd done his best with the missing patches, moving the rest around and masking the loss with gel, but anyone with a sharp eye could see this was the Gen-X version of a combover.

He had acne-scarred skin and protruding dark eyes with remarkable lashes. I debated whether the scruff of three-day stubble was a nod to current trends, a work in progress, or a symptom of laziness. Noting stains on his blue and white Western shirt with snaps, discoloration on his brown corduroy pants, and holes in the white socks he wore underneath sandals, I settled on laziness.

He ate with gusto, swallowing inches of his handheld burrito with every gulp.

Halfway through the wrap, I approached him.

I dropped my business card on the counter, catching him midbite.

I hoisted myself onto the stool next to him as guacamole, rice, corn, cheese, and other unidentifiable food items dribbled down his chin and fell from the overstuffed tortilla.

"Todd Lynch," I said, reading the identification tag pinned to his chest. "You work at Colorado Credit Company."

Mouth full, he mumbled, "Yeah."

By the start in his eyes, I could tell he recognized me from Gina Hernandez's cubicle.

"Lauren Vellequette. I'd like to hire you."

He pushed my business card across the counter. "I have a job."

"Consider this a sideline gig. I need five minutes of your time." I smiled and placed a large bill under his Coke.

He eyed me warily as he wiped salsa from his chin with the back of his wrist. "I shouldn't be talking to you."

"Someone's hacked into CCC's system, and I need to know who."

He shook his head vehemently, dislodging morsels from his face. "No way. Couldn't have happened."

"It did. Do the names Deidre Johnston and Dee Jackson mean anything to you?"

"Huh-uh."

I bluffed by handing him the report Sasha had prepared for me after scanning the real estate transaction records in the *Denver Post.* "Someone at CCC, or someone using CCC's name as a front, has produced credit reports for these women."

Despite my request for accuracy over speed, Sasha had completed the report in one hour, toiling without complaint. It might have helped that she'd treated herself to a piece of last year's Halloween candy every time she found a property purchased by someone with the initials DJ.

All told, she'd eaten twenty-eight pieces of stale candy.

After we'd had about as much as we could stand of each other—she on her sugar high and I in my perimenopausal low—I'd sent her out for a walk around the block. When she returned, she prepared a spiffy Excel spreadsheet detailing dates, addresses, and names.

Todd Lynch stared at the list, and his face turned a pasty color.

That's when it dawned on me that I could save my hundred bucks. I didn't need this IT worker to sniff around and lead me to the culprit. He was the culprit! Without a word, I picked up my money and pocketed it.

He got the message, because he began babbling. "I was fooling around, all in fun. The credit reports were fictitious inventions. They can't harm anyone. You want to know the truth, I've been helping a buddy do good work."

"What buddy?"

Todd took a sip of his Coke and cast a sideways glance at me. "Why should I tell you?"

"Because if you don't, I'll tell Gina Hernandez."

His cheeks reddened, but his tone remained cocky. "I haven't done anything wrong."

"Fine. Explain that to Gina as she's firing you." I stood, grabbed the list, and turned to leave.

He rotated on his stool and clutched at my arm. "I swear, it's no big deal. Nothing illegal. I make up credit histories for women who need help. Widows, divorcées, immigrants. They're not bad people, but they can't buy houses or cars if they don't have high credit scores. This is like my volunteer work."

"You didn't find it a bit coincidental that all these needy women had the initials DJ?"

"Now that you mention it . . . "

"C'mon!" I said, with a hard stare.

"Okay, I did notice something, but the money's good."

I sat down. "How much?"

"Five hundred."

I shook my head in disgust. "Who's your buddy?"

"Richard."

Eureka! The same name Freddie Taylor had mentioned as the boyfriend of Deidre Johnston, the woman who had bought Jessica Stankowski's house.

"Last name?" I said, neutrally.

"I don't know. I only met him twice. He mails a lady's name, lender info, and cash to my post office box. I do my thing."

"How do you contact him?"

"I don't. I can't. He didn't give me a phone number or e-mail or address or anything."

I sighed and gave him a frozen smile. "Where did you and Richard meet?"

"At an investors' meeting."

I eyed Todd suspiciously. "What were you doing at one of those?"

"Learning everything I can. I want a passive income stream. As soon as I get my own apartment building, I can quit my job." There was a distinct delay before he added, "And move out of my sister's basement."

"Which investors' group?"

"The one that meets in Aurora, in that storefront with the bingo hall that's boarded up."

"Investors International?"

"That's it."

My face betrayed no emotion, but I felt a surge at the mention of the venue where Deidre Johnston had met Freddie Taylor. "How often do you attend?"

"Every month."

"You've only seen Richard twice?"

Todd nodded. "I wish he'd come again, because I want more money. I've stashed $31,500 for a down payment, but I need at least $50,000 to buy a decent building. I'll bet he'd give me an advance, or maybe come in as a silent partner."

I refrained from shaking my head. This guy's naiveté was off the scale, and apparently, the scope of the scam was bigger than I thought if he'd accrued more than thirty grand, at five hundred bucks per fake credit report.

"How did Richard approach you?"

"We sat next to each other at a meeting. I told him I work for CCC, and the next time he came to a meeting, he asked if I could use a little extra money for doing charity work."

"What does Richard look like?"

"I don't know, like a regular guy."

I took a deep breath. "Height?"

"Taller than me."

"Weight?"

"Skinny."

"Hair?"

"Gray. Long."

"Eyes?"

"Round."

"This is worthless," I said angrily. "Are you intentionally trying to be an ass?"

"No," Todd replied frantically, spewing burrito. "I don't notice stuff. Not ever. Not with people. They don't look at me, and I don't look at them."

In that comment, I understood, not so much from what Todd Lynch said, but from how he said it, how a stranger named Richard had gotten him to do his bidding.

I adopted a more patient tone. "Do you remember anything from your two encounters?"

Todd Lynch thought for a moment. "His ring. It was like one of those Super Bowl rings."

"Big, with lots of jewels?"

"Yeah, yeah."

"Are you making this up?"

"No, no. I noticed it because he hurt my fingers when he shook my hand."

"We need to talk about this," I said, indicating the report Sasha had compiled.

Todd Lynch gripped the page tightly. "Where did you get it?"

"Are these real women?"

"Yes," he insisted, his voice tinged with panic.

"You met them?"

"No, but Richard told me they're his clients. They have to be real. He had social security numbers, dates of birth, Colorado driver's licenses, work histories, everything. I wouldn't mess with that shit. I just made up the rest."

"What rest?"

"I plugged in fake credit card numbers and mortgages and car loans, mostly information I took from other client files. Sometimes, I gave them a few dings on their reports. By the time I finished tinkering, they all had credit scores in the high 700s. That's what Richard wanted."

"You sent the fake credit reports and scores to him?"

"No, directly to the lenders he chose. I came in after hours and transmitted them from my work computer so they'd look legit."

"The same lender?"

"Different ones."

"On a legitimate CCC report, don't you gather information from three credit bureaus? What if a lender checked one of these women's credit histories with Equifax, Experian, or TransUnion?"

"They'd come up blank. The women Richard gave me didn't have data, none, which was weird."

"You didn't go in and change data in the Equifax, Experian, or TransUnion systems?"

Todd relaxed a little, enough to resume eating. "I couldn't. No one can hack those systems. I didn't need to."

"You're not worried one of Richard's lenders might catch you?"

"Never. They're too lazy. That's why they hire CCC to compile the reports. All they care about is one number, the credit score. We send other information for their files, but no one reads it. That's what Richard says. In case he's wrong, I have a backup plan."

"For what you'll do if you get caught?"

Todd nodded. "I'll tell my bosses it was a software glitch. I've already erased everything. They'll have nothing but a ghost trail."

"What about the copies in the lenders' files?"

"Richard said they destroy files after thirty days. Electronic and hard copies. I'm cool."

"Your buddy Richard's wrong."

Todd Lynch choked on his burrito and could barely speak. "They don't?"

"Lenders never throw away anything. They store it off-site and hold on to it in case of litigation or audit . . . " I said softly, before raising my voice for the finale, "forever!"

I took great pleasure when his face lost all color again.

CHAPTER 11

No big deal. Who did Todd Lynch think he was kidding?

This was modern-day robbery, on a potentially massive scale. His scheme was the equivalent of blowing open a bank vault and stepping into a room full of gold bullions.

Fiddle with credit scores—the magical numbers generated by mathematical formula—and the possibilities for fraud became endless.

Whereas lenders used to rely on applications, face-to-face meetings with borrowers, and their own credit history research, over the past twenty years, they'd come to depend almost exclusively on a system that assigned a three-digit number to each consumer.

Known as FICO scores, they were supposed to be indicators of how likely consumers were to repay loans. Three reporting agencies gathered and maintained data and determined scores by giving weight to up to thirty influencing factors. The five biggies were: payment history, amount of debt owed, length of credit history, pattern of credit history, and types of credit in use. FICO scores allowed creditors to evaluate applicants on a consistent, impartial, and timely basis, often facilitating on-the-spot credit approvals.

As a less attractive result of automation, computers, not loan officers, made forecasts as to who was capable of managing money and who wasn't. I tried to impress this upon the people I served. The almighty credit score would determine not only whether a loan would be approved or declined, but also the interest rate and down payment.

Some lenders requested scores from all three bureaus: Experian, Equifax, and TransUnion, and used the average, low, middle, or high score, depending on their internal rules.

However, other brokers, such as the lenders who worked with Deidre Johnston and Dee Jackson, trusted companies like Colorado Credit Company to compile one easy-to-read report.

In doing so, Prime Service Lending and Capital Quest had based their decisions on Todd Lynch's fabricated credit histories and scores. Lenders were supposed to use FICO scores to support their decisions, not make them, but in most cases today, humans didn't even glance at credit reports.

Which is what made Todd Lynch's scheme nearly flawless.

Nearly.

His plan had worked until a woman named Jessica Stankowski happened upon two of his separate computer creations in the form of one woman's body . . . until someone decided the encounter was enough of a threat to necessitate running her over . . . until her mother cared enough to keep pursuing the hit-and-run driver when the police wouldn't . . . until I gave my word that I would do everything in my power to find the killer.

Now Todd's parallel universe of meaningless numbers and inflated credit scores had collided with my world of fraud, murder, and grief.

Believe me, that pip-squeak hadn't seen the last of me.

• • •

"That's a look," I said to Sasha the next morning, inclining my head toward her green polo shirt with the embroidered Vista Hills Golf Course logo.

"Kip gave it to me."

"After he ran over it with a lawn mower and washed it with a cup of bleach?"

Sasha had chopped off the sleeves, collar, and bottom twelve inches of the shirt, creating something more akin to what members of the World Wrestling Federation might wear. The cut exposed her midriff and showed off a thick white belt. Tight low-slung white jeans, red high-tops, and a Vista Hills visor, cocked sideways, rounded out the outfit.

She glared at me. "That's not very nice."

"After your consultation with Becky, you consider this appropriate office attire?"

"You're in sweats," she said, defending herself by attacking me.

"I don't have any appointments this morning," I replied, with a cool smile.

Not to mention, I had eaten an entire thick-crust pizza the night before, started my period at four in the morning, and woken up in a cruddy mood. Plus, I planned to change clothes before my afternoon appointment with Verneeda Brown, the contact Mary Jo Channing had given me at the Department of Motor Vehicles. But enough about me.

"How did it go with Kip?"

"Pretty good. Want to hear what I found out?"

I leaned back in my chair, hands folded behind my head. "Aren't you going to type up a report, like we discussed?"

"I will, but can't I tell you the good stuff now?"

Who could resist such youthful exuberance? I sighed and said charitably, "Just this once."

Sasha sat across from me, on the edge of her seat. "Kip is really nice. He let me spend a bunch of time with him, but I only put the hour of the interview on my time sheet, right?"

"Right. That's all we can charge on the invoice. What did you two do?"

"We rode around in the golf cart and told people to speed it up. Kip taught me how to use positive vocabulary and conflict resolution techniques. We used those to discourage people from taking mulligans."

"From cheating? That was my favorite part of the game the one time I played."

"Practice swings, Lauren," Sasha said, with a patient smile. "Kip let me carry the clipboard and use the walkie-talkie. He said I'm a natural as a marshal."

"I'll bet." I could see Sasha persuading old guys to step it up. In a nice way. In that appealing manner only nubile teenage girls can pull off.

"I drank four Mountain Dews from the beer cart, and I didn't have to pay for them. On the sixteenth hole, he showed me where a guy died."

"From golf?" It was hard to believe the least athletic sport on the planet could kill anyone.

"From a heart attack. He fell down when he was putting, and his friends played through. They skipped from the fifteenth to the seventeenth hole."

I didn't bother to contain my disdain. "While he lay there?"

"The dead guy was covered with a sheet. Kip said it didn't surprise him. He's seen it all in golf."

"Including Bud Cauldron's 520-yard ace?"

Sasha waved me off with both hands. "Not that, no way. Bud wants to have the hole in one certified by the U.S. Golf Register, and he has affidavits from the three people he was playing with . . . what are those?"

"Oaths. Written statements signed by a notary."

"Kip has to sign one, too."

"He doesn't want to?"

Sasha shook her head solemnly. "Kip doesn't believe it could have happened, and he doesn't want everyone laughing at him and saying bad things abut Vista Hills. He loves his job. His wife says he likes golf more than her. I don't get it."

"Why people become addicted to such an asinine sport?"

"No, how Bud could have hit a hole in one. You should see it, Lauren. There's no way."

I studied Sasha closely. "Absolutely impossible?"

"Maybe a one-in-a-trillion chance. They have these yard markers on the ground, like rocks, only flat, not standing up. The ball could have hit one or two of those and kept rolling, but . . . I don't know."

"No one saw it happen?"

"You couldn't. The hole bends around this marshy part. When you stand on the tee box, you can't see the flag. Not even with binoculars. I tried."

"You took binoculars with you," I said, proud of her resourcefulness and preparation. "Where did you get them?"

"From the cabinet." Responding to my chastising glare, Sasha said defensively, "I put them back. In the case and everything. I didn't break anything."

I almost went into convulsions. "The silver or the black ones?"

"The black ones. The silver ones were too heavy."

I relaxed. Sasha had grabbed the pair I'd picked up for $49 at a sporting goods store, the Audubon 8x40s. A basic pair of binoculars that weighed about a pound and had magnification of eight times. Fortunately for her—and her job security—she'd passed over my pride and joy, the Miyauchi

Apochromatic binoculars, 20x100. These wonders had set me back $4,400, not including the optional 26x and 37x eyepieces. There was nothing better on the market for delivering sharp, high-contrast images, but they weighed almost thirteen pounds. It wasn't easy holding those puppies up to my eyes for extended periods, but I hadn't bought the tripod yet. The weight was my insurance against old lady arm flab.

I wrenched my attention back to the matter at hand. "The only witnesses to the hole in one are this guy Bud Cauldron and the other players in his foursome?"

"Brent the groundskeeper, too, but not really. The night it happened, he was playing by himself, and they let him pass. Kip had me talk to him. He's really cute. He mows the fairways, and he's tan all over, and—"

"Sasha, focus!"

"You're no fun," she pouted. "Anyway, Brent said he didn't see anyone else around, and he didn't leave a ball in the hole. He was using a different kind, a Titleist. Bud had a Lady Precept."

I scratched my chin. "What was the weather like?"

"I asked that," she said excitedly. "Brent told me there was a forty-miles-per-hour tailwind, and it was hot and dry. The fairway was hard, like concrete."

"What time did Bud hit the ball?"

Sasha smacked her fist on her forehead. "I forgot to ask. I'm so dumb!"

"No big deal," I said reassuringly. "Call Kip."

"I know it was about an hour before dark."

"That's a start, but you'll need to pinpoint the precise time before you interview other witnesses."

"What should I do next?"

"What do you think?"

Eventually, she said, "Should I talk to Bud Cauldron first?"

"That'll work."

Sasha looked unsure of herself. "Is that what you would do?"

"I would."

"Right on," she said, pleased. "Then I'll do those other three people who were with him."

"Separately," I reminded her.

"I know. In person, not on the phone or through e-mail."

I mirrored her sizable grin. "You're learning. Is there anyone else who might know something? Are there any streets, office buildings, or homes nearby?"

Her voice rose. "There are houses, huge ones with big windows. Right by where the ball goes in."

"How about talking to the neighbors? Find out if anyone noticed anything. This sounds like a fun prank for a kid," I said, fondly recalling ring-and-run episodes from my youth.

"I have another idea," Sasha said tentatively.

"Let's hear it."

She crossed her eyes. "It might be lame."

"Nothing's lame when you're brainstorming."

"Maybe a hawk picked up the ball and put it in the hole."

"A hawk?"

"I told you it was lame."

"Not at all," I said, trying to mask my incredulity. "Did you see any birds flying around the course?"

"No, but maybe they do later in the day. Lots of animals stalk their prey at dawn and dusk."

"Good point," I said, impressed with her leap in logic. "How would you follow through with that?"

She answered immediately. "As soon as I find out the exact time, I could go back to the golf course at that hour and watch."

"Better yet," I suggested, "how about calling the Colorado Wildlife and Game Division. Ask about migratory patterns and whether a hawk or some other animal might have ball-moving tendencies."

Sasha's eyes widened. "You're really smart."

"Experienced," I said modestly. Also, inspired to avoid paying mileage on the gum-ball car. "Did Kip have any theories?"

"He knows exactly what happened, but he doesn't know how to prove it."

"What?"

She narrowed her eyes. "Kip says Bud Cauldron had a hole in his pocket."

• • •

I didn't sleep well that night.

I went to bed consumed with thoughts of golf, real estate scams, and credit scores.

I woke up in the middle of the night thinking about the second serious relationship I'd had in my life. Undoubtedly, it was the credit scores that triggered the memories.

Partner #2: Blackhawk, that's what happened to her.

Located just thirty miles west of Denver, Blackhawk was an old ghost town that had turned into a gambling mecca.

We'd been together for two years when I realized I was no competition for my partner's true passions: poker and slots.

She loved the card game and played it well enough to be hired by one of the larger casinos as a prop. They paid her eleven dollars an hour to fill their tables. She thought she'd died and gone to heaven. I'd never seen a closer approximation of hell. She lost between fifty and a hundred bucks every sixty minutes, as far as I could tell.

When I put a stop to that, she transferred to slots. Nickel slots. Harmless enough? Wrong. She played five coins, nine lines, which meant $2.10 a spin. Her whole being changed when she talked about the game within a game, the sounds, the different machines, the bonus rounds.

In less than six months, she'd cleared out her life savings, my life savings, our life savings, and decimated our individual and joint credit.

Once I made the decision to leave her, I severed all ties in less than two months, but I'm still repairing parts of my credit history. I've given up on protesting the charges. When an ancient debt rears its ugly head, I utter a few choice words and settle it immediately. Thanks to paying off a lot of bills that didn't really belong to me, my credit score has risen to 789, a nice number that allows me to borrow at will.

A score that I'll never again jeopardize by commingling funds or jointly purchasing assets.

Funny how relationships can do that to you. Grind down your trust, making you connect less and less with other human beings.

CHAPTER 12

A pension prisoner.

That's how Mary Jo Channing's sister-in-law, Verneeda Brown, introduced herself when we met at a Vietnamese restaurant near her place of work. She'd served twenty-seven years of a thirty-year sentence at the Department of Motor Vehicles, most recently at the Five Points branch, and soon would retire at 80 percent of her salary.

No time off for good behavior.

She used the promise of opening a retail store in a warmer climate as motivation to drag herself into work each morning. She'd drawn up a business plan for a location in Atlanta that would carry hair products for African-American women. Only daydreaming allowed her to tolerate the toxicity of Colorado citizens yelling at her as they waited in the long lines brought on by Republican tax cuts.

Verneeda was tired of "working for the man" and discouraged by the recent witch hunt at the DMV offices.

"Folks come in and look at us like we're thieves," she said, examining her fingernails, which were works of art. She wore them a full inch past the tips of her fingers and had decorated each with clear polish and stars-and-stripes art. The festivity matched her hair, which was braided with extensions, beads, and bells dangling from the ends of each rope.

"Did you know the clerk who was arrested for issuing false IDs? What was her name?"

"Felicia Nguyen. She was like a daughter, praise Jesus."

"Did you suspect her?"

"I asked her last year, 'Child, where you gettin' all that money?' I saw that new house of hers and knew good and well a clerk starting at DMV only makes $26,687. She was a hardworking woman, raising three girls on her own, but I knew she was in over her head. A gentleman friend was helping her out, that's all she'd say."

"Some friend," I said ruefully.

"Ain't men dogs?" Verneeda laughed loudly, before turning serious. "Felicia could get three years in prison for selling drivers' licenses for $100. God willing, she'll make it through this."

"She'd risk her job for $100?"

"Not $100, girl. One hundred per license, three to five times every week, for months, you understand?"

My eyebrows shot up. "That's a lot of cash."

"You know it."

"Do you think this gentleman friend was the one buying the licenses?"

"Must have been. A girlfriend from the cubicles told me Felicia's fella was selling them to people who wanted to finance cars."

"Why would they need fake licenses?"

"I hear tell they were part of the package, with phony social security numbers, verifications of employment, and credit reports, you know what I'm saying?"

I nodded distractedly, lost in thought, struck by how much this mirrored Todd Lynch's scam at Colorado Credit Company.

Verneeda rambled on, until a partial sentence recaptured my attention.

". . . at the Havana Street branch, too. We're not looking so good these days. Two more employees are in hot water for selling truck drivers' licenses. Ain't that scary? Eighty thousand pounds of truck and cargo, with dummies at the wheels. Lord help us all on the highways."

"How did you hear about that?"

"Our supervisor clipped an article from the paper, in case any of us menial workers forget our place in the system. Morale's never been lower."

"You've never had these issues before?"

"Here and there, we'd hear about someone fired for issuing a false ID or driver's license to an illegal, but nothing like this. It's a whole new world out there, with computers and such, you know what I'm talkin' about?"

"I do," I said, as another piece of the puzzle fell into place.

• • •

Friday morning, I awoke to a bolt of lightning.

I saw the flash through the slats of wooden blinds that covered my bedroom window. This was a rarity in Denver in late June, or any other month, for that matter. The morning thunderstorm, complete with lighting spectacle, made it hard to get out of bed.

I regretted that I'd stored my electric blanket in the basement locker in April, and I spent thirty minutes searching for an umbrella I never found.

Maybe I didn't own one.

I drove to work slowly, through deep puddles and small rivers, with the lights on, arriving shortly before nine.

Sasha attacked me with a burst of enthusiasm as soon as I came through the door, before my first mocha.

"I'm finished with that assignment you gave me. I drove by all twenty-eight properties. Aren't you proud of me?"

"Very," I said, barely coherent.

"Guess how many are vacant?"

I hated conjecture, especially first thing in the morning. "Just tell me."

"You're not very nice," she said petulantly. "It wasn't easy driving all over the place, you know. You owe me for gas and lunches."

"Submit the receipts, and I'll cut a check."

"You owe me $69.50 for gas, $83.22 for lunches, and I need money to fix the air conditioner in my car."

Now I was awake. I looked at her steadily. "That wasn't part of our deal."

Sasha didn't blink. "You know how much I sweat."

"Actually, I don't."

"I sweat a lot, and that won't look professional. You wouldn't want me to ruin my new blouses, would you? You told me to make a good impression on people, didn't you?"

I gritted my teeth. "How much?"

"Probably $700."

"That's more than the car's worth," I blasted in frustration.

"You could buy me a company car," she said, with an ear-to-ear grin.

I opened my top desk drawer, rifled through a pile of business cards, and handed her one with a big wrench on it. "Give this guy a call."

"Thanks, Lauren."

To her departing back, I shouted, "Tell Stan to send the invoice directly to me. And you forgot to tell me . . . how many properties are vacant?"

She came back to the doorway and danced as if she were in an end zone, making circles with her closed fists, as she chanted, "All of them. Every one. Sasha rocks. To-tal-ly."

• • •

Twenty-eight properties, all vacant, all purchased by women with the initials DJ.

Or more accurately, one woman who had qualified for the mortgages using different identities, thanks to Todd Lynch tinkering with the credit scores.

Had the IT guy told me the truth when he claimed that he couldn't reach Richard, the man who paid him to create false credit identities and histories?

The more I thought about it, the more I doubted it.

Would the head of information technology at Colorado Credit Company risk his job for packets of cash? Obviously, but for cash that came in the mail from a man he'd met only twice? That wasn't as clear.

The description Todd had given for Richard was ridiculous, generic enough to match half the male population, which was probably his intention. Only one useful iota had emerged—the description of the clunky ring, probably a class or fraternity ring. Was this a truth that had escaped from Todd's pack of lies, or another lie?

I debated following Todd Lynch for a day or two, to see if he'd set up a meet with Richard. Almost as soon as the idea occurred to me, though, I nixed it as a time-consuming long shot.

Too taxing on me, and too expensive for Bev Stankowski.

Which reminded me to place a call to the bereaved mother, something I had done at least once a week, even when I had nothing to report.

The verbal updates, brief snapshots of my progress, had seemed to comfort her. The written details, compiled in a report, would come at the conclusion of the case.

My news that Keelie Dunham's tip about Ramon Garcia and his Maxima hadn't panned out had been met with profound disappointment the previous week.

I reached Bev on my first try, and in this briefing, I couched my words.

I told her that the possibility of a real estate scam still existed, but that I'd eliminated Dan Reed, Freddie Taylor, and Rebecca Bishop from my list of suspects. To my way of thinking, all had been innocent pawns of a distant master. Dan Reed had the ambition, but not the brains. Freddie Taylor had the insider know-how, but not the amorality. Rebecca Bishop had no time or inclination.

I couldn't rule in or out Jack Barton, the buyer's agent who had represented Dee Jackson in her purchase of Holly Stamos's house. I'd stopped by his office earlier in the week, only to have a suite mate inform me that he was in Europe for the summer. Jackass might have bothered to mention that on his outgoing voice mail message, saving me the trouble of multiple calls and an office visit, but poor customer service wasn't a tip-off to fraud.

My best leads—Todd Lynch and his cohort Richard—I presented cautiously to Bev.

There was no question I'd stumbled across a labyrinth of corrupt and illegal activities, but I couldn't tie them directly to Jessica's death.

The coincidences were foreboding, but not yet incriminating.

Bev took the news in stride and thanked me for all my hard work. Near the end of our conversation, she told me that she and her husband were about to leave for the cemetery, to supervise placement of the stone at their daughter's grave.

She invited me to join in the private ceremony, but I declined.

Not for the first time, I wished that I'd overridden my parents' wishes and buried them.

On solitary hikes, I had spread my mother's ashes near Vail and my father's near Tabernash, but I longed for a place to visit. I needed a ritual for dispersing grief when it threatened to fill me.

My brother would have supported my desires, but I couldn't betray my parents. Not a second time.

I'd already double-crossed them at the funeral services. Both had requested open caskets, but I'd refused.

If their friends and extended family had felt the urge to view bodies, they should have visited my mother and father on their last days in the hospice.

My brother agreed, and we shut the lids, without compunction or second thoughts.

As I looked out the window at the light drizzle, I resolved to bring closure to Jessica Stankowski's loved ones.

I had to come up with a concrete connection between Todd Lynch, Richard, and Jessica.

Deidre Johnston, the recipient of Todd's credit-forging largesse, seemed as good a place as any to start.

Fortunately, I knew where to find her, thanks to the calendar Sasha had extracted from Jessica's PDA.

Jessica had made a notation, DJ/685SIRV, on the eleven o'clock time slot for a Wednesday morning in January.

This Wednesday happened to fall six days after she met Holly Stamos for drinks to celebrate the house sale and two days before her death.

I'd studied Jessica's schedule at least once an hour for days and could tie most of her abbreviations to engagements that made sense. In the days leading up to her demise, she'd visited the dentist, lunched with her mom, and shopped with Holly. She'd closed out her bank account, picked up gear at REI, and cut her hair.

All of these were normal activities as she prepared to spend months out of the country doing missionary work.

What about DJ/685SIRV, though?

Why did it toggle something in the back of my mind every time I read it?

I knew the DJ had to stand for Deidre Johnston, but how did 685SIRV factor in?

Then it hit me!

I raced to the filing cabinet where I'd stored the papers Bev Stankowski had given me from her daughter's closing, jerked out the folder, and flipped through the pages as fast as I could.

On the third addendum to the sales contract, I found what I was looking for, the same piece of information that might have cost Jessica Stankowski her life.

There, handwritten on the form, was 685 South Irving Street, Deidre Johnston's real address.

Not the contrived one that appeared on every other document in the file, the one that matched the bogus credit report Todd Lynch had manufactured and sold to his buddy Richard.

Not that one.

This one, I suspected, was the real deal, a slip, written from habit.

Just once.

Once was all it took for Jessica to catch the discrepancy and track her down for a confrontation.

I confirmed my suspicions with a quick peek at Denver County real property records.

A Denise Johnson owned a 1,050-square-foot house at 685 South Irving Street, one she'd purchased eleven years earlier.

I sprinted out of the office, determined to retrace Jessica Stankowski's last movements.

• • •

I found Denise Johnson's house in the Westwood neighborhood, a few blocks west of Federal Boulevard and south of Alameda Avenue.

When no one in his right mind should have paid more than $40,000 for these tiny frame and siding, one-story structures, Denver's out-of-control market had driven the prices to the mid- to high-$100s. A crime, in a crime-ridden area. Today, sheds were designed with more striking architectural features.

I'd never bought or sold a house around here, but I'd toured my share over the years, successfully avoiding taking a listing or writing up a contract.

Most of the homes were constructed after World War II, slapped together as inexpensive housing for returning veterans. They had no basements and were bordered by dirt alleys.

In a move designed to improve the appearance of Denver's poorest neighborhoods, the mayor of Denver had promised to pave all 1,042 city-owned dirt alleys with a four-inch layer of asphalt, a $20 million commitment over a ten-year period.

The six-ton asphalt roller had yet to reach this area, as evidenced by the deep wheel ruts that were full of standing water and debris. Paving alone, although "meaningful and symbolic" (to quote an elected official), couldn't begin to solve the neighborhood's problems.

For instance, one good summer of rain wouldn't make up for the fact that the home owners and renters rarely watered their lawns and had lost most of their grass to previous years of drought. The lots fell into one of four categories: yellow grass, thinning grass, bare dirt, or waist-high weeds.

None was green and lush, including Denise Johnson's.

She'd avoided the horticulture problem altogether by spreading pink and white rocks from the street to her front porch, where I now stood, banging.

The doorbell was on the ground, next to the warped step.

A tall woman came to the screen door. "Whatever you're selling, I'm not interested."

"You might be," I said, sounding like a chirpy solicitor or a Jehovah's witness. "I understand you recently purchased two properties in Washington Park." Before she could retreat, I handed her one of my Lauren Vellequette real estate cards.

She opened the door to take the card, and when she studied it, her eyes contracted. "I don't know what you're talking about."

"You purchased 1206 Josephine Street on December 11 and 1283 Elizabeth Street on January 22. I'd like to make an offer on those properties. Are they still available?"

"You must be hard of hearing," she shouted. "I'll say it again, I'm not interested."

"What are your plans for the houses?"

"None of your business."

"I know they're still vacant."

"I'm putting together an investors' group," she said, with a concentrated effort, as if she'd been coached in the proper use of that line.

"May I come in, Denise? Or would you prefer that I call you Deidre or Dee?"

She slammed the screen door and locked it, which wasn't as effective as it could have been, due to the damaged parts. I reached through the torn opening in the screen and turned the door handle. "We can do this in a civilized manner, or I'd be happy to scream my questions from the porch if you shut the inside door."

"Get out of here," she said, her words slightly slurred.

"Were you this rude to Jessica Stankowski when she came by?"

"Who?"

"The young woman who sold you 1206 Josephine Street, the one who had the misfortune to recognize you again after her friend's closing."

By now, I stood in the entryway, a fact she'd finally absorbed. "If you don't leave in the next five seconds, I'm calling the police."

"Please do." I calmly handed her my cell phone. "I'd love to show them these." I thrust copies of the drivers' licenses Mary Jo Channing at Guaranty Title had made for me—the ones that clearly depicted her photo with the names of Deidre Johnston and Dee Jackson on them.

She caved in.

Without a word, she turned and shuffled away, dragging her left foot behind her.

Not shy, I took that as an invitation and followed her.

In the living room, which was surprisingly tidy, she dropped into a recliner and lit a cigarette. By the look of the overflowing ashtray, this wasn't the first or the last of the day.

I steeled myself against the inevitable puffs of smoke, rationalizing that they might mask the stale garlic smell coming from the kitchen. The light, streaming through the small front window, shone on Denise like a spotlight, highlighting her facial features.

In her late thirties, she had a large mouth, with slight spaces between all of her upper teeth. Below a high forehead, her small eyes were spread far apart, and she had thick eyebrows and a beak-like nose. Her long neck showed premature signs of aging in its wrinkled folds, and her dark hair, combed up and away from her face, seemed brittle. Yet, somehow, all these exaggerated features combined to form a striking beauty, albeit one that injury, addiction, or both had ravaged.

On her left cheek, she had the telltale mole Mary Jo had spotted in the license photos.

Denise didn't bother to offer me refreshment, but she took her time with a long sip from a Diet Coke can. "How did you find me?"

"You mean the real you, not one of the twenty-eight identities your partner Richard furnished?"

I detected a slight flicker in her eyes. "I don't know anyone named Richard."

I let that lie pass, for the moment. "How about Freddie Taylor?"

"Who?"

"The agent you used to buy Jessica's house. She tried to contact you, to pass on the name of a personal injury lawyer, for your workplace accident," I said, gesturing at her gimpy leg. "But all your numbers had been disconnected. Didn't you want your thank-you gift?"

Denise didn't reply.

"Is Jack Barton your friend?"

"No one's my friend," she said cynically.

"Jack's in Europe now, supposedly. He probably paid for the trip with the commission he made on the house he helped you buy from Holly Stamos. Or does he even exist? Maybe Jack has multiple names, too. Is he really Richard?"

"I want to know how you found me," she said, groping for each word.

"The same way Jessica Stankowski did. On one of the papers you signed when you were buying her house, you accidentally wrote down this address. It must be habit, if you've lived here eleven years."

She took a drag from the cigarette. "No one's perfect."

"I guess not."

"None of this is your business. Or her business. I told that girl until I was blue in the face. She got the money she wanted for her house, full price, but she wouldn't get out of my life."

"You didn't count on Jessica Stankowski being such a righteous person, did you?"

"More like a stuck-up bitch, I'd call it."

"You probably didn't realize that she couldn't stand to be wrong. She knew you were lying when she ran into you in the lobby after Holly's closing, and she had to prove it. You should have admitted you knew her."

Denise sucked her teeth. "Don't talk to me like that. She should have left well enough alone."

"That was one of her traits—to a fault, according to her mother and her best friend. Jessica couldn't be wrong."

"She was, and I showed her."

"You did, didn't you?" I said mildly. "Where's the car now?"

"What car?"

"Two separate eyewitnesses saw you do it." I leaned forward to capture her attention. At varying intervals, she seemed to drift off. I'd need to make a note in my report that Denise Johnson probably was under the influence of drugs and/or alcohol during our interview.

"Saw me do what?"

"When I show them these driver's license photos, they'll confirm your involvement. I'll take their signed statements to the police."

"If you're so tight with the cops, why aren't they arresting me? Because it was no big deal, that's why," she said, crowing.

"They're not here because I'm not done with you, and I don't work for the Douglas County Sheriff's Department."

"You sure as hell ain't a real estate agent. Not in those clothes," she said, with a smirk.

She should talk. At least I had on pants, nice gray linen ones, and decent underwear. She, on the other hand, was dressed in an oversized Bette Midler T-shirt, no bra, and panties with holes. Not a pleasing sight.

"I'm a private investigator. I report to Bev Stankowski."

Denise stared at me without blinking, her eyes watery. "Who?"

"Jessica's mother."

Denise laughed, a low, mean sound. "You've been watching too many cop shows."

"Maybe you could say it was an accident," I offered helpfully.

She snorted. "No, I did it on purpose."

"Too bad you told me that," I said, my voice even. "The accident angle could have reduced your sentence from life in prison without parole to twelve to twenty-five years, out in six with good behavior."

She laughed again, more boisterously than the first time. "You're crazy."

"Not as crazy as you," I retorted. "I'm sure you'll be a big hit with the jury. The woman who assumed twenty-eight identities and bought twenty-eight properties through fraudulent means."

"Have you seen a jury pool? Twelve of my so-called peers couldn't convict a shoplifter caught on videotape, much less unravel this. At least that's what—" She stopped suddenly.

I finished the sentence for her. "Richard says?"

She crushed her cigarette in the ashtray, sending ashes flying. "I'm done talking to you."

That was an invitation to leave, but I didn't move a muscle. "You—and Richard—don't give juries enough credit. When they find out Jessica Stankowski was about to embark on a missionary assignment in Costa Rica when she tripped over your devious plans, they'll deliberate for about ten minutes."

"It figures she was a do-gooder."

"They'll take your life away for having taken hers."

"If that girl gave up her Christian pipe dream because I called and yelled at her, she must not have had much devotion."

I did a double take. "You made harassing phone calls to Jessica?"

"Not calls. A call. Didn't I admit that five minutes ago?" Denise said, her eyes glazed as she tried to recall. "So sue me. Or call the cops. Or run and tell her mommy. Or whatever you need to do, but I don't want to talk to you anymore. Get out of my living room."

"That's what you did on purpose?" I said, starting to feel as if I were losing my own mind. "Threatened Jessica in a phone call?"

"How many times do I have to tell you? Yes, I called the girl and told her to butt out or else."

"Or else what?"

"Or else nothing. I didn't think that far ahead. I just wanted her to get off my neck so I could get on with my life. It worked. She hasn't bothered me since."

"When did you make the call?"

"The same day she came here. The more I thought about her interfering, the madder I got. I called her in the middle of the night, to piss her off. She had no right to mess with my deals. She got her money. Full asking price. Her friend did, too. They weren't entitled to anything else."

"How about the right to live?"

"Sure, why not? Live and let live—what were they, lezzies? I can't do anything about that," Denise said, her face twisted in condescension. "It's a free country."

Were we having two different conversations, or was she trying to divert my attention? She didn't seem bright enough for subterfuge. Time for bull's-eye clarity.

"Jessica Stankowski is dead."

She stared at me impassively. "Sorry to hear that, but what goes around comes around."

"Two days after she came to your house, she was the victim of a hit-and-run accident."

Denise Johnson's eyes blinked rapidly as she tried to focus on what I was saying. She recovered her wits for one more denial. "That's got nothing to do with me. She should have been more careful. She was probably jaywalking."

"Jessica was off the road, on the far side of the bike path, when a burgundy Maxima mowed her down. Were you driving, or was Richard?"

My suspect swallowed three times in succession. When she eked out words, they sounded as if they'd been rubbed raw with sandpaper. "I can't drive a stick shift. Not with my leg."

That's all she said.

Every time I posed another question, she repeated through a clenched jaw one of three refrains: Buzz off, I know my rights, or that's none of your business.

I left her to her smoking.

• • •

The rest of the day and night, I kept feeding facts into the computer in my mind.

A gang of people had gone to a lot of trouble to buy up houses, only to leave them vacant.

Why?

What was up with Denise Johnson's stick shift slip, when I hadn't said a word about the Maxima having automatic or manual transmission? Was that meant to trick me?

Although Denise had seemed unaware of Jessica's death, she recognized the description of the car that had been used in the hit-and-run. I couldn't be positive Denise was the driver, but I knew she was up to her bleary eyeballs in this.

As was Todd Lynch. He'd risked his job at Colorado Credit Company, but I didn't see his motivation or involvement extending beyond the envelopes of cash he received at his post office box.

Richard, the buddy Todd had met at the real estate investors' group, now he was a more likely candidate for mastermind and murderer.

What was the scam?

I pushed on the sides of my head, trying to will the answer out of my brain.

When that yielded nothing—the harder I tried, the more my mind wandered—I gave up and went to bed, the site of my truest epiphanies.

While most people used sleep for rest or escape, I relied on it as a means to retrieve information and connect dots.

This slumber was no exception.

In the morning, in the waking moments between grogginess and full alert, I had my answer.

CHAPTER 13

I couldn't wait to test my new theory at the Denver City and County building. I rushed to the basement of the government headquarters, where the real property records division was located, and spent hours with the recording clerk.

I waited my turn, again and again, as other people came and went, but the tedium paid off.

By the time the clerk went to lunch, I'd made it through nineteen of the twenty-eight vacant properties Sasha had identified.

As the morning progressed, I could barely contain my excitement, and at record nineteen, I decided I had enough information. Forget about the other nine. I didn't need to spend any more time proving an already irrefutable point.

The nineteen shared a trait that made my skin crawl.

All of the properties purchased by Denise Johnson, under her various aliases, had significant second liens filed against the deeds of trust.

Translation: She had purchased the properties and then immediately borrowed substantial amounts of additional money, using the properties as collateral.

Found money.

Todd Lynch, for all his pride in $500 of easy money for dirty IT work, had shortchanged himself. If this were a bank robbery, he would have been the gang member filching from the lollipop tree in the lobby while his cronies ran out the back door with the bullions.

I didn't have a calculator with me, but adding figures in my head, I almost burst when I arrived at a total well in excess of three million dollars.

The price of Jessica Stankowski's life.

• • •

Arriving back at the office, I shared my good news with Sasha, but she seemed disinterested.

Maybe she didn't understand the financial ramifications. More likely, she was absorbed with her own case.

"I didn't see an account for Vista Hills Golf Course or Kip Livingston in our database. Want me to make one?"

"No. I'll take care of it."

"Do you want my time sheets? Don't you need to send a bill or something?"

"Er, yes," I said vaguely. "Put them in a folder and leave it on my desk."

"When do clients pay us?"

"Whenever I get around to billing them."

Sasha responded to my a snappish tone with a mellow, "Chill, Lauren. I was only trying to help. Want to hear what I've found out on my hole-in-one case? I interviewed Bud Cauldron and one of the other golfers, Cal."

"Remember our procedures? You're supposed to submit a written report."

Her face went slack. "They're boring, and they take too long. Can't I tell you now? Please!"

"One sentence only."

"Only one?"

I closed my eyes. When I opened them, I refused to give in to her forlorn expression. "Take your time. Make it a good one."

After a short pause, she blurted out, "Kip's wrong."

"Okay."

"Don't you want to know more?" Sasha said, crestfallen.

I flashed a meager smile. "Yes, but I don't want to influence the outcome. Write up what you know. We'll talk about it after you've interviewed the other two players in the foursome."

"Do I have to?"

My smile widened. "The sooner you contact them, the sooner we can talk."

• • •

A few minutes later, as we shared lunch at my desk, Sasha spoke up, between bites of a Quizno's sub. "You should get a new office."

I chomped down on a potato chip. "Why?"

"Because this one's gross. You don't have anything on the walls. It's like you're not even here."

I looked around, surveying my surroundings, as if for the first time.

On the downside, I could see the stained gray carpet, the narrow windows, and the fluorescent lighting. I'd never been pleased with the stale smell of smoke that permeated the building, most of which came from the grizzled CPA down the hall. She prepared my corporate and personal returns every April, and I had to air out the papers for a week before I could sign them. If I asked nicely, she'd spray a citrus deodorizer and close her door, but the stench traveled past the manufactured smell of oranges and through the ventilation system.

On the upside, I loved the central location at the corner of Colorado and Mexico, a stone's throw from I-25. The four-story building had ample parking, and I'd been on a month-to-month lease for seven years. Best of all, the executive suite was the cheapest space I could find to house my files. That's about all I'd done prior to Sasha's arrival, flitting in and out for an hour at a time, the rest of my day spent in my traveling profit center, my Subaru Outback.

Sasha had a point, though.

Maybe I needed a more vibrant environment. For her, for me, and for my new private investigation business. "I'll think about it."

Her face lit with joy. "I could research office space for you."

"What do you know about it?"

"A lot," she said, her lips pouting. A sign I'd hurt her somehow, a signal she flashed at least ten times every shift.

"Okay," I said grudgingly. "That'll be your project this month."

"What are your boundaries?"

"Boundaries?"

"North, south, east, west?"

I scratched my cheek. "Hampden to Colfax, Broadway to Monaco."

"I can make a spreadsheet, take digital photos of the properties, and give you a cost analysis."

"A cost analysis?"

"Quicken pie charts, showing overhead as a percentage of total revenues."

I looked at her with open admiration. "Where's this coming from?"

Sasha smiled shyly. "I'll compare prices per square foot, common area maintenance charges, utilities, leasehold improvements, lease duration. You'll have to tell me your criteria."

I was too floored to do anything other than mumble, "Criteria?"

"Do you prefer an upper floor or lower floor, do you need conference space, what kind of tenants do you want to share space with, would you like a view?"

"I'd love a workout room. A nice one," I added.

On a banner above the front door, the manager of this building bragged about its "state-of-the-art" fitness center. False advertising. I'd used the decrepit equipment only once—after spraying it down with Lysol. The sauna, let's just say no amount of solvents could have persuaded me to enter that chamber.

"If I'm going to check out spaces, the mileage might add up," Sasha said, alluding to her own profit center.

"For the Vespa?" I countered hopefully.

"The gum-ball car."

"Don't forget to park at the edge of the lot, or leasing agents won't take you seriously."

She took a giant bite and said, with her mouth full, "I will."

"How do you know so much about this stuff?"

She chewed slowly and cast her eyes back and forth, but didn't answer at first. When she did reply, her voice faded with every word. "My father's a commercial broker."

"I thought he was an electrician."

"Not my foster, my blood."

I looked at her inquiringly. "Your father's still alive?"

Sasha met my eyes squarely. "Yes."

"You said he was dead."

"He's dead to me."

I bristled. "Where does he live?"

"Somewhere."

"Close by?"

Sasha drew in an extended breath and let it out slowly. With the exhale, I could feel her distaste. "A mile from here. In Observatory Park."

Her steady gaze unnerved me, but I pressed forward. "Alone?"

"No-o-o," she said loudly, stretching the word out to three furious syllables. "With my mother and three brothers."

• • •

That ended our lunch.

Sasha wadded up the wrapper with half her sandwich in it, grabbed her Mountain Dew, and returned to her desk. She was too busy to talk, she claimed.

Two could play at that game.

I vacated the office and drove to Washington Park, where I sat by the lake, in full sun, and ate the rest of my lunch. After that, I read the newspaper until it was time for my meeting with Mike Schmidt, the foreman at Kitchen and Bath Remodels, the one I suspected of stealing from his boss, Kelly Hesselbach.

Posing as a nitpicky real estate agent renovating a house for a quick profit (which wasn't a stretch), I spent more than an hour with him, every minute of which I secretly tape-recorded.

We met at a vacant house I'd borrowed from a general contractor who owed me a slew of favors.

Eager to please, Mike took measurements of the kitchen island and promised he could install a Black Galaxy slab on Saturday, a miracle in construction days, as countertops generally require six to twelve weeks' lead time.

My first choice was solid black, but he showed me a four-by-four-inch sample square and convinced me the Black Galaxy would remind me of a "starlit night." I requested straight edges, but he talked me into a double bull-nose, which would "keep eggs from rolling off the counter." I preferred a honed, satin matte finish, but he corralled me into polished, with a mirror shine. He assured me the thirty-six-by-sixty-inch countertop would have industry-standard thickness, two centimeters, with a four-centimeter laminated edge.

Best of all, he quoted me $500 for the slab and $300 for installation, a steal.

The countertop should have cost between $1,000 and $2,000, but he explained the savings with, "My boss lets me take scraps and one-of-a-kinds, because he's too cheap to give me a raise."

Touching. Not exactly how Kelly Hesselbach would have described his missing inventory or himself, but perception was everything. As for the break on installation, well, that came compliments of Mike's kid, the "beef" of the operation, who would assist him for a couple bucks and a six-pack.

That worked for me.

We wrapped up the deal with a handshake, because (not surprisingly) Mike Schmidt wasn't a fan of paperwork.

• • •

I spent the balance of the afternoon on Bitterweed Court, leaning on Jackie Cooper.

Sort of.

I drank tea, ate sweets, and played gin rummy with my hit-and-run witness and her mother. With Jackie intentionally throwing away good cards to Pearl, to shorten the game, I didn't have a chance of winning.

That pissed me off, almost as much as the lack of new information.

At one juncture, when Jackie left the room to gather more refreshments, her mother made a point of telling me that her daughter had an uncanny memory for numbers, informing me in a loud whisper, "Always has. If she saw that license plate number, she knows it."

While Jackie was packing me a to-go container of homemade cookies and brownies, Pearl Cooper let me in on another secret. She knew Jackie let her win at gin, and she didn't care. She didn't like the game either.

An interesting afternoon, all in all. Quite enlightening if my intention had been to gain insight about a dysfunctional mother-daughter relationship. But the two hours had done nothing to move me closer to learning who had killed Jessica Stankowski, which meant I couldn't add them to Bev Stankowski's bill.

Damnit!

And my stomach hurt like hell, thanks to an overindulgence in sweets.

When would I ever learn?

• • •

I drove from Jackie Cooper's home to a mid-rise office building at Dry Creek and Broadway, where I climbed the stairs to the eighth floor.

I'd managed to secure the last appointment of the day with Jim Nalen of Prime Service Lending, the mortgage broker who had provided the money for Deidre Johnston (who I now knew was Denise Johnson) to buy Jessica Stankowski's house.

I arrived about five minutes early, and thirty-five minutes later a receptionist told me Mr. Nalen would be along shortly. I passed the time with mints, devouring half the sweets in the bowl in the middle of the twelve-person conference table. I also pocketed a handful of pens, compliments of Prime Service Lending, as slight recompense for my time. Both of these transgressions went unnoticed in the glass room, because the mini-blinds had been closed on all sides, floor to ceiling.

I was about to get up and leave when a tall, broad-shouldered, heavyset man appeared. He offered no apology, and I wouldn't have accepted one anyway.

Nearing sixty, Nalen had a full head of whitish-blonde hair and beady eyes that were almost lost in the folds of his eyelids. Clearly, he'd bought in to the meterosexual look, because he was clean-shaven, with short sideburns and manicured nails. He wore a pale green monogrammed shirt, a baby blue thin tie, and dark blue tailored pants. However, no cut of clothing could disguise the belly that spilled over his leather belt by a large margin.

Citing Mary Jo Channing of Guaranty Title as a reference, I stood and handed him one of my private investigation business cards, which he tossed on the table without a glance.

I returned to my seat in the plush chair at the middle of the table, but he remained standing.

"Does the name Deidre Johnston ring a bell?"

"Yes, she's a client."

"She's bought an extraordinary number of properties this year."

He said deliberately, "I wasn't aware of that."

I took another mint and slowly peeled away the wrapper. "You processed her loan for a property at 1206 Josephine. Do you remember that?"

"I do. Two actually. A no-down first and a home equity line of credit. Why does this concern you?"

"Did Deidre use the line of credit?"

He stared at me fixedly. "I have no way of knowing. Once we close a loan, it's transferred. We don't service loans."

I popped the candy into my mouth. "You couldn't make a call?"

"I could, but . . ."

I duplicated his thin, pained smile. "If you would, it might save me a trip to the district attorney's office."

His features hardened. "What are you driving at?"

"I haven't finished gathering all the facts, but it looks as if the woman posing as Deidre Johnston bought at least twenty-eight properties this year, using different names and credit identities. Her real name is Denise Johnson."

Jim Nalen's eyebrows shot up. "Fraud?"

"On a massive scale," I said, with a fleeting smile.

He cringed. "I'll be right back."

Not right back.

I waited twenty minutes before he returned with a thick file in his hand. His tan had faded to a sickly yellowish color. He dropped into a seat at the head of the table and let out his breath in a slow sizzle. "It seems as if we lent Deidre Johnston $289,500 in December, when she purchased the home on Josephine. In February, we extended a $95,000 line of credit."

My jaw dropped. "How did she manage to borrow that much, that soon? Nothing could have appreciated like that."

"Yes," he said slowly, rifling through papers in the folder. "It could if the condition of the house changed significantly, which it did. According to these notes, she gutted the house, down to the studs. She updated the electrical, finished the basement, installed copper piping, and remodeled the kitchen and baths."

"Did Deidre Johnston make her payments on time?"

"Yes, on the first loan."

"Right up to the point she closed on the second, I'll bet. She hasn't made a payment since, has she? Not on either loan."

He coughed into his hand. "That would be correct."

"FYI," I said offhandedly, "the house hasn't been touched."

"That can't be," he said plaintively. "I have before and after pictures of the kitchen and baths."

"See for yourself." I reached into my purse and pulled out a stack of digital photos.

Not bad photography, for a teenager. Sasha had borrowed the key to Jessica Stankowski's house from Holly Stamos, gained access to the property, and spent an hour shooting pictures of the interior and exterior. She'd done a splendid job for her first assignment. Nice composition, good clarity, sharp focus.

Jim Nalen, however, was not interested in the quality of the snapshots. It was their content that made his yellowish complexion morph to a dark reddish color. "This can't be," he sputtered.

"That's the kitchen, as it was twenty-four hours ago. If you don't believe me, drive by yourself. No one lives there, and the curtains are open. You can peek in and see the entire layout."

The mortgage broker fumbled through his paperwork at such a rapid pace, half of it fell to the floor. He handed me a set of photos. "This is the kitchen."

I studied the maple cabinets, stone floors, granite countertops and backsplash, and stainless appliances. A wry laugh came bubbling out of me. "This is a beautiful kitchen, but it's not inside the house you used as collateral for the home equity line of credit you gave Deidre Johnston. Where did you get these?"

"From the appraiser. They're part of the permanent file."

"The appraiser you sent out for the $95,000 loan?"

He bobbed his head. "Kurt DeWitt, of DeWitt Appraisals."

"Is he a guy you use regularly?"

Nalen removed his reading glasses and rubbed his eyes. "No."

"Who recommended him?"

"The broker," he muttered.

"Which broker?"

"Freddie Taylor, of Fine Homes."

Freddie Taylor. Deidre Johnston's agent, the woman I'd trusted and bonded with over tea at the Brown Palace. "You used an appraiser the borrower's broker recommended?"

"Yes," he said, his voice scarcely audible. "But his report was in direct line with the first appraisal."

"Which was conducted by . . . ?"

"Don Kimborough, of Front Range Appraisal."

"Did it ever occur to you that Kurt DeWitt's appraisal might have been in line with Don Kimborough's because you gave a copy of the first appraisal to Deidre Johnston at the time of her closing?"

Jim Nalen shrugged his shoulders in despair.

"All DeWitt had to do was make a few adjustments to the numbers and include the kitchen photos," I said, unable to resist adding to the mortgage broker's misery.

"I also have receipts to prove the quality of workmanship," he said feebly.

"Receipts?"

"Invoices from Home Depot and subcontractors." He gestured toward the pile of papers lying on the floor. He didn't bother to retrieve the relevant ones, apparently having accepted that they were now irrelevant.

"Did you look closely at the receipts?"

"Of course," he said, but I knew he was lying.

"Do you know how easy it is to fake receipts? Any high school kid with a computer can rig up a phony invoice."

I knew this because Sasha had tried to pass one off on me, after she'd forgotten to ask for a receipt at a downtown parking garage.

I continued. "My showing you a $10,000 Home Depot receipt for appliances doesn't mean I installed them at 1206 Josephine Street."

"That's why I relied on the photos," he said, dazed.

"Taken at someone else's house?"

"If what you're telling me is true, yes, but this is an aberration."

"Don't you people ever get in your cars and go see the properties you're using as collateral for loans that run in the hundreds of thousands?" I said, knowing full well the answer.

Clients often resented real estate agents for our hefty commissions, numbers we couldn't hide because they appeared in plain sight on settlement sheets. Buyers rarely directed their barbs at mortgage brokers, but they should have. These weasels often made as much or more than we did on deals, without ever disclosing their compensation.

They didn't have to drive men and women with too much aftershave and perfume all over tarnation and back, only to discover they had no intention of buying anything.

Jim Nalen must have picked up on my resentment, because he practically shouted, "We rely on an effective system." He momentarily regained his composure, long enough to trot out a threadbare speech. "People apply for loans, and we check their credit to assess our risk. If their credit scores are high, we assume, by their proven track record, that they'll continue to manage debt responsibly."

"If they don't, you always have the property to fall back on. Which means you're never really exposed to risk, because you always make sure the property is worth substantially more than the amount of money you lend."

"In most cases, yes."

"Foreclosures aren't even really a pain in your ass. In enough instances, you walk away with a profit, compliments of other people's misfortunes or mismanagement."

"That's not fair," Jim said, frazzled.

"For this effective system to work," I said, my sarcasm unmistakable, "you rely on independent verification that the property is worth as much as the amount of the loans against it or, ideally, a good deal more."

"Well, yes," he said, casting a look of disgust at the papers all around him.

"This time, from a so-called independent appraiser recommended by the borrower?"

"Houses in Washington Park command those prices," Jim Nalen protested, although not vigorously. "I've seen similar deals in the past year, all at price points above $400,000."

"You're absolutely right," I said agreeably. "Neighborhood comps will support appraisals in that range. But not for the house that Deidre Johnston bought from Jessica Stankowski. Between the first and second mortgages on 1206 Josephine Street, you're carrying $384,500 worth of paper on a property that's worth $289,500. The system might be broken, wouldn't you agree?"

He pushed away from the conference table in anger.

"Maybe you're not that far into it," I said cheerfully, gathering my belongings. "The $95,000 was a line of credit, right? With any luck, Deidre Johnston hasn't touched it yet. Maybe she's only borrowed a little bit of it. How much has she used, do you know?"

When Jim Nalen didn't reply right away and didn't scramble for the truth in the mound on the floor, I answered myself. "Deidre Johnston used it all, didn't she? Every cent, as soon as she could."

The discomfiture in his eyes confirmed my guess.

• • •

Jim Nalen's frustration couldn't begin to match my exultation.

It served these crooks right that they'd been swindled.

Headline news proclaimed home default rates were at an all-time high, and for good reason.

Industry sycophants blamed the state's struggling economy and the low annual housing appreciation rate for the rise in foreclosures, but they were paid to tell half-truths.

The other half, the uglier side that no one in the real estate industry wanted to own up to, was that underwriting guidelines had become more lax in the past decade. Qualifying ratios had become an amusing tool of the past, thrown aside to make room for FICO scores. For years, industry standards had dictated that monthly housing expenses (principal, interest, taxes, insurance, and home owners' dues) couldn't exceed 28 percent of gross monthly income, but that benchmark had become obsolete.

As lenders threw limits out the window, they opened the door to a dizzying array of choices. In a short span, we had gone from one product (the good old-fashioned, thirty-year, fixed-rate mortgage) to more than 150 mortgage products.

Try explaining this to buyers. I'd used all variations of words, but people only heard the good news—that they'd be moving into the home of their dreams. Never the rest—that with one misstep, they'd lose it.

Lenders said they knew what they were doing, relying on statistical averages from FICO scores, but I'd never seen a banker or broker attend an eviction, and such an event should have been a prerequisite for employment.

No-money down mortgages meant buyers didn't have to save for a down payment, which in turn, lowered their commitment to the property. No-documentation loans (affectionately known as liar loans) ushered in new levels of fraud. When buyers didn't feel comfortable lying on their loan applications, mortgage brokers did it for them. Lenders didn't give the pretense a second thought, knowing they'd collect hefty commissions long before the properties went in to foreclosure. Other lending options available to the unsuspecting public included adjustable rate mortgages, interest-only mortgages, balloon payment mortgages, option ARMs.

Etcetera, etcetera, etcetera.

With every one of these squirrelly innovations came more risk to the borrower. Yet, how many borrowers were fully aware, at the time of their closings, of the gambles they were taking? None.

For buyers needing mortgage advice, which, let's face it, was almost everyone, I became the de facto mortgage consultant, an unpaid and often unpopular position.

I couldn't count the number of times I'd broken hearts by advising against deals that looked possible, but were trouble in disguise. Most of my colleagues celebrated the permissiveness of lenders, but I felt differently. I'd seen too many broken budgets, foreclosures, and bankruptcies to join in the jubilation.

If payback was hell, I hoped Jim Nalen of Prime Service Lending was feeling every singe of the flames.

Industry studies suggested that between 10 and 15 percent of all home loan applications involved fraud or misrepresentation, but after spending seven minutes with that man, I suspected an audit of his files would reveal a much higher percentage.

High enough to red flag his involvement in a massive fabrication that involved scores of credit identities and millions of dollars in loans?

That, I couldn't say.

CHAPTER 14

Two hours and one margarita later, my mind had stopped whirring with all the possibilities for scams, even though I had to admit, I was in the thick of one.

"What did you think of my e-mail?" I said to Rollie, who sat across the table from me on the patio at Fiesta's, our favorite Mexican restaurant in west Denver. I'd forwarded the MLS description for a condo on Park Avenue West. "Should I schedule a showing?"

"No, no, and triple no."

I tried my best to appear surprised. "What didn't you like?"

"The men in rags, doll. If I wanted to step over a drunk, I'd have stayed married to my last ex."

I let out a long sigh. "I'll keep looking."

Rollie patted my arm. "Don't worry, sweetie. It's out there."

Outwardly, I seemed disappointed. Inwardly, I was thrilled.

For the better part of two weeks, I'd been tracking a condo on the top floor of the Norman, an elegant, Spanish Colonial Revival on South Downing Street, near Washington Park. Built in 1924, the six-story, forty-eight-unit building was surrounded by tall trees and lush gardens and had stupendous views of the mountains, downtown, and the Denver Country Club.

Because units in this Denver landmark rarely came on the market, sellers received contracts as fast as agents could write them. There would be no time for Rollie Austin's usual hemming and hawing. The penthouse I had in mind hadn't come up for sale yet—the divorcing couple was finalizing details of their dissolution—but a colleague had given me advance warning, an offer of a private showing, and right of first refusal.

This was my chance!

I couldn't wait to see the gourmet kitchen with cherry cabinets, silestone countertops, top-of-the-line appliances, and an eating bar. I knew Rollie would be captivated by the natural light streaming through the windows in every room. I'd never helped anyone buy or sell a condo in the Norman, but I'd been through a number of the units and had always dreamed of it.

First, I had to follow through with "Operation Sabotage."

My plan was to prepare Rollie by first showing her the types of properties she claimed to have an interest in, but only those with serious defects. The one we were discussing suited her in every respect (down to the Italian marble tile in the bathroom), except for the homeless shelter across the street.

Every morning, the shelter released the men and locked them out until dusk. The less mobile slumped against the building, staggered to the corners, or propped each other up on the sidewalks. I knew people who changed their routes to avoid driving through the depressing gauntlet on Park Avenue West, and no one dared walk through it.

Hardly a welcoming archway to a luxury highrise, but blame the developer. He had obtained the vacant land for a ridiculously low price, considering its proximity to downtown, Coors Field, and the chi-chi blocks of Larimer Square and LoDo. He'd developed it into a product only the wealthy could afford, then had the audacity to complain publicly about the "rampant scourge of the homeless."

Shame on him, but at the moment I appreciated his stupidity.

It played straight into my strategy, and I had a few other beauties up my sleeve. A spectacular fifth-story rooftop loft on Blake Street . . . with no elevator. A twelfth-floor condo in the Golden Triangle with a wraparound balcony . . . from which the previous owner had jumped. An East Cherry Creek townhome with unparalleled views . . . of the concrete parking garage to the south.

By the time the couple at the Norman had worked out their differences enough to separate for life, I'd be ready to move Rollie into their condo.

• • •

The next morning, my head felt fuzzy. From one lousy margarita.

Six years earlier, I'd given up alcohol and only recently had begun allowing myself the pleasure. The less I drank, the less I could tolerate the aftereffects. At this rate, I'd be choosing abstinence again.

Sasha's voice grated on my brain. "Did you read my report?"

"Not yet," I lied. "Give me the summary."

"Now? I don't know what to say."

"Start with, did Bud Cauldron hit the longest hole in one in U.S. golf history?"

"No."

"Did he fake it and convince three people to lie for him and sign false affidavits?"

"No. Cal must have put the ball in the hole."

"Who's he?"

"One of the guys who played with Bud."

"How did he do it?"

Sasha shrugged.

"Why pin it on him?" I said, my stress rising, as it had each of the three times I'd read Sasha's sketchy report.

"Because he acted guilty. He wouldn't look at me, and his hands shook."

"Some people have nervous mannerisms."

"He wants the promotion."

"What promotion?" I said, suddenly alert. This explained why Sasha's written report totaled less than half a page. She'd left out all the juicy details.

"Bud is the sales manager for Dexter. They sell supplies to veterinarians. Cal, Bob, and Anita, the three players, work for him. Bud is going to promote one of them next month."

"Last names?"

"I can't remember, but they're in the report you never read."

I ignored the snippy tone. "Spelled correctly, I assume. Who told you about the promotions?"

"All of them. Little bits. I asked them how they knew each other, and they told me all this other stuff."

I nodded with satisfaction. "Good."

"Bob doesn't want a different job. He likes the one he has. Anita's quitting next week, but she made me promise not to tell anyone. I know it's Cal. He had the same kind of ball as Bud."

I released a slow smile. "The two men played with the same ball that day?"

"Not that day. Bud made the hole in one with a Lady Precept ball that had Dexter's logo with a pink ribbon imprinted on it. They gave them out at a company golf tournament in April."

"Cal was at that tournament?"

"Yep," Sasha said triumphantly. "Bob and Anita weren't. Bud sent them to a Purina meeting in St. Louis."

I rubbed my hands together. "As far as you know, Cal was the only one with opportunity?"

Sasha nodded proudly.

"Other than Bud," I said pointedly.

She shook her head. "Bud didn't do it."

"What makes you certain?"

"He was nice to me. He said he liked my hair, that it reminded him of a rainbow."

I sighed. "Sasha, you can't rule out someone because he pays you a compliment."

"He talked to me like I was a real person."

"Again, a nice quality, but no proof of innocence."

"He's a good golfer, and this is bugging him," she said earnestly. "He wishes he'd never hit the ball. He lives on a golf course in Thornton and plays every day. He started golfing when he was eight. He was a helper or something at the Denver Country Club when he was twelve."

"A caddy?" I offered.

"Yeah, that. He used a Big Bertha club," Sasha said, her words spilling forward faster than her breath. "He has a four handicap, whatever that is, but Kip told me it's good. Kip told me he'd heard about a three-year-old boy who hit a hole in one with a Snoopy driver and a nine-year-old girl who hit one the first time she swung a golf club. If little kids can do that, why can't Bud hit one 520 yards? He's had eight in his life, why would he make one up?"

"To register the longest one in history?" I said reasonably.

"Bud didn't know he'd set a record," she cried defensively.

"Says who?"

"Bud. He looked for the ball forever, then he gave up and hit another one."

"A drop shot," I commented to myself.

"He was totally surprised when they found the first ball in the circle."

"The cup. Says who?"

"Bob, Cal, and Anita. They all saw his reaction. He almost fell over, he was so excited. Bud wants to send the ball to the FBI for fingerprints, but—"

I cut in. "Let me guess, too many people have handled it."

Sasha's jaw dropped with surprise. "How did you know?"

"Experience."

"You don't believe Bud?"

"Do you?" I countered.

"Yes," she said angrily.

"Why?"

"Because."

After I waited for the words that should have followed but never did, I began slowly. "In this field, Sasha, you have to be more suspicious. You're starting with trust. I want you to begin with distrust."

"I don't want to be like that," she said, with a glare. "That's why you don't have a girlfriend."

"Focus on Bud," I said tersely. "Convince me."

"Bud hasn't told anyone about the hole in one. He's afraid they won't believe him. They'll think he's crazy or he's lying."

"Yet, he intends to register the feat?"

"Only because a friend told him about the national organization. He'd never heard of it."

"Ah, ha!" I said loudly. "Bud did tell someone—at least one person."

"Yes. No. That's not fair. You're confusing me. Stop it," Sasha said, frustration in her voice.

"I want you to see that you have to stick with facts. Do any facts help eliminate Bud as a suspect?"

"No," she said, one small word, in a small voice.

"Keep digging."

"Okay," she screeched.

I changed tactics. "If you're sure Cal is the guilty party, produce a credible witness to back up your theory."

"What's that mean?"

"Someone believable, someone with nothing at stake."

Sasha pushed air out her cheeks. "This is hard. How am I supposed to do that?"

"You said there were houses near the golf course . . ." I prompted.

"So?" she said sluggishly.

"Knock on doors."

A look of fright crossed her features. "What am I supposed to say?"

"That you're a private investigator hired by the Vista Hills Golf Course to independently verify a hole in one that occurred on June 3 at the seventh hole."

Sasha scrunched up her face. "What if people won't talk to me?"

"Go to the next house."

I stared at her, but her expression never changed. I uncrossed my arms and said eventually, "If we have to, we'll go back together."

"You'd help me?" Her features softened, but there was something in her eyes I couldn't read.

"Of course I would," I said quietly.

• • •

Several hours later, Sasha loomed over my desk. "I don't have money for lunch. What's in that blue bag in the freezer, the one marked with an R?"

I reached into the petty cash envelope in my top desk drawer. "A breast."

"Of what?"

I handed her a ten. "Of me."

She turned pale and couldn't speak. I could see the wheels turning, as if she wanted to say something, but nothing came out.

I continued casually. "Six years ago, I was diagnosed with cancer. I had both breasts removed."

"Eww," she squeaked. "Why did you keep it?"

I ignored her open stare, directed at my chest. "Because I didn't know what else to do with them."

She seemed stunned. "Where's the other one?"

"My left breast is in the freezer at my apartment."

"Wouldn't this one fit there?"

"Yes," I said deliberately, "but then I'd have all my breasts in one place. This way, I've split the risk."

"Of what?"

"Of a power outage destroying them."

Sasha kept gawking. "How long are you going to keep your breasts?"

"Until I'm done with them," I said mechanically. "Why? Does it make you uncomfortable?"

"No," she said uneasily. "I've just never met anyone with cancer."

"You have now." I turned back to my work, hoping she'd take the hint.

She didn't stir. "Lauren?"

"What!" I snapped reflexively.

Her words came out in a meek trickle. "Are you going to die?"

I cocked my head upward until I met her eyes. I answered in a steady voice, "Not from cancer."

She shuffled around the desk to give me a glancing hug. "I'm sorry your breasts are in the freezer."

• • •

When Sasha left the room, my palms started sweating, and I had to blink hard to avoid tears.

How could this teenager I barely knew be the first person to say something that made sense? I shook my head in quiet disbelief and took deep breaths, trying to still my heart.

Maybe I shouldn't have lied to her.

The truth I'd told her: Breast cancer wouldn't kill me. The truth I'd withheld: Suicide might.

Maybe I was lucky the cancer hadn't spread to my lymph nodes or lungs or brain, but I didn't feel lucky.

Most days, I felt tired and alone and finished.

I felt like saying "fuck you" to everyone who said it was a miracle the doctors caught the cancer at an early stage, to everyone who told me I was fortunate to be alive, and most of all, to everyone who said they'd pray for me. Those people annoyed me beyond expression. I had my own deal going with God, and thus far, it hadn't included gratitude—in any way, shape, or form—for saddling me, my mother, and my father with malignant cells.

I hadn't actively thought about suicide in a long time, but through my parents' illnesses and immediately after their deaths, it was all I thought about.

What a notion: I could die all at once, not by degree. The thought cheered me immensely.

From my parents' prescriptions, I stashed enough sleeping pills to fell an ox and threw in antidepressants and heart medications for good measure.

I took great comfort in feeling as if I had a choice. About something. Based on the amount of suffering I could tolerate versus the joy I felt, I could select the day, the time, and the circumstances. The decision would rest entirely in my hands, not in those of strangers.

I could die in the woods or on a playground, next to the ocean or in a stream. I could die before sunrise or after sunset, on a full-moon night or under a sliver. I could die in an alpine meadow or on a sunbaked deck. I could die in a pouring rain or a gentle snowfall.

I could die today. Or tomorrow. Maybe the day after.

Once I came to that realization, everything changed. For the first time since the doctor averted his gaze and I heard the words "abnormal clusters of calcification," I felt completely alive.

I no longer had to suffer through tests and rechecks, clinging to technicians' every word, searching for clues in the undertow of their voices. I didn't have to live with the lie that cancer was forever. Once stricken, never again healthy, only time bidden between doctors' appointments and death. I didn't have to wait for results of when and how I would die.

Cancer would never kill me. I'd kill myself first. As soon as I arrived at that decision, a few others followed, including the big one: a career change.

Whereas before, I'd been afraid to risk, nothing seemed risky anymore. Lay my life on the line, and everything else paled. Fear of what? Failure, rejection, humiliation? Tiddlywinks compared to what I'd already wagered.

The thought of death, on my own terms, had jump-started me back to life.

Emotionally, my heart hadn't quite caught up to my actions. Most days I still felt like an outsider, wishing the world would slow down enough for me to jump back on, but at least I'd done something.

I had my new private investigation business and all my gadgets. Not to mention an intern, now my paid employee, singing off-key to her iPod in the next room.

Tangible evidence of my new life.

Just to be safe, though, I'd hold on to the breasts.

For a while longer.

• • •

"Lauren, this is a voice from your past."

My heart raced, and I could have strangled Sasha.

She'd transferred the call to me, without the screening or introduction that I'd told her, over and over again, was part of her job. "Valerie."

"How are you?" Valerie Edbrooke said, drawing out the words.

"Good, and you?"

"Same as ever. How long has it been?"

Two lifetimes. "Who can remember?" I said nervously.

"How's your health?"

"Perfect. How are the kids?"

"They're a handful, as usual. Kimber's playing basketball at St. Mary's, and Leila's in the band at St. Vincent's, playing the tuba, if you can believe it."

I smiled at the image of the twiggy girl wrapping her arms around the giant brass instrument. "I miss them," I said quietly.

Valerie's voice rose in hyper-perkiness. "They'd love to see you. How are your parents?"

I paused for a split second. "They died a few years ago."

"Oh, Lauren, why didn't you call?"

"I don't know . . ." I said, my voice disappearing.

Silence followed. "I hear you're a private eye now. Are you out of real estate?"

"Not entirely, but I'm moving in that direction."

"Good for you. You talked about quitting ten years ago."

"Did I?"

"Constantly. Freddie Taylor told me you two had tea at the Brown Palace."

"We did." I smiled at the memory. "Have you been there with her?"

"Several times, and it never gets old."

"Mmm," I said in agreement.

Another dead space, which made me ache.

At one time, I'd considered Valerie Edbrooke my best friend. For years, we'd shared the same cramped office, sense of humor, and addiction to chips and salsa.

Out of the first floor of a Victorian house in the Uptown neighborhood, we operated separate real estate firms, sharing administrative services, marketing, and phone coverage. When Valerie's husband dumped her, leaving her with two toddlers and a hefty mortgage, she turned to the structure and guaranteed income of a larger real estate company. Without the burden of business, our friendship had deepened. For years, I felt as if I were a member of her family, a proud "auntie" to her girls.

That all ended the day I was diagnosed with breast cancer.

Valerie was the first person I called, on my way home from the doctor's, and for some reason, the news instantly created a rift between us, one I never understood well enough to bridge. I'd thought of her often over the years—almost obsessively at times—but I'd never picked up the phone or stopped by, and neither had she.

Valerie spoke eventually. "I'd like to hire you, if you're interested."

"Okay," I said hesitantly.

"I'm the president of the Southeast Board of Real Estate Brokers. Our top priority is to address open house thefts. We've had eighteen crimes in the southeast corridor this quarter alone."

Valerie Edbrooke hadn't been a joiner, much less a leader. What else had changed? Had lines formed around her mouth from her pack-a-day habit? Had she started wearing bifocals? Had her breasts sagged? Had her black hair ceded to gray?

I couldn't bear to imagine myself through her eyes. All I could say was, "Hmm."

"Unfortunately, I have a vested interest in the situation. They hit one of my listings in Regal Pointe last weekend."

"The gated community in Greenwood Village?"

"That's the one. I have a 5,300-square-foot, Spanish two-story listed at $2.25 million. While one of my associates, Barb, hosted an open house for me on Sunday, someone left with prescription drugs from the master bath."

"No jewelry or other valuables were taken?"

"The home owner had those locked in a safe. Unfortunately, two bottles of Vicodin and Percodan were in a drawer, not under lock and key, but certainly not in plain sight. One hundred and twenty pills are missing."

"Did you call the police?" I said, fully aware that most of these crimes were never reported.

"The seller did on Monday. The police came and lifted fingerprints. They're searching the Colorado Bureau of Investigation and the FBI databases for a match."

"Was the thief a man or a woman?"

"Barb guessed it was a woman, but she can't be sure. She had twenty-three people come through the open house. She's working with detectives to produce a sketch, but we need to be more proactive. At our last board meeting, someone suggested we offer a $5,000 reward, but I'd rather put the money toward hiring you."

"You don't trust the police to catch the criminal?"

"I don't believe they understand our dilemma. Last year, we invited an officer to attend a general membership meeting, and his suggestions were laughable. He wanted us to keep all buyers in view."

"You can't," I said simply.

"We're supposed to take down driver's license numbers on our sign-in sheets."

"No one would agree to that."

"He'd also like our sellers to strip all personal belongings out of bedrooms and bathrooms before the open houses."

"That's not practical."

"My favorite: We aren't supposed to go into basements alone with prospective buyers."

That tip, I knew, had arisen from a harrowing episode in Park Hill the previous year. An agent had been sexually assaulted in the basement of a house in the middle of a Saturday afternoon showing. "Yet, the officer wants you to keep visitors in view? How does that work?"

"You see my frustration."

"You might want to contact the Denver Real Estate Board. They sent a flyer recently to all active members, with a warning. Maybe it's the same woman."

"That's a good suggestion. I don't know what else to do. Open houses help sell properties and attract unattached buyers, but agents are becoming wary. We have to make them safe again. If my board will approve this, would you be interested in the job?"

"I would. When's your next meeting?"

"In three weeks."

"Let me know."

Another awkward pause followed, before Valerie said, "If the board doesn't go along with the idea, we should get together for old times' sake."

"I'd like that," I said, with a catch in my voice.

"If you have the time . . . is there anyone special in your life?"

"No, you?"

"Not this year. I took a vow of celibacy."

I kept my tone light. "How's that working out?"

"I think about sex all the time."

I tendered the obligatory laugh. She added, "It's made me less frantic, more centered."

"That's good."

I'd never known Valerie Edbrooke not to be "in a relationship," a perpetual state she assured through conscious overlap. I couldn't imagine the toll the revolving door had taken on her daughters, much less on her. As her friend, I'd suffered under the strain of it. Early on, I'd learned never to say a disparaging word about any man departing from her life, lest he return to an elevated status.

There was a lengthy pause, before she said casually, "We might meet for coffee or margaritas sometime."

"Either sounds good."

That was how Valerie Edbrooke and I ended our call.

Exactly as we had six years, three months, and fourteen days before, with the illusion of closeness and interest, but no commitment.

After I replaced the phone in its cradle, I cried softly.
For what I'd lost, or what I'd never had?
I couldn't have said, and what did it matter?
The release, more a hiccup than a sob, nonetheless felt cathartic.

CHAPTER 15

After a short time, I regained my composure and stepped into the outer office.

Sasha looked up at me, expectantly. "Why are you wearing sunglasses?"

"My eyes hurt. Why didn't you tell me who was on the phone before you transferred the call?"

"Chill, Lauren. She said she was an old friend, and she wanted to surprise you. Was it a surprise?"

"Yes," I said, with more resignation than anger.

"By the way, do we get Friday or Monday off as our paid holiday for Fourth of July?"

"Neither."

"That's not fair. What's the company policy?"

"I have no idea," I said wearily.

"Where's the employee manual? I'll look it up."

"You'll have to write it first."

Sasha stared at me and said in a loud whisper, "You don't have one?"

I shrugged. "Why would I? I've never had employees."

"You need an employee manual," she said firmly. "We studied human resource management in my business class last year, and you could get in big trouble. I'll write one for you."

When I rolled my eyes, she added hastily. "I'll go online and research what's standard. We're going to be big, Lauren. We'll need consistent policies and procedures for all of our employees."

"Fine," I said distractedly. "Throw something together, and I'll review it."

"I get to make all the decisions?" she said, rubbing her hands together gleefully.

"You make the recommendations, and I'll make the decisions."

Sasha scrunched up her face, deep in thought. "This year, we're too busy to take time off to celebrate Independence Day."

"Sounds good," I said heartily.

"I'd recommend we receive overtime pay on Monday, at time and a half."

I scowled.

"Or," she said swiftly, "we could take a comp day sometime before the end of the year."

I smiled. "That's better."

• • •

The next morning, I called Freddie Taylor to clear up a point.

After we exchanged pleasantries, she told me she'd never met Kurt DeWitt, the appraiser who submitted the inflated figure that allowed Deidre Johnston to secure a $95,000 home equity line of credit.

Claiming she wanted to help out a friend, Deidre had given Freddie a stack of Kurt's cards and had asked her to pass them on to people in the field. Ever the networker, Freddie had obliged, turning one over to Jim Nalen of Prime Service Lending.

That was Freddie's story, and I believed her.

Just in case, though, I erred on the side of caution and lied when she asked if I'd located Deidre Johnston.

Nothing could be gained from telling Freddie that I'd met her client, real name Denise Johnson, and that I was well on my way to proving her guilty of fraud, conspiracy, theft, forgery, and possibly murder.

• • •

In the middle of the next morning, I was clicking through MLS listings, looking for more properties with serious flaws that I could show Rollie, when I heard rustling in the outer room.

I called out to Sasha, then remembered that I'd sent her to the printer's.

I rose, cautiously walked through the door, and saw a woman fiddling with items on Sasha's desk.

She wore a deep purple blouse with detachable ruffle, a lightweight polyester lavender jacket, and matching contour-waist pants. No need for a belt with those slacks, or a static waist size. I'd sworn to never wear pants like that unless I was in a nursing home. This woman, around my age, apparently didn't suffer from the same vanity. She had mousy brown hair with one-length bangs that extended past her eyebrows and blended into the helmet of hair surrounding her round face.

"May I help you?"

She barely looked up. "I'd like to discuss Sasha."

"Why?" I said, with trepidation.

"She's my foster daughter."

"Oh."

"Do you have a moment?"

"Of course. I'm Lauren. Lauren Vellequette." I reached to shake her hand.

She returned my grip with a fingertip squeeze. "I assumed that. I'm Gayle Bidwell."

I gestured to my office. "Come in."

She situated herself on the edge of the folding chair across from me, her posture erect, her hands clasped around the purse in her lap. "I'm concerned Sasha may have misled you."

I tilted back in my chair. "About what?"

"Her circumstances," she said, forcing a smile on her sour face.

I stiffened. "Which are?"

"Sasha wants to believe she's normal, but she's not. She desperately tries to fit in, but never will."

"Sasha Fuller?" I said, in disbelief. The one with circus-like makeup, a nose ring, and blue and yellow hair?

"I'm equally troubled that you may be misleading her."

I felt the blood rushing to my face but calmly replied. "How so?"

"By working here this summer, she might get the wrong idea. She won't be able to continue when the school year resumes. Her studies come first."

"August is two months away," I said levelly.

"You're satisfied with her work?"

"Extremely." Other than the coffee pot she ruined while heating up her Cup-a-Soup lunch.

"What does she do?"

"She's my personal assistant."

"She can't be trusted. I hope you know that."

"She's a teenager."

"She's a pathological liar."

I frowned. "I hadn't noticed that."

"Who has no friends."

My furrow deepened. If Sasha didn't have friends, who helped paint the gum-ball car? An imaginary friend?

Gayle Bidwell continued her litany. "Who has a driver's license but won't explain how she obtained it."

"Hmm," I said, not about to implicate myself.

"Who suddenly has a brand new wardrobe but won't reveal how she funded it. Who stays out until all hours of the night, if she bothers to come home at all."

"Isn't this typical of her age . . . and the age we live in?" I said lightly.

"It most certainly is not," she huffed. "My husband and I were pure when we married. We're raising our foster children with the same family values. Not everyone has to drown in the swamp of this culture, but Sasha seems to be headed that way. By her behavior, I can only conclude she's involved in sex or drugs, or worse."

I tried to hide a smile. "Worse?"

"Cults or criminal activities, and I won't allow that influence in my home. Sasha Fuller may not have felt repercussions from her biological family, but she will from me. There will be serious consequences if she doesn't shape up."

"I don't think she'll respond well to threats," I said mildly.

"With children, you have to curtail inappropriate behavior before it gets out of hand, which is why I'm here. I can't understand Sasha's sudden interest in real estate. Why is she eager to work for you? Can you explain it?"

"Maybe she has nowhere else to go."

"I hope it's not a front for something else."

"Like what?" I said, surreptitiously shooting my eyes across the desk, ready to cover up anything that tied me to a private investigation business. Fortunately, Sasha must have tidied the office earlier in the morning. That was one of her finest attributes—converting piles into files.

Gayle Bidwell eyed me with suspicion. "You don't keep cash on hand, do you?"

"Never."

"There must be something," she said stubbornly.

"Sasha likes the challenge. She's using her computer skills and her organizational talents, and she's learning how to run a small business. She could do a lot worse with a summer job."

Gayle's eyebrows arched judgmentally. "You're paying her?"

"I used the term loosely," I said rapidly. "In her internship program."

"You'd better not count on her continued involvement. She has a habit of disappointing people."

"She's a smart, confident young woman, and I look forward to seeing her every day," I said, surprising myself with a rare spurt of honesty.

She snickered. "Apparently Sasha hasn't told you much about herself."

"Only that she lives with you and your husband."

"Nothing about the three other children in our care?"

I shook my head.

"Did she tell you that her parents are dead?"

"At first, but—"

When Gayle let out a mirthless laugh, I raised my voice. "Sasha told me the truth, that they live in Observatory Park."

"I suppose that's progress," she said, studying me with a grudging respect. "Did she tell you about her years in psychiatric care?"

"No, but she's told me that she's thought about suicide." Not quite true, but reasonably close. Anyone with half a brain could have surmised that from our initial job interview, after Sasha had asked about suicide and my reaction to it.

"Did Sasha tell you she had to be homeschooled because of her catatonia?"

"No."

"Did she tell you about the fire?"

"The scar on her leg," I said impulsively.

"Did she tell you she started the fire with fireworks?"

"That could happen to anyone," I said, my face betraying no emotion.

She sneered. "Did she tell you she set them off in her bedroom?"

A small cry slipped from my throat.

"Did she tell you that she received third-degree burns?" Gayle Bidwell said matter-of-factly. "Or that a doctor in the emergency room told her that she was lucky she hadn't tried to put out the flames with her face?"

• • •

Five minutes after Gayle Bidwell departed, her foster daughter came strolling into my office.

As Sasha sniffed around the room, her face hardened. "The witch came to see you, didn't she?"

"I have no idea what you're talking about," I said innocently.

"Stop lying. I can smell her. Why did she come by?"

I dropped the pretense. "She's concerned about you. Why didn't you tell me about the rest of your family, that you live with three sisters?"

"They're not my family. Those girls are bitches, and the witch and warden hate me."

"I'm sure that's not true."

"They'd dump me if they could, but they need the $900. That's why they keep taking in kids, for the monthly checks the state sends them. The witch doesn't have to work anymore."

"You're not close to your sisters?"

"Foster sisters, and no! They're preprogrammed robots. Did the witch tell you about her views on sex, about the purity covenant she makes everyone sign? I'm the only one who refused. I can't bring my friends to the house, or she attacks them with her Religious Right platform. Did you hear about it?"

"A little," I said, a gross understatement.

"Don't you think it's sick?"

"It's extreme, but she has a few other points."

"Like what?" Sasha said, combative.

"Where do you go at night?"

Sasha avoided my gaze. "Away."

I searched for a way to connect with her but came up empty. After a long pause, I said, "Are you safe?"

"Y-e-s," she said, stretching the word for maximum effect.

"Will you ever tell me about it?"

She let out an exasperated sigh. "Maybe."

"When?"

"When you're forty-five."

I tightened my shoulders in a stretch, took a deep breath, and let it go. "Did you see your foster mom leaving? Is that how you knew she'd been here?"

"No. I'm psychic," Sasha said viciously. "Did the witch call me a pathological liar?"

"She did," I said blandly. "Are you?"

She shrugged. "Sometimes."

"Why don't you tell the truth?"

"Because they wouldn't believe me anyway. You're the only one who believes me."

"You're not into drugs or cults, are you?"

She grunted but otherwise didn't answer.

"Your foster parents aren't physically or sexually abusing you, are they?"

Sasha dropped her head. "No, but they're emotionally abusing me."

"How?"

"By making me live by their values."

"That's all?"

"It's a lot. I'm oppressed every day. They're killing my spirit."

"Most parents do that," I said, with an easy smile, "whether they're foster or biological."

She pouted. "I hate them."

"That's pretty standard, too."

Sasha folded her arms across her chest and sulked. I stood and patted her on the shoulder as I passed, strolling over to the doorway and sniffing. "You weren't kidding. You can smell your foster mom's perfume when you stand here. That's how you knew she was here."

"That's what you think," Sasha said, laughing carelessly. "I spied on the two of you using the fake smoke alarm." She pointed to the detector attached to the ceiling above my desk.

I felt a moment of panic. "You did not!"

"I should have." She laughed more hysterically. "That would have been hilarious."

This girl scared me. Maybe she was psychic. She'd just guessed the next device on my list of coveted electronics. I'd debated between the smoke detector and the wall clock, both priced at $899. Each came with the same undetectable camera hidden in its innards, with wide angle pinhole lens, micro-electronic sensors that adjusted with light changes, independent power supply, and wireless setup. I was leaning toward the smoke detector, which was fully functional, because people never noticed them. Wall clocks faded into environments, but smoke alarms disappeared.

"How do you know about the smoke detector video camera?"

"It was the last page you visited on the Spy Company website," she said, before adding savagely, "You better not use it on me."

"It's not for the office," I assured her. "It's for a friend."

"If you say so."

"A friend I've known since high school, Nancy. She wants one for her parents."

"Nice details," Sasha said sarcastically.

"Nancy's mother thinks the cleaning lady's stealing food."

"Uh-huh."

"Honestly. Nancy's father is a diabetic, and he's on a sugar-restricted diet. He may be sneaking snacks. Her mother doesn't want to make accusations until she has proof."

"Whatever."

The more I spoke the truth, the more it sounded like a lie. I persisted. "Sasha, look at me."

She raised her head. "What?"

"I trust you," I said softly but urgently.

When she met my gaze, the sorrow in her eyes hurt my heart.

"You shouldn't," she said, stomping out of the room.

CHAPTER 16

I had one last item of business to conduct before the holiday weekend.

The day before, I'd made an appointment with Kurt DeWitt, the appraiser Jim Nalen at Prime Service Lending had used on the house on Josephine Street.

Kurt had agreed to meet me at a vacant property he needed to appraise in Congress Park.

When I arrived at the designated house at noon, he stepped down from an F-250 truck that displayed not only his corporate identity and tagline, but also a caricature of himself.

He handed me a mini Mag-Lite branded with the company logo.

In person, he was as arrogant as he'd sounded on the phone. Dressed in khaki pants, gleaming work boots, and a short-sleeved black cotton shirt with DeWitt Appraisals stenciled on the pocket, he had the build of an offensive lineman gone to seed. His deep voice matched his bulk. He had thick black hair, bushy eyebrows, and a postage-stamp-sized swatch of whiskers below his lower lip.

As he shook my hand, he glanced at my chest, but it didn't hold his interest. When I'd had boobs, the lingering male stare had always unnerved me; now that I'd lost them, the dismissive scan bothered me more.

"How did you hear about me?" he said conversationally, as he grabbed a digital camera and laser tape measure from the front seat.

"Jim Nalen gave me your name."

Kurt DeWitt nodded. "A good guy. We've done some deals together. He'll give you a reference for my work."

"He's not too pleased with one appraisal you did recently," I said good-naturedly. "A house in Washington Park, 1206 Josephine Street."

Kurt's eyes narrowed, but his smile never wavered. "What seems to be the problem?"

"Based on your appraisal, Jim's company extended a $95,000 line of credit, on top of a first mortgage he'd already closed."

"What's your point?"

"The first appraisal . . ." I pulled a small notebook from my purse and paused to study a page in the middle, a trick I'd learned from the SOB instructor. "Let's see, the first appraisal in December of last year came in at $289,500, the purchase price of the house. Yours, in February, came in at $384,500."

"Again, what's the problem?"

I raised an eyebrow. "That's quite a spike."

"Happens all the time."

"What would make a property's value skyrocket like that, in such a short period of time?" I said, with a demure smile.

"Any number of situations could account for it. Mold abatement, zoning change, room additions, new kitchens or baths. You name it . . ."

"Fraud?"

His eyes narrowed. "I don't like your tone."

"Or the implication, I'm sure, but there it is," I said pleasantly.

"Who did you say you were with?"

"I didn't, but I'm conducting an investigation on behalf of the Federal Housing Authority," I said, dropping the big bomb.

At the mention of the FHA, Kurt dropped all pretense of charm. "Did Nalen sic you on me?"

"I can't answer that."

"Screw him," he said, in a menacing tone. "Screw all of them. They hire me to do a job, they tell me a number, and I'm supposed to hit it."

"Who's they?" I said mildly.

"Mortgage brokers."

"Is that what happened with the Josephine property?"

Kurt DeWitt shook his head slowly, restoring his calm. "To be honest, I can't remember. In a good week, I do thirty appraisals. If this one was in February, like you say, that was four months ago. I'd have to look at my records."

"But you're admitting that you do inflate the values?"

"Slightly. From time to time," he said, clenching his jaw. "For the referrals. If I don't, the jerks won't hire me again. Every guy working in this business does it."

I made a mark in my notebook. "Did Jim Nalen pay you more?"

Kurt DeWitt stopped fiddling with the tools in the box on the cab of his truck and raised himself to his full height. "Hell no! He's never given me more than the standard fee of $175, which he marks up to $350 for the client. None of us appraisers is getting rich."

"When there is a legitimate jump in the values because of renovation, how do you demonstrate it?"

He swung a collapsible ladder from the truck bed and almost hit me with it. "With interior photos, if the lender wants proof, but most don't. In a standard job, we take exterior shots and street views. Unless they ask for more, that's it."

"Did you provide photos of the house on Josephine?"

"Again," Kurt said tightly, "without my notes and the file, I can't answer that."

"Does a solid granite slab and cherry cabinets in the kitchen ring a bell?" I offered helpfully.

He let out a wry snort. "That describes half the kitchens going in today."

"Do you visit every property you appraise?"

Kurt hesitated. "Not necessarily. But neither does any other appraiser, no matter what he tells you."

"In other words, you may have taken a shortcut on this property?"

"Possibly."

"Could you have relied on photographs you never took, at a house you never stepped foot in, for a quick fee?"

He eyed me warily. "I might have."

"Did Jim Nalen give you the photos?"

Kurt DeWitt's eyes flickered, but he didn't say a word.

"Or someone else? C'mon, Kurt, I understand your position—you were screwed if you made up a number and screwed if you didn't. You obviously didn't benefit from a fraudulent appraisal, but someone did. Give me a name, and you'll be in the clear."

"No more hassles?"

"Not from me."

"I can't say what happened in this particular situation," he said, in a slow drawl, "but when someone pressures an appraiser and tells him how to do his job, it's usually someone with a vested interest."

"Say a real estate agent or a mortgage broker?"

"Could be."

"Maybe someone named Freddie Taylor?" I suggested.

"Maybe," he said vaguely.

"Or Jim Nalen."

"I didn't say that."

I unleashed a conspiratorial smile. "Never."

"We understand each other?"

"Perfectly. What about Denise Johnson?"

He started. "Who?"

"The woman who bought the house on Josephine."

"Never heard of her."

"You may have known her as Deidre Johnston or Dee Jackson."

"Lady, you're confusing me," he said, his smile reappearing in full illumination. "Let's talk about something else. What do you like to do for fun?"

"Fun?" I couldn't think of a single reply.

"Maybe we could meet for drinks sometime."

"I don't think so."

"Are you in a relationship?"

"Yes," I said, in a clipped tone.

With myself. And it wasn't going well.

• • •

What did I like to do for fun?

As I sat home alone on opening night of Fourth of July weekend, without fireworks, only TiVo and See's Candies for company, I contemplated Kurt DeWitt's question.

How pathetic was it that I couldn't come up with a decent answer?

If my life had depended on it, what would I have chosen for fun?

Nothing that involved messy entanglements. Not with my track record.

Partner #3: Cheating, that's what had broken us apart.

We met in a hiking club and gradually became best friends who did everything together. Then girlfriends. Then partners.

We had a close circle of friends who were similarly coupled. We entertained every weekend and traveled the world. We sea-kayaked in Alaska, snorkeled in Cozumel, and heli-skied in Banff. We even talked about having children.

I put an end to all that in the Satire Lounge.

Three years into our relationship, I served a term on the Colorado Board of Real Estate Brokers and met a woman I liked. Our innocent flirting accelerated one night when we joined a group of agents and brokers at a bar on Colfax. I teased this gal about why she didn't have a girlfriend, causing her to blurt out that she was attracted to someone who was unavailable. I wouldn't stop hounding her until she revealed the object of her desire. Only a part of me was surprised when she leaned close and mouthed my name.

I can still remember the excitement of that whisper.

The rest is a blur. I have vague recollections of sex at odd hours, in strange places. Thrilling at first, routine in no time, a chore by the end of the year. I broke it off before I'd passed through four seasons of deceit, but I couldn't live with the guilt.

On Valentine's Day, my fourth anniversary, I told my partner about my lover.

We separated in the early morning hours of February 15.

We ended as we began, with little intensity.

On St. Patrick's Day of that year, I found out I had breast cancer.

I didn't necessarily view it as punishment, but I'd often thought about the cause and effect between living two lives and two living tumors.

I never told my ex-partner about the cancer.

She read about my parents' deaths in the obituaries and attended both funerals, breaking my heart all over again.

Although her new partner and twin daughters probably wouldn't appreciate hearing it, I still missed her on a daily basis.

For the past six years, I'd been single.

Breast cancer could do that to you.

If you weren't in a relationship when you got the blow, you sure as hell weren't eager to join an online dating service.

Something about dry mouth and metallic tastes, a surgically disfigured chest and bald head—none of these made you want to make love. The downside to a bilateral mastectomy: It ripped out your sexuality. The only upside I'd discovered: It made jogging easier.

After what I'd been through, I couldn't summon the energy to dream of a candlelit dinner or the sun streaming across my bed the morning after.

Romance, to me, wasn't about light at all.

It was about how people coped when all the light went out, about holding hands across a hospital bed or keeping a positive attitude when all hell broke loose.

When I found a woman who understood that, maybe I'd feel something again.

• • •

"Smile," I said, rolling tape at nine o'clock Saturday morning.

Mike Schmidt grinned broadly, exposing a chipped front tooth. "How's this?"

"Priceless," I said.

Not exactly true.

There would be an exact cost.

His job. Maybe a felony conviction.

Like a Hollywood bigwig, I'd borrowed a stage set for the day. My general contractor friend, who was renovating the house in Denver's Country Club neighborhood, had agreed to clear out all his workmen and lend me the property for the day. For a fee. Burgers piled high with fixings at My Brother's Bar.

I'd told Mike that my sister was also interested in a kitchen makeover for her house in Littleton but that she was out of town and couldn't attend the installation.

"Could I tape the morning's activities for her?" I'd asked, in my sweetest voice.

Mike had agreed readily. In fact, he'd seemed tickled by the attention.

For the next three hours, I taped evidence of employee theft, while he mugged for the camera and offered a running commentary.

He and his teenage son, Razor, maneuvered the granite slab into the house, using a refrigerator dolly. They pushed and pulled it up a makeshift ramp, through the entryway, down the hall, and into the kitchen. At 12.5 pounds per square foot, the Black Galaxy masterpiece weighed in at just under 200 pounds.

The wiry son's youth compensated for the pot-bellied father's age. At every strenuous juncture, Razor shouldered three-quarters of the burden.

On top of the island cabinet, the two men installed a three-quarter-inch sheet of plywood and plastic sheeting, before laying the slab. With two-part epoxy, they cemented the granite into place.

The countertop had come from Granite's Edge Art. The California company purchased stones in huge blocks from quarries and shipped them to China, where they were sliced, like loaves of bread, into modular-sized slabs that fit standard cabinet widths. After polishing, they were freighted to distribution warehouses in the United States, along with precut pieces for backsplashes and edges.

This particular stone was "first quality," a designation based on its color, type, composition, age, structure, and character. The anomalies, Mike assured me, added elegance. This was an especially rare gift of beauty, he swore, with its variations in color range, veining, motion, and striation. While some customers preferred a consistent, homogenous product, significantly driving up the price of the stone, he felt artistic, creative types, such as myself, could appreciate imperfections. Not to worry about the stone's fissures or fractures—those were commonplace, more reminders of nature's gifts.

In the end, I had not only the proof to convict Mike Schmidt of employee theft, but also an educational documentary on granite.

Too bad its world premiere would consist of an audience of one: Kelly Hesselbach, owner of Kitchen and Bath Remodels.

My overall feeling at the end of our afternoon together was one of sadness. Why would this man, with such obvious experience, skills, and passion, risk it all for a few bucks on the side?

After Mike and Razor carted their tools and supplies to the truck, Mike returned for one last look.

My guilt skyrocketed when he said, with a proud smile, "Ain't she a beaut? I told you I'd take care of you."

• • •

The uneasy feelings carried over in my phone call with Kelly Hesselbach, Mike's employer.

Obviously Kelly had been primed for the news I delivered, but his silence extended to an uncomfortable length.

When I added that Mike had offered to tile my kitchen with Cherry Blossom marble tiles, at a fraction of the cost of retail, Kelly let out a hiss.

The sound intensified with my revelation that Mike also had offered me a machine-carved Ivory White marble mantle for $800.

When Kelly spoke at last, to thank me for my services, his voice sounded thick.

I told him I'd mail the video recording and final report, and I disconnected quickly.

I couldn't bear to hear a man cry.

• • •

Monday morning, as soon as I arrived at the office at nine, Sasha had a chilled mocha waiting for me.

The drink was the treat I needed as I began to type notes into the computer, sentences Hesselbach could use in a court of law, if he chose to press charges against Mike Schmidt.

After concluding my report and generating an invoice, I turned my attention to the progress I'd made on the Jessica Stankowski case.

Between sips, I thought about the appraisal process.

Ethical licensed appraisers were supposed to protect the interests of everyone involved in a real estate transaction, by giving an unbiased estimation of the property's market value. To support this, they submitted reports outlining their methods of approach and the reasoning behind their valuations. Despite using the same logic and tools for research, two honest appraisers wouldn't necessarily turn out identical reports, because data were always open to interpretation.

In a residential appraisal report, an appraiser took the property in question and compared it to three comps that had sold recently in the neighborhood. Simple enough, until the appraiser tried to define "comps" and "recently" and "the neighborhood." Depending on the interpretation of comparable, how far back the appraiser dug, and how wide he spread the boundaries, the results varied.

Measuring square footage, drawing a floor plan, and describing the interior and exterior, foundation, basement, and insulation were easy tasks. Adding or subtracting for amenities, high-end finishes, and condition of the property was still a fairly straightforward process. However, start pulling in comparables, and this is where the numbers began to diverge.

Because no two buyers agreed on what constituted comparable, it was unfair to expect precision from appraisers. Yet exacting numbers were vital.

Who cared about an accurate appraisal? The banker who didn't want to lend more money than the asset was worth, the buyer who didn't want to pay more than the property's true value, the seller who wanted to be paid full price, and the real estate agent who worked to ensure a fair deal for everyone involved.

That said, I'd given up on the accuracy of the system in my first year as an agent. Every year since, perhaps unwittingly, I'd lowered my standards. The most I could hope for now was approximate. Say a property was marketed for $200,000. If the appraisal came in within 5 percent either way, good enough, call it a day. Never mind that a $10,000 error represented a fortune to most buyers and sellers. I'd become accustomed to settling for anything that didn't scream fraud.

The industry should have been driven by clients and agents, but it wasn't. We all sat in the backseat while lenders and their flunkies careened around on a collision course.

Was it any wonder that I was trying my best to get out of this field? Private investigation—despite all the lying, subterfuge, and pretext—seemed noble in comparison to real estate.

With little effort, shady appraisers could make data represent anything they pleased, and obviously Kurt DeWitt had, but at whose behest?

Did he lie for Denise Johnson/Deidre Johnston, the buyer of Jessica Stankowski's house, who had passed a stack of his cards to Freddie Taylor? For Freddie Taylor, the buyer's agent who represented Denise/Deidre in the transaction and gave one of Kurt's cards to Jim Nalen? For Jim Nalen, the mortgage broker who supplied the money for the original purchase and gladly extended a line of credit? For the mysterious Richard, who was Denise's boyfriend and Todd Lynch's secret source of income? Or for Todd Lynch, the IT guy who invented false credit identities that allowed Denise to purchase dozens of properties?

Maybe all of the above, maybe none.

Maybe Kurt DeWitt had lied for himself.

• • •

Sasha interrupted the rambling nature of my typing with a yell from the other room. "Some lady's on line one. She won't give her name or the reason for her call. Should I hang up on her?"

I rose and walked to the doorway. "Did she ask for me specifically or for whoever's in charge of maintenance on our office equipment?"

Sasha must not have felt hospitable, because she replied tersely, "I know how to do my job."

"Surprise me! I'll talk to her."

Sasha patched through the call, but I could barely hear the caller's whispered remarks over the classical music playing on my Bose. I reached for the remote and hit mute.

"Could you please repeat that?"

"Leave me alone."

"Who is this?" I said, snapping to attention.

"I needed the money to hire a lawyer who would take my workers' comp case, but all I did was sign papers."

"Denise? Is that you, Denise? Denise Johnson?"

It was about time.

I'd left five messages after my meeting with Jim Nalen and added five more after my encounter with Kurt DeWitt. She probably didn't appreciate my calling. After all, she hadn't given me her phone number. But she had made the mistake of using the bathroom during our interview at her house, and I'm not ashamed to say, I borrowed her cordless phone without asking permission. I called myself, trapping Denise's number with caller ID.

"Quit calling me," she snapped. "I didn't hurt anybody. I signed papers, and there's nothing wrong with that. I love him, and he loves me. He's angry that you keep calling. You shouldn't have done that."

"Who's angry?"

Before she could answer, I heard a male voice in the background.

"I have to go," she said, rushed.

Those were her last words.

CHAPTER 17

I dialed Denise Johnson's number, but the call went directly to voice mail, indicating that she'd turned off the phone.

As I spent the afternoon filling out nine tax forms for the second quarter, thoughts of her intruded. How could I prompt her to admit her guilt? Would I have to go visit her again? Should I conduct a stakeout at her house, hoping for a lead on Richard or the Maxima?

I mulled the possibilities.

At five o'clock, Sasha bounded through the door, her cheeks red. "Lauren, I have a witness in my case. A believable one."

"Okay, calm down," I said, alarmed by her shortness of breath. "Who is it?"

"Mrs. Morton." Sasha sat in the chair opposite my desk and almost fell off in the excitement. "She lives next to the golf course, and she's home all day."

"A stay-at-home mom?"

"No, she's really old and partially blind."

I groaned. "How well can this blind woman see?"

"Not very. She thought I was a boy when I came to the door, but maybe it was the color of my hair. She sits in a big room in the back of the house, and guess what she looks at?"

"Birds and squirrels?"

"Those, too. She has a bunch of feeders. Mostly, she stares at the seventh hole." Sasha paused for effect. "With binoculars."

I smiled broadly. "That's what I like to hear."

"Good ones, too. Her son gave them to her, and they cost $300. They'd be powerful like yours, right?"

I nodded. "For that price, they'd do a decent job."

Sasha continued, her words spilling out in a torrent. "One whole wall of this big room is a sliding glass door and windows. Mrs. Morton sits there all day. No one visits her anymore, and she doesn't go anywhere. All she does is watch golfers. Some of the regulars wave to her. She says she's lonely in the winter, when the course closes. She wants to die before the snow falls again."

"Is she sick?"

"She has one of those things you put in your nose, with a cord that's attached to a thingy-ma-jiggy."

"An oxygen tank?"

"Yeah. Hospice workers come in three times a week. What do they do?"

"They help people die with dignity. Without pain," I said, my voice catching.

The color drained from Sasha's face. "Do you think Mrs. Morton's dying? She's really skinny, and her skin is sort of a weird color, but I don't want her to die. Is she serious about leaving for good before October?"

"She might be," I said gently.

"I'll go visit her again," Sasha said, cheering up. "I liked her a lot. She let me sit in her chair and borrow the binoculars. I could see everything."

"What does Mrs. Morton claim she saw?"

Sasha scooted to the edge of her seat and said triumphantly, "She saw one of the men put the ball in the hole."

That grabbed my interest. "Is she certain?"

"Mrs. Morton says her husband used to play golf, and she knows a cheater when she sees one. When the other three players were looking in the bushes on the side of that short grass—what's that called?"

"The green."

"Yeah, that. When they were over there, the fourth one cut across, past the flag to the weeds and stuff—"

"The rough," I corrected reflexively.

"On his way to the rough, he dropped a ball in the hole."

"Is Mrs. Morton positive it was one of the men?"

"He was wearing plaid pants and a golf cap."

"Which one?"

Sasha shrugged. "I don't know. It couldn't be Anita. It must have been Cal, Bob, or Bud," she said, naming the players in the foursome.

I tried to keep my voice even. "In your interviews, didn't you ask the golfers what they were wearing?"

Her face fell, and she slumped in the chair. "No. Would you have?"

"Probably not on my first case," I said, to bolster her spirits. "It's easy to let something slip. As soon as possible, you'll have to contact all four players again."

A whine escaped. "Not in person, can I call them?"

I sighed. "This time, call. But remember, witnesses can disappear or die. They may refuse to speak with you again, or forget, or change their stories. You won't always have a second chance. You have to be thorough the first time."

She bit her lip. "Did I mess up?"

"Not at all. You cracked the case."

Sasha beamed. "I did okay?"

"You've done a phenomenal job, but I have one more question."

The lines across her forehead telegraphed anxiety. "What?"

"Why didn't Mrs. Morton come forward on her own?"

"I know that answer," Sasha said, pleased with herself. "She didn't know about the hole-in-one record until I told her. After they found the ball, she saw everyone jumping up and down, but she sees that a lot. She only remembered this group because of the plaid pants and the cheating."

"She doesn't read the newspaper?" I said, recalling a mention of the achievement in the sports pages.

"Not anymore. She can't see, Lauren, remember?"

"Just checking," I said brusquely. "Did any television stations cover the story?"

"Nope. Channel 9 called Kip, but he told them they'd better wait, that he had a private investigator looking into it." Sasha stopped suddenly. "He meant me, right?"

I smiled. "Right."

"Cool. I'm an investigator," she said, rising to celebrate. "I'm so cool. I'm so cool."

I cut short the touchdown dance. "Don't get cocky. You need to prove it now."

In an instant, she deflated. "How am I supposed to do that?"

"Come here," I said, beckoning with my finger.

When she came closer, in a conspiratorial whisper, I explained what she should do next.

As she comprehended the scope of the task, Sasha grinned. "Sweet."

• • •

Several hours later, I couldn't get a strike to save my life.

In fact, I could barely stay out of the gutter.

Rollie had talked me into joining her for Monday Night Madness, half-price everything at the 300 Club, an upscale bowling lounge off South Broadway, near I-25.

After three games, I had yet to crack the 100 club. Maybe I needed a more traditional environment to fine-tune my game, one without blaring rock 'n' roll. I found the nightclub atmosphere of the 300 Club a bit distracting. The forty lanes had wide plasma screen TVs mounted above the pins, and an enormous video wall flashed images from emerging artists.

I thought the upscale retro décor was excessive, but nothing in comparison to the dress code. Among the prohibited fashions: hats worn to the back or side; sweats or athletic gear; baggy clothing; torn or soiled clothing; clothing with offensive writing; shirtless vests or jackets; sleeveless shirts for men; sports jerseys; exposed intimate apparel; excessively long shirts, Ts, sweaters, or jackets; and chains.

Geez, what was left?

Apparently, not much, because despite the deep discount off the $45-per-hour lane rate, Rollie and I were the only patrons on the hardwood, and we'd barely slipped by. Rollie wore a gold sparkling jacket, black halter top, and tight blue jeans, and I'd had to hide a tear in my front pants pocket with my purse.

Only a handful of people were scattered across the fifty-foot sports bar, seven billiard tables, and restaurant, certainly not enough to warrant turning anyone away at the door.

After three games, my thumb felt sprained, and Rollie agreed we'd better give it a rest.

As I stuffed the ball and shoes she'd lent me into her personalized carrying case, I apologized for my scores. Rollie deflected the apology with a grace that came from a 183 lifetime average. To improve my game, she said diplomatically, maybe I needed to bowl more often than once every thirty years.

In the restaurant, while we waited for our BBQ chicken pizza with tomatoes, red onions, and smoked gouda, we clinked glasses.

She took a sip of her Amaretto di Saronno and eyed me keenly. "What's on your mind?"

I swallowed my iced tea. "What do you mean?"

"You've had a look of gloom and doom all night."

"Is it that obvious?"

"To a professional," she said, with a gentle smile. "Give!"

I propped my elbow on the table and leaned my cheek against my palm. "It's Sasha."

"Oh, no, sugar. Is it serious?"

"Her foster mom, Gayle Bidwell, came to see me. She and her husband are considering giving up Sasha."

"What's the girl done?"

"Gayle claims she's a bad influence on their three other foster kids."

"We corrected the problems with her appearance. What more do they want?"

"I don't know—" I began.

"I must say, Becky did wonders with her," Rollie interjected, in a gossipy tone. "The velour off-the-shoulder sweaters are an improvement over ruffled tank tops. You have to love the fedora and the newsboy caps, much classier than the skull caps and the trucker's caps. She's found pants she likes without waist ties, and she doesn't wear that 'Spare me' shirt anymore. She has—"

"Rollie!" I interrupted loudly, "Sasha's fashion statements are the least of their worries. The foster mom says she's a pathological liar, she sleeps too much during the day, she doesn't have any friends, and she might be in a cult or on drugs."

Rollie's eyebrows shot to the ceiling. "Do you believe the mother?"

I shifted in the booth. "I don't believe any of it, but Gayle says Sasha's disappearing at night."

"Where's our charge going?"

"That's what I want to find out."

Rollie's eyes sparkled. "You have a hankering to tail her, don't you?"

I nodded grimly, not nearly as tickled at the prospect. "Do you think I should?"

She snapped her fingers. "Without a doubt."

"What if she catches me? We're just beginning to build trust. If she finds out I'm spying on her, she'll probably quit."

"Which would mean you'd miss those mochas she makes every morning."

"C'mon, Rollie!"

"You're not in the mood for a little ribbing, okay. We'll get serious. Are you thinking Sasha might be in some kind of trouble?"

"Yes."

"You put that at the forefront of your mind. Teenagers don't deserve the right to privacy. Not when they're building pipe bombs or snorting coke or meeting perverts on the Internet. You dig like you're tunneling to China. Don't let up until you know her every movement and can rest assured she's not at risk."

I groaned. "Couldn't I talk to Sasha instead?"

"Would that work?"

"Probably not," I admitted, feeling defeated.

"Why don't you borrow my GPS system? She'll never know you're out there slinking around."

I perked up. "You'd lend it to me?"

"For a few days. Drop by the office tomorrow. Carla can give you a run-through."

"You won't need it?"

"Take it," she said insistently.

"You're sure this will work?" I said, full of misgivings about the betrayal.

"Listen, honey, if by some fluke Sasha catches you, tell her you're borrowing the system from me and checking it out to see if you want to purchase one. She'll fall for that."

"I hope so," I said faintly. I added, with more urgency, "We can't let the Bidwells kick her out. Gayle Bidwell is definitely a downer, and she might annoy Sasha with her religious zeal, but who knows where Sasha could end up next? You wouldn't believe the mess the foster care system is in."

"Not good?"

"Horrible. Some of the businesses that oversee placements have long histories of violations."

"Nitpicky, missing paperwork flaws, I hope."

"Try foster parents with arrests for drunken driving, domestic violence, and sexual assault. More kids in a home than state limits allow. Molested children molesting other children in the family."

"You seem to know a lot about this subject," Rollie said, flagging our server for another round.

"When I was working for the SOB private eye instructor, he assigned me to a case he thought needed a woman's touch. One of the smaller foster care businesses was paying its owner $125,000 per year to oversee two foster families. In one of those families, a girl who was placed in foster care because of habitual running away was sexually assaulted in a gang initiation."

"Touching," Rollie said, her wrathful tone conveying the opposite.

"Before I could complete the investigation, the foster parents' adopted son slashed the girl's throat," I said, my voice deepening. "The day the girl died, I walked out of the SOB's office and never came back."

"That's a bugger of a case to dump on a trainee."

"The SOB still owes me my last paycheck."

"Let's go wring it out of him!"

I shook my head, my thoughts far removed from money. "You wouldn't believe the conditions in that girl's home. Holes in the walls. Broken windows replaced with garbage bags. Filth everywhere. Standing water in the basement. You tell me why the state would take these kids from neglectful parents and send them to worse places."

"Did the state take Sasha from her family?"

"From what Gayle Bidwell indicated, Sasha's biological family gave her up voluntarily."

"Is there any chance they'd take her back?"

"I doubt it. She set their house on fire."

Rollie didn't bat an eye. "On purpose?"

"Maybe. She set off firecrackers in her bedroom, but she did try to stomp them out."

"Ah, the scar," Rollie said, making the connection with the damaged tissue on Sasha's leg. "Have you considered contacting her parents?"

"I'm not sure she'd go back to them. She acts like they're dead."

"Ain't family great?"

"Shit," I said as I laid my head on the table. "This is so depressing. Do you think I should contact Sasha's parents?"

"Let's approach her circumstances with professional detachment," Rollie said briskly. "The same as we would any other case. There's no reason to fret over multiple scenarios. You follow Sasha, and I'll get the background on the birth parents before you approach them."

"I can run the check," I said, my spirits temporarily elevated. "Sasha gave me her legal name and social security number."

Rollie put up a hand to slow me down. "That's all we need, but who are you fooling? You can't investigate Sasha's family. You'd have to use your computer for that, and I'm betting she tracks your every move."

"She does, but maybe I could—"

Rollie waved me off. "My treat."

"I appreciate you helping me out," I mumbled.

"Not everything is about you, sweetie," she said gruffly. "I'm rather fond of the girl myself."

• • •

The next morning, shortly after the mailman dropped a stack of correspondence in the outer office, Sasha came strolling up to my desk.

"Is this for real?" she said, pointing to the photo of a cat that my sister-in-law had sent. "Or is it one of those Internet pranks?"

"That's my brother's cat," I said mildly.

"Why does he have a blue ribbon around his neck?"

"He's the fattest cat."

"Obviously," she said, her tone patronizing. "But what's the award for?"

"The fattest cat," I repeated. "He's won it twice."

Sasha stared at me in horror. "Who gives out that kind of prize?"

"I try not to ask," I said, with a dismissive wave. "Someone in Utah. Are you in the habit of opening people's mail?"

"Yeah," she said, without a trace of shame. "Usually I seal it back up so they don't know. Do you want me to do that with yours?"

I looked at her with faint surprise. "No, but while you're at it, could you throw away all the junk mail, including this crap?"

"If I have to." Sasha couldn't take her eyes off the photo. She smiled at the cat and petted its head. "Can I keep this? He's sort of cute."

"It's yours," I said briefly, not bothering to inform her that Tank bore a strong resemblance to my sister-in-law.

• • •

By noon, when I hadn't heard from Denise Johnson, who had cut short our call twenty-four hours earlier, I decided to borrow an investigator from Rollie's firm to accompany me on a home visit.

One of the first pointers Rollie had stressed when we began working together was: If you feel uneasy, go in pairs. At the time, she'd made a standing offer that I could call for reinforcement anytime, anywhere, for any reason.

I felt self-conscious summoning backup, but within the hour, the immutable Carla met me at a gas station at the corner of Federal and Alameda.

We drove together to Denise Johnson's house, and to her credit, Carla didn't try to muscle me out of my own case.

She followed my lead as I nonchalantly strolled to the front porch and knocked on the door. When no one answered, we traipsed to the side of the house. She gave me a boost up to the kitchen window and patiently waited while I climbed through it and let her in the back door.

She even covered my mouth when I screamed at the sight of a dead body.

CHAPTER 18

Someone had killed my killer.

Which meant another killer lurked.

Damnit.

Denise Johnson's body lay on the bedroom floor, battered and bloodied.

I wanted to run out of the house, as fast as my wobbly legs could carry me, but Carla persuaded me to stay for five minutes.

We split up and conducted a superficial search of the house.

Unfortunately, neither Carla nor I could locate a shred of evidence leading to Denise's boyfriend Richard. After the bludgeoning, he'd probably removed everything that belonged to him.

We didn't find the weapon from the first killing either, the burgundy Maxima. We found the key to the garage hanging on a hook in the kitchen, and we peeked in the outbuilding but saw only junk and space for a car.

When we returned to the living room, I lingered in a beam of light shining through the small window and thought about Denise Johnson's series of bad decisions, the worst of which might have been an intentional swerve on Highlands Ranch Parkway.

However, Carla was in no mood for lingering.

Before she shoved me out the door, I stole a photo of Denise, cheap frame and all, and we hurried back to the gas station where we'd left my car.

As we parted, Carla assured me that she'd call the police from a pay phone several miles away.

That should have taken a few minutes, but I swear I heard sirens as I pulled out of the lot.

• • •

Now that there was a second murder—one which had occurred while I was still investigating the first murder—I needed to kick into high gear.

I decided to take another run at Jackie Cooper, my eyewitness to Jessica Stankowski's accident.

This time, I vowed, I would not be swayed by tea or cookies. I would not play gin rummy. And I would not leave her house without a positive ID of Denise Johnson as the driver of the car. I knew Jackie had seen the driver, and I was determined to get an accurate, complete, written statement out of her.

As a balm for my stressful day, I stopped at Krispy Kreme and picked up a six-pack, then headed to Fatburger for my usual: double bacon cheeseburger, onion rings, and strawberry shake.

Good thing I didn't live in the suburbs. Too many fattening franchises.

At Jackie's house, I nursed my shake through opening remarks before coming to the point. "I've tracked down the driver of the car that hit Jessica Stankowski."

She wrung her hands. "You have?"

"Yes, and I'd like to show you a photo for confirmation."

"I didn't have a good look," she stammered.

"I think you did, but you've been too frightened to point the finger. Am I right?"

She bit her lower lip. "Maybe."

"I understand your apprehension, but there's no threat. No one can hurt you. The driver has passed away."

"Died?"

"Gone," I said, hoping she wouldn't ask about the circumstances of the demise. "Will you please take a look at this picture? It would mean a lot to Jessica's family to have closure."

"I don't want to get involved," Jackie said nervously.

"You're already involved. You guaranteed that when you called the reward hotline. If I have to, I can subpoena you to produce information, but I'd rather not make it complicated. How about a quick look?"

In the pause, I was glad her mother Pearl was asleep in the other room and had missed my idle threat. I had no grounds for a subpoena but was banking on Jackie's ignorance of the law.

"I'll try," she said, trembling.

"Thank you." I turned over the photo of Denise Johnson.

Jackie let out a warbled cry. "That's not him."

"Him?" I said, astonished. "The driver was a man? You're certain? Why didn't you tell me before?"

"He had a ponytail, but it was a man. What if he saw me?" she shrieked. "How did this woman die? Did he murder her, too? Oh, my, why didn't I keep my mouth shut? Why, oh why?"

I stayed with Jackie for a long time after the outburst but only managed to calm her down a notch below raving.

I couldn't get her to say anything more about the driver, and the delay meant I hit early rush-hour traffic on the way home.

• • •

I had every intention of following Sasha that night, but after eating suburban fat food and strong-arming Jackie Cooper, I'd lost my desire.

Plus, I figured I deserved a night off after my time with the corpse.

The next evening, though, I was well rested and ready, and tailing Sasha turned out to be easy.

Maybe too easy.

My newfound occupation was bound to bring temptation into future relationships. Prone to distrust since birth, I was headed down a slippery slope with the tools I'd acquired. I may as well have been a recovering alcoholic teaching a mixology class. I'd have to curb my impulses, in a major way, for love to work again.

Not yet, though.

This night was for marveling at the wondrous technology Rollie Austin had lent me.

Before GPS was made available to the public, private investigators had to rely on the risky practice of surveillance at dangerous speeds, through red lights and blind intersections. I, on the other hand, could watch my full-color computer screen map for movement of the target vehicle and print out reports at will.

The good life.

I'd attached the GPS device to the gum-ball car earlier in the afternoon when Sasha thought I was in the bathroom down the hall. A string of belches, compounded with a simulated emission, followed by a frantic bolt past her desk with a toss of, "I'm not feeling well. Answer the phones, I'll be right back," had assured she wouldn't follow me to the ladies' room. An annoying tendency she'd developed recently.

When she left for the night around six, we exchanged our usual good-byes, and I gave her a five-minute head start.

Once I knew she was on her way, I sprinted to my car and fired up the GPS system. Happily, it lived up to my expectations, and more.

When I came to a standstill, outside Sasha's foster home, I felt a pang of disappointment that she hadn't led me to a seedy location.

But I couldn't complain.

Private eyes in years gone by had to survive long hours in the car with only talk radio and greasy food to break the boredom, but I had the modern comforts of technology at my disposal.

The casino game Carla had loaded onto the laptop (probably without Rollie's knowledge) provided me with endless entertainment as I waited for Sasha's next move.

In my favorite feature of the game, I created my own likeness by choosing head shape, eyes and brows, nose, skin tone, color and style of hair, mouth, glasses, facial hair, shoulders, and clothes. From a distance, my computer clone bore a passing resemblance to me, but upon closer scrutiny, she looked more like a petite, clean-shaven Asian man.

Next step, I populated my table with fantasy players—all good-looking women. Too bad life didn't work this way.

I played Texas Hold'em and turned $5,000 into $3 million in the hour I waited around the corner from Sasha's house.

From time to time, I looked up at the one-story house where Sasha lived with her foster family. A mid-century modern, the house was in good shape but showing signs of benign neglect. I couldn't imagine how Sasha and her family functioned in what looked like about 1,600 square feet. Maybe the large Tuff shed situated on the side lot housed all the usual household clutter, but fitting six people into the tiny three bedrooms must have been a challenge.

I'd begun to believe that Sasha might be in for the night, and that I'd have to repeat this exercise another evening, when the little car on my computer screen moved.

And moved and moved.

As I followed Sasha for more than twenty miles, to a neighborhood in Broomfield, one of the northwestern suburbs, I vowed to have a chat with her about speeding. At the rate of travel she preferred, she'd have her driver's license revoked before her seventeenth birthday.

When her car stopped moving, I waited a few minutes before approaching the address near 136th and Lowell. As I drove by, I had no trouble spotting the gum-ball car, parked in front of a two-story contemporary home. The house had white shutters on every window, a covered porch with railings, siding designed to resemble tan brick, and an oversized two-car attached garage.

I circled back and parked a few houses down, between a truck and a car, with a direct sight line and minimal risk.

About thirty minutes later, as the sun was setting, Sasha emerged from the house with a strangely clad figure and a golden retriever.

I did a double take and raised my Miyauchi binoculars.

In my haste to leave the office, I hadn't been able to locate my ATN Night Scouts, the $600 pair of night-vision binoculars I'd purchased the week before, and the Miyauchis were a poor substitute.

However, even in the dim light, I could see that Sasha's foster mother might have been accurate about her cult accusation.

• • •

It had to be ninety degrees outside, yet Sasha's friend wore a getup more suitable to bee-keeping than Frisbee-tossing, which is what the two were doing in the front yard with the dog.

The outfit looked all the more comical in relation to Sasha's choices: shorts that wouldn't have covered my underpants and a tube top that fit like a sausage casing. Nothing else. All skin.

The girl—I assumed it was a girl, but who could tell?—had on long floral-print pants, tennis shoes, socks, a long-sleeved cotton shirt, and white gloves. She also wore a headdress with a broad visor and material that draped down her neck and across her shoulders. Beneath enormous sunglasses, white tape covered her nose.

After about ten minutes of Frisbee, Sasha gathered items from her backpack, and they walked down the sidewalk, side by side. At the end of the block, they took a sharp turn onto a path that cut across a schoolyard. Backyard fences lined one side of the path, with tall hedges on the other.

There was no way I could follow them.

I'd scare them to death if they saw my shadow, and no doubt I'd lose Sasha's trust for good if she recognized me.

I must have repeated the word "damnit" a hundred times, at least, as I observed their light beams fading from my view.

I was cursing because I'd recognized one of the flashlights as my X3 Xenon light, a $100 model I'd picked up at a flea market, and I'd also located my ATN Night Scout binoculars.

They were dangling from Sasha's neck.

Why did this miscreant have to borrow my equipment, without asking? My high-intensity light designed for SWAT teams and my alloy construction binoculars developed for the military—why was Sasha taking them on a walk, when trinkets from Wal-Mart would have sufficed?

Damnit.

I had a feeling I knew where Sasha and her companion were headed, but that did me little good.

One block down, the path cut across a wide street and joined with another before coming to a dead end at an open space dog park at 136th and Meade. I'd visited the field once—on a first date with a dog owner who couldn't spend an hour without her chocolate lab. The date had ended abruptly, but none too soon, when the dog bit me.

I cussed again, because it made me feel better, as I helplessly watched Sasha and this person in strange garb walk into the darkness.

• • •

The next morning, I stepped outside to a gray cover of clouds. On the morning news, a chipper meteorologist had promised the sun would peek through before day's end, but I knew better.

I may not have had Doppler radar at my disposal, but I had forty-two years of experience.

With the exception of my one college year in Boulder, I'd lived in the Denver metro area my entire life, and when gray sky persisted in every direction, the day never improved.

Ever.

I arrived at the office to find Sasha at her desk, yawning.

My beloved ATN Night Scouts were back in the metal cabinet, where Sasha had returned them.

On my way in, I'd paused in the parking lot to remove the GPS device from Sasha's car. It felt like too much of a violation to leave it in place out of mere curiosity. I'd found out what I needed to know—where she was going at night—now I had to stop.

All morning, I heard loud yawns coming from the vicinity of Sasha's desk. She was supposed to be putting labels on the newsletters that I sent to my twelve hundred real estate contacts, and the two times I checked on her, she looked wiped out. She slowly opened and closed her eyes, like a cat caught in the middle of a morning nap.

I was worried about all the newsletters arriving at their correct destinations, but I was too tired to supervise.

Or more like too depressed.

From a three-line notice in the *Denver Post* obituaries, I'd learned that services for Denise Johnson would be held that afternoon at St. John's, a cathedral near downtown, at three o'clock.

Over lunch, I went home to change.

From the back of my closet, I retrieved the outfit I'd worn to my mother's funeral and my father's funeral: black silk pants and blazer, light pink linen shirt.

As I dressed, I thought about the kindness of the saleslady, Pamela, who had helped me make the selections the day my mother died.

I'd come into the store with a credit card and no clue. I knew I had to have something dressier than my usual real estate outfits, but beyond that, I was lost.

In the best of times, I hated shopping, and these were the worst of times. I had ten million things to do that day—order flowers, pick out music, call friends and family, meet with the funeral director, hire a caterer, cancel doctors' appointments, console my father, write an obituary, clean out my mother's room in the hospice, wash my hair—and no energy to do any of them.

When I entered the Ann Taylor store in Cherry Creek, Pamela greeted me, and I informed her that I had five minutes, no more, to buy clothes for a funeral.

As I crouched on a bench in the dressing room, she brought me handfuls of clothes, all of which I summarily rejected because they made me look ugly. Two hours later, I settled on the first combination she'd brought into the stall.

On this day, I put on the solemn clothes with slow, stunted motions.

For a moment, I lost my breath when I pulled a Mass card from my father's service out of the pocket of the blazer.

It reminded me of the blur.

My memories of his funeral and reception were foggy, but I couldn't forget the aftermath.

After the memorial service, I'd gone for a walk, to clear my head.

Wracked with sorrow, I decided I'd keep walking until I reached a better place.

I walked for the rest of the day and into the night before I stopped. Not because the place I'd reached was so much better than where I'd started, but because I couldn't bear the pain anymore.

After hours of deep crying on a park bench in Westminster, I took a cab home. My arches hurt for weeks.

No wonder I'd never worn these clothes again. They reminded me of death and dying. I vowed to donate them to Goodwill the next day.

For the moment, though, they would serve a purpose.

I had a funeral to crash.

CHAPTER 19

At St. John's, I blended in with the fifty or so people paying their respects at Denise Johnson's funeral Mass.

I'd slipped into the back of the small vestibule, purposefully a few minutes late. From my seat in the last pew, I could observe without being observed. Thank God the casket wasn't open. No amount of artifice could have masked the frenzied beating Denise Johnson had suffered.

I studied the mourners during the ceremony, making mental notes as I tried to guess at people's connections to the deceased.

Unfortunately, I didn't see a likely candidate for Richard/boyfriend/killer.

I confirmed his absence by eavesdropping at the reception following the service.

Because most people were strangers to each other, there was nothing remarkable about me standing alone in the church hall, moving around awkwardly, and introducing myself to family, friends, coworkers, and acquaintances.

About an hour into my circulation, I hit paydirt with two women who were stationed at the end of a banquet table in the corner. I brought my paper plate, piled high with cold cuts, potato salad, deviled eggs, and baked beans, to an empty table nearby and sat with my back to them.

As I sipped punch and munched, I picked up every word.

"I can't believe Richard didn't have the guts to show his face," the one with the raspy voice said. With a quick glance, I matched the words with a heavyset, jolly-faced older woman, who wore a dark brown pants suit that looked like it came from J.C. Penney's.

"He didn't come, because he probably did it," the one with the squeaky voice replied. She had a massive swoop of platinum blonde hair and was dressed in a dark red suit with matching high heels.

"I never thought they went together, did you?"

"He wasn't her type. Before her accident, she dated manly men, like my Roger. I don't know why she hooked up with him . . ."

I leaned against my folding chair and strained to capture the details.

The squeaky voice continued, ". . . such a strange guy."

"Denise probably needed the money, if she hadn't worked since the accident."

"She changed after the fall, didn't she?"

"Wouldn't you, if you were in that much pain?" the voice rasped.

"I'm sure losing her job and having to sue the company for lost wages and medical costs didn't help. All she talked about was how they did her wrong, letting their workers' comp coverage lapse. What a rotten way to spend your last days, with lawyers and depositions."

"Would she have won?"

"Her lawyer assured her she'd get a settlement, but the company was dragging its feet, and the lawyer kept upping his retainer," said the squeaky-voiced one.

"What a bum deal. What was she living on?"

"Richard."

"Richard didn't have any money!"

"He most certainly did!"

"Then tell me why he drove that old Maxima?"

"Who knows, but Denise told me he was really rich. They were planning to leave the country as soon as she won her court case. They were going to the Cayman Islands, or maybe Belize."

"Where did she meet him?"

"At a real estate seminar. He swept her off her feet."

"With lies, no doubt. If Richard had all that money, why didn't he fix his car? All winter, it sat in Denise's garage, smashed up. It's probably still there."

"No, he towed it away last week."

"Really? I didn't see that. Last Thursday, I waved to him on my way to the grocery store, but he ignored me."

"Lucky you. I avoid him whenever I can. I never told Denise my impressions, but I don't trust him. A man in this day and age wearing a beret, with his gray, stringy hair in a ponytail? Ugh!"

"Did you ever see him with his hair down?"

"Lord, no!"

"He was a fastidious dresser," the one with the raspy voice mused.

"Obsessive/compulsive, if you ask me. He couldn't stop playing with his ring."

"Why do men wear those? They're clunky and ugly."

"Maybe they feel they add vigor."

"Richard used his as a weapon. He shook my Fred's hand one time and almost crushed it."

"He always acted like he was better than everyone else."

"He did enjoy correcting people."

"He was fresh."

"Lecherous, but he seemed to make Denise happy."

"He was supposed to be some kind of star polo player. Do you believe that?"

"Denise told you?"

"She went to all his matches. He should have showed her that kind of support. I don't think he drove her to one doctor's appointment."

"You were a good friend to her. I don't know what she would have done without you in January and February, when she was on crutches. You went out of your way to help. How many times did you take her to the doctor's or bring her groceries?"

I started in my chair at this piece of news. If Denise Johnson couldn't drive in January, this tidbit confirmed that she couldn't have run over Jessica Stankowski. My sudden movement caused the folding chair to scrape across the linoleum floor, emitting an alarming noise. Fortunately, the two women paid no attention.

"Too many to count, but it was the right thing to do. Denise would have done it for me. She was a good friend."

The raspy voice lowered. "Do you think Richard did it?"

"Yes," came the squeaky whisper. "Do you?"

"It had to be him!"

"Did you tell the police?"

"No. Did you?"

"I couldn't even give them his last name, and I was Denise's closest friend. Could you?"

"You know, I'm not sure I ever heard it."

"Poor Denise. At least she's not in pain anymore."

"Poor Denise. May she rest in peace."

• • •

Poor Denise. Lucky Lauren.

I was getting closer in time and space.

I had found the killer of Jessica Stankowski and Denise Johnson.

Richard, Denise Johnson's boyfriend.

I had the Maxima to tie Richard to the hit-and-run. I had the class ring to tie him to the meeting with Todd Lynch at the investors' club. I had the plans to leave the country to tie him to proceeds from the real estate scams.

Best of all, I had a distinctive physical description that would separate him in a crowd, and I had a bead on where to find him.

Case solved.

Almost.

To celebrate, I grabbed five chocolate cream puffs on my way out of the church hall.

• • •

I drove back to the office through pouring rain.

According to news reports, clogged and overwhelmed storm drains had caused flooding throughout the city and every suburb, but I avoided the worst of it by carefully picking my way down side streets.

As soon as I dashed inside and shook the drops from my funeral outfit, I cornered Sasha at the computer.

"I need you to interrupt whatever you're doing to look up something."

"I'm writing my report on the golf case."

"That can wait," I said, in a rush. "I need you to research everything related to polo in the Denver metro area. I'm looking for a guy named Richard—"

She was at the cusp of a pout. "I'm busy."

"Now!" I said, my tone leaving no room for misinterpretation.

Instead of our usual power struggle, she fled the room, leaving me flustered.

I debated whether I should jump on the Internet and waste an hour or apologize to Sasha, who could complete the task in five minutes.

I decided it wouldn't kill me to be gracious, except I couldn't find her. Our office suite contained two rooms, hers and mine, a short hallway, and a large closet.

The hallway was empty, which left only the closet. I tapped on the door. No answer. I knocked again, more forcefully. No reply.

I tried to open the door, but it wouldn't yield. This was getting tiresome. "Sasha, will you please come out of the closet."

Nothing. I tried again to get in. No progress.

"Sasha, unlock the door."

That evoked a mumble, but I couldn't make out the meaning. "What?"

"It's not locked," she wailed.

"Fine," I said quietly. I pushed with all my might this time, managed to move the door a few feet, and poked my head into the dark space.

I found my employee lying on the floor, in the fetal position, sobbing uncontrollably. I knelt on the carpet, near her feet. "Look, let's start over. I didn't mean to snap at you. Could you come back and help me find this guy?"

The crying continued.

"You know how inept I am at the computer. Won't you please help me? I brought you some cream puffs."

Between struggles for breath, she made a noise.

"Was that a yes?"

She didn't answer.

"Could you move your left leg if that was a yes?"

She raised her left foot an inch.

I touched her leg. "What's wrong? Can you accept my apology?"

"It's not you," she sobbed. She reached back to touch my hand. I held hers tightly, but she didn't squeeze back.

"Whatever it is, we can work it out. We're a good team. Maybe not today, but usually. I'll give you the cream puffs, plus five bucks, if you'll get up."

Sasha made a sound without words.

"That was a laugh, right?"

She moved her left foot.

"You're not crying again, are you?"

She sat up. "No, I'm dry," she said, but that wasn't true. Tears had streaked her cheeks and neck. She'd worn jeans and a hooded sweatshirt to work, and at the moment, she had the hood tied to strangle-tightness around her face, pushing out her cheeks.

I touched one of her cheeks gently. "If it's not me, what is it?"

She dropped her head and shrugged.

"Is something bothering you? At home? With friends?"

"I can't talk about it."

"Sure you can. Try me."

After a long pause, she choked out, "I drove by, and they were having a barbecue."

"Who?"

"Nobody," she sniffled.

I racked my brain. "Why would a barbecue upset you? Was it your friends, someone didn't invite you to a party?"

She raised her head and stared at me, eyes puffy and vacant. "I don't want to talk anymore."

That's all she'd say.

No matter.

I had my own sources of information.

• • •

The next morning, I left a message for Sasha, telling her I had errands to run and would be in the office by midmorning, and I headed to Broomfield.

Back to the house where Sasha had met up with her strangely clad friend two nights earlier.

I parked on the street and walked to the covered porch, which was surrounded on all sides by giant sunshades.

I rang the bell.

When a girl answered, I peered into the darkness. "Is your mom home?"

The waif, with white skin and long, wavy red hair, turned and retreated. Allowing for her frail stature, I put her at about sixteen.

In moments, an older, healthier version of the girl appeared, apparently the mother. She had a pale complexion, an oval face, and strawberry blonde hair that had begun to turn white. Her locks were straight, parted in the middle, all one length that fell to just above her waist. A burnt orange sundress hung loosely from her bony shoulders.

She looked at me with curiosity and apprehension. "Yes?"

"I'm Lauren Vellequette. I was wondering if you have a minute to talk about Sasha Fuller."

The woman's face lit up. "You're Sasha's boss."

"I am."

"I'm Meredith, Molly's mother. Please, come in," she said, clutching my arm. "Sasha talks about you all the time."

"She does?"

"Incessantly. Lauren did this, Lauren said that. She worships you."

"That must get tiresome," I said mildly.

"Not at all," Meredith replied, with a warm laugh. "It's quite charming. Working for you has completely changed her."

"Really?" I said, embarrassed when the word came out as startled instead of casual.

"A hundred and eighty degrees. Molly and I were worried about Sasha, especially this spring. She was moody and detached, and she stopped visiting as often. We tried to reach her, but it was as if she wanted to withdraw. I'm pleased she's more engaged again. Molly really missed her. My daughter doesn't have any other friends. Not any that come by. Most of her connections are with people on the Internet, which doesn't seem . . ." Meredith's voice trailed away, as she searched for the right word.

I supplied one. "Real?"

"Maybe," she said, with an open smile.

I followed her into the kitchen, where thick shades blocked all outside light, and we sat at the table. After she poured coffee, she added, "Sasha might have told you—Molly has Gorlin syndrome."

"No, she hasn't said anything."

"That's kind of her. She's one of the few people who treats Molly as if she's healthy."

"What is Gorlin?"

"An allergy to sunlight. Her skin can't tolerate ultraviolet rays. She's twenty-one, and already she's had nine surgeries to remove cancerous skin cells from around her eyes, the bridge of her nose, her cheeks, and her neck."

"How did she and Molly meet?"

"In a chat room. They corresponded for months before Molly felt comfortable inviting Sasha over to the house. She has trust issues, as you might imagine, having grown up with taunts and stares. And not everyone is willing to socialize in the middle of the night."

"Molly never goes out during the day?"

"Only to doctors' appointments. Recently, she told me that nothing else is worth the risk, but I wish she wouldn't give in to people's cruelty."

"Maybe she'll change her mind."

"I don't know about that. She has a UV monitor she takes everywhere, to test light levels inside buildings. Doctors have told us she can't be exposed to more than one hundred microwatts per square meter."

"How much comes from the sun?"

"In Colorado, about eight thousand on an average day. Molly can cover up, but that brings on a different set of challenges. When she was younger, she dealt with the physical losses, the pain, the surgeries, the change in lifestyle. Lately, she seems to be struggling with the judgment of other people and the permanence of her situation."

"When was she diagnosed?"

"In fifth grade. At a routine checkup, our dentist discovered cysts eating away at her jaw. Once testing pinpointed the cause, Molly had to give up everything she loved. Swimming, bike riding, soccer, trips to the mall."

"Did you pull her out of school?"

"No. With support from her teachers and administrators, we made it work. She continued with her class, despite all the time she spent in Children's Hospital, but she lost her friends."

"When did Sasha start coming around?"

"About a year ago. They're lucky to have each other. Sasha reaches Molly on a level I can't. They have an unspoken bond."

"Because of their physical disfigurements?"

Meredith nodded. "And the emotional isolation."

"What does Molly do all day?"

"She spends time on the Internet. She enjoys drawing, reading, watching TV, playing videos." Almost as an afterthought, Meredith added, "She sleeps a lot. Less so since she met Sasha. She's really helped pull Molly out of her shell."

"And vice versa, apparently."

"Certainly. They rely on each other. In March, Molly wanted to attend a twenty-four-hour comic book event but was scared to go on her own. Sasha volunteered to go with her. They contacted the organizer ahead of time and made sure the space would be safe."

"Was this a convention?"

"No, an invitation-only drawing session. Ten other artists attended, and they spent one full day, from four o'clock Saturday until four Sunday, producing their own comic books. They had to complete a twenty-four-page book in twenty-four hours. All original work, from scratch, no bringing in sketches, designs, or plots. Molly loved the feeling of community she shared with the other illustrators."

"They worked through the night?"

"Molly did. A few others took naps."

"What did Sasha do the whole time?"

"Ate junk food, by the sounds of it," Meredith said, with a chuckle. "She was a sweetheart, giving up her weekend like that, but they both had a grand time. I haven't seen Molly that animated since before we found out about the Gorlin. The comic book weekend inspired her to apply for a job with a video game company. As soon as they saw her drawings, they hired her on the spot. She's now part of the development team for a company in Louisville."

"What a great job!"

"Full-time and high-paying. They like the way she fleshes out characters, and they allow her to work at home. None of this would have happened without Sasha. I can't thank her enough."

"She's a good kid," I agreed.

"Enough of my bragging, you must have come for some other reason," Meredith said expectantly.

I nodded unhappily. "Sasha's foster mother stopped by my office last week, and she told me she and her husband are thinking of returning Sasha to a group home."

Meredith gasped and covered her mouth with her hand. "Does Sasha know? After four years? Are they allowed to do that?"

I answered only the last question. "Evidently."

"Why don't they want her anymore?"

"They claim she's disrupting the family. One of Gayle's concerns is that Sasha is out all night."

"Of course she is. She's at our house, under my supervision," Meredith said, with a bitterness I knew all too well—the dangerous side of caretaking.

"Could you please call Gayle Bidwell and tell her that?"

"Would it help?"

"It couldn't hurt."

"I'd be happy to give her a piece of my mind," she said, which didn't exactly reassure me. "What's wrong with mothers these days? Can you imagine, after what Sasha's been through? Enjoying barbecues and acting as if nothing happened?"

"No," I said honestly. How could I, when Sasha had told me next to nothing?

"That family cast her as a scapegoat."

"The Bidwells are strange."

"Not the Bidwells, the Fullers. Can you picture anything worse than being put in foster care while your mother, father, and three brothers stay intact as a family?"

"No," I said, becoming more quiet as her rant gained steam.

"They should be ashamed of themselves."

"I agree."

"It wasn't her fault."

"Never."

"She was a sensitive child. Maybe she had to burn down the house to get their attention."

"Maybe," I said distantly.

"To begin with, I don't know how they could have stayed in that house, not after what happened."

Silence fell.

I'd run out of neutral responses, and the suspense was killing me. I had to drop the charade. "What did happen?"

Meredith measured me. "Sasha hasn't told you?"

"Not yet."

"When Sasha was ten years old, her mother was raped in their home. After the assault, the family went on as if nothing had happened."

"But Sasha crumbled," I said, before I could catch myself.

CHAPTER 20

When I arrived back at the office, I couldn't look at Sasha without feeling the urge to hug her.

Happily, she didn't seem to need any bolstering at the moment. She bounced on her feet. "Guess what?"

"What?"

"I finished my report on the 'Investigation of the Alleged Hole in One at the Vista Hills Golf Course.' Do you think that's a good title?"

"Marvelous."

"Will you read it soon?"

The excitement in her eyes persuaded me to break from policy. "Why don't you summarize it for me, verbally."

"Thanks, Lauren," she said, ebullient. "Cal did it. Mrs. Morton was right. He put the ball in the hole."

"Just like you thought. You have good instincts."

"Guess what else?"

"What?"

"Bud Cauldron fired Cal. That's just wrong."

"For what?"

"For telling the truth. That sort of sucks, huh?"

"Cal came to Bud?"

Sasha nodded. "Cal saw how much it was hurting Bud, not knowing. People were treating Bud like a criminal, and he felt bad about it."

"Maybe Bud fired Cal for lying, not for telling the truth. Why did Cal put Bud's ball in the hole in the first place?"

"He meant it as a joke, but when he saw how excited it made Bud, he couldn't say anything. He did something dumb, but Bud didn't have to fire him, did he? Cal didn't mean to make such a big deal, and he told the truth eventually."

"But not necessarily voluntarily. Maybe your investigation made Cal come clean."

"Really?"

"Probably. He had five weeks to speak up, and he never did. You interviewed him and the other golfers. Still nothing. Finally, after you followed my suggestion—you did make the calls, right?"

"I did," she said breathlessly. "I called Bud, Cal, Bob, and Anita and told them I had a witness who had seen a man drop a ball in the hole. I told them exactly what you said, that my witness thought it was a groundskeeper, but I needed a better description before Kip fired him."

"That was a good one," I said, temporarily caught up in admiration of my own work. "It can't be coincidence that Cal confessed after your call. You did it, Sasha. You solved your first case."

"Yippee!" Sasha shouted, dancing around the room like a toddler, feet flying, arms waving.

I could do nothing but stare.

Who was this creature, part girl/part woman, with the percentages changing by the hour?

When she showed no signs of winding down, I had to scream over her jubilation. "Where do you think the ball is?"

She stopped in the middle of a cheerleader kick and almost toppled over. "What ball?"

"The Lady Precept ball that Bud Cauldron hit, the one that never made it into the hole."

"That's easy," she said, leaving the room. When she returned seconds later, she held out her hand. In her palm, she cradled a golf ball imprinted with a Dexter logo and a pink ribbon.

I laughed. "Where did you find it?"

"Mrs. Morton told me to look in the tall grasses, in that mushy part of the course."

"The wetland reeds and marsh?"

Sasha pointed her finger at me like a gun and nodded. "Those.

They're about two hundred yards from the place where you hit the ball."

"The tee box?"

"Sure. Around that corner—"

"The dogleg?"

"Whatever. Mrs. Morton says lots of people lose their balls in the swamp, but no one wants to look there. They always go farther up. I found like twenty balls. You want some?"

I matched her irresistible smile. "No thanks."

Sasha rubbed the famous ball, which, after all, had taken a quite ordinary flight. "Should I give this to Bud?"

I raised one eyebrow. "It's your call."

After a pause, she said, "No. I'll let him think that *maybe* he could have hit the longest hole in one in golf history. That'll make him happy."

"You think?"

She nodded. "I know he wanted to believe, even though he said he didn't. Like Santa Claus. You know it's your parents, but you still believe. Let's let Bud believe. Is that okay?"

"Good call," I said, rising to shake her hand. "You're turning out to be a top-notch investigator."

"Am I?" she said, doubt expressed in her frown.

"Y-e-s," I said, stringing out the word in a spot-on imitation of her. "You're smart, you're patient, you're a problem solver, you're a whiz on the computer, and that last decision showed me that you have the most important quality, one that can't be trained."

"What?" Sasha said, shyly. "What else am I good at?"

"Compassion."

• • •

Hours after Sasha left, Rollie Austin came stumbling through the darkened outer office.

"Time to go home, honey."

"Soon. I promised myself I'd stay late and catch up on paperwork."

"This is late enough. Call it a night."

"What brings you by at this hour?" I said, glancing at the clock that would soon strike ten.

"I reckoned I'd better grab you when Sasha wasn't around. I tried your apartment, but when you weren't home, I decided to swing by here."

"What's so urgent?"

"What I found out about Sasha's biological family is disturbing, to put it mildly. I wanted to break the news in person."

"I already know," I said glumly.

"About the mother's rape?"

I nodded. "I found out from the mother of one of Sasha's friends."

Rollie scratched her forehead. "Why did we believe that Sasha didn't have any friends?"

"Because her foster mom doesn't know what the hell's going on in her life. Sasha does have friends, at least one: Molly, and she's allergic to sunlight. That's why Sasha visits her at night. As far as I can tell, they play Frisbee and go on walks."

"That doesn't sound sinister."

"No kidding. How did you come across the mother's sexual assault? Victims' names are never published, and the rapist was never caught, according to Molly's mother."

"Mr. and Mrs. Fuller split two years ago. The divorce showed up in my background check, and I paid a visit to the county clerk."

Few people were aware of this, but virtually every Colorado divorce proceeding was open to public scrutiny. High-profile people had the sense to request that their records be sealed, but for the rest of the population, open season prevailed on the darkest squabbles of their lives. All it took was a simple request of the county clerk, and anyone could read the file.

"Wait a minute, you're sure the Fullers are divorced?"

"Split in two."

"Sasha thinks her dad lives in Observatory Park with her mother and three brothers."

Rollie shook her head. "She's kidding herself or you. The dad and boys reside on South St. Paul Street, but the mom has an apartment in Lakewood."

"Hmm," I said, trying to absorb the information and its ramifications. "What was in the divorce records that indicated her mother had been raped?"

"As part of the settlement, Dad has to pay Mom $500 per month for counseling, for three years."

"Even though the rape took place seven years ago?"

"Even though."

I took a deep breath. "What should I do now?"

"You haven't talked to Sasha?"

"Not yet. I haven't had time. I'm in the middle of this hit-and-run."

"You better make time."

"I will," I promised. "Soon."

"Good. Now fill me in on your case."

With that, I spent the next thirty minutes updating Rollie on the progress I'd made.

In the end, she congratulated me and gave me a few pointers.

As she rose to leave, I said, "Care to join me at a polo match tomorrow night?"

"Polo? In Denver? The sport of kings?"

"And killers," I said, sending my eyebrows up and down as an evil invitation.

Rollie declined.

She had to take her bedding to the Laundromat, but she assured me I'd be safe among the society crowd.

Lucky for me, her sports car wouldn't hold all of her dirty comforters.

We agreed to trade cars for the weekend.

• • •

As I drove home in Rollie's 350Z, never reaching a speed above thirty, I rejoiced that I'd decided against holding an open house for a two-story Denver Square I had in Congress Park.

I'd promised the owner I would do it the following weekend, which bought me time, but only postponed the inevitable. Another lost Sunday. I didn't know how many more I could afford to give up.

There was one small consolation.

The world was safe for real estate agents again.

In the middle of the week, the Denver Real Estate Board had sent out an e-mail, claiming credit for having apprehended the notorious open house burglar. In a sting operation coordinated with the Denver Police Department, the woman had been caught rifling through the master bathroom of a home in Capitol Hill.

Brokers everywhere could breathe a mint-tinged sigh of relief. The police had trapped the culprit, and we could go back to trapping buyers.

I told Sasha to forward the e-mail to Valerie Edbrooke.

Valerie called to thank me and to tell me authorities had linked the same woman to the string of thefts in the southeast corridor.

She left the news on my voice mail. I hadn't allowed Sasha to transfer the call.

• • •

Shortly before six the next evening, I arrived at the Elmhurst Riding Club in style.

As I stepped out of the Nissan 350Z and stretched, I was reminded of why I could never leave Colorado—the beautiful weather.

According to Sasha's online research, the polo match would be played, rain or shine.

I was grateful for shine, particularly after two days of drizzle. I couldn't have asked for anything more idyllic: temperature in the low eighties, a blue sky unbroken by clouds, no humidity, and a light breeze.

At that moment, it seemed as if there were no better place on earth than this serene oasis in the middle of Denver, an emerald carpet bordered by mature cottonwoods and elms.

The Elmhurst was home to the Rocky Mountain Division of the International Polo Federation, a group of sixty active members who lived in Colorado or southern Wyoming. Two local teams would be squaring off in a few minutes.

Tickets for the event, which was sponsored by the Denver 30-40, a social club for rich men and women ages thirty to forty, cost $250, open bar and culinary spread included.

I'd had no idea how to dress for an outdoor polo match, but I assumed I couldn't be far off with casual choices. Wrong! Ladies in gowns and men in tuxedos mingled in tents alongside the ten-acre pitch.

I joined a cluster of people away from the tent who were dressed like I was—in jeans, button-down shirts, and cowboy boots. It took me a few minutes to realize I'd attached myself to the grooms, trainers, and instructors who served the players on the field.

No matter.

They accepted my presence without question, and before the official match began, an elderly man made a beeline for me. For his age, he was quite spry. He had cropped white hair that stood on end, a neatly trimmed mustache, and twinkling eyes.

With the comportment of a man accustomed to getting his way, he spoke in a cultured voice. "Is this your first time?"

I smiled. "It's that obvious?"

"Not at all." He extended his hand, which was surprisingly soft. "Walter Devonshire."

We shook. "Lauren Vellequette. How did you know I was new to this?"

He chuckled. "You have the 'deer-in-the-headlights' look."

I inclined my head toward the field, where play had begun in a flurry of horses, mallets, riders, and a tiny ball. "I can't believe they go that fast."

"This is slow motion compared to a professional match. Those are a sight to behold."

I noted his white jeans, team Alexi jersey, knee guards, boots, spurs, and helmet. "Are you playing tonight?"

"Only in the event of an injury."

"You've been benched," I teased.

"You could say that, but I don't mind. At seventy-five, the bones are a little creaky, and my wife worries about the spills."

"Does that happen often?" I said, watching as teams of four raced up and down the field, players seemingly near disaster with every swing of the mallet.

"Most of the ponies are trained well enough to overcome operator errors. The best keep their eye on the ball and anticipate. That helps prevent collisions."

"I love the pageantry and the color."

"Most women do."

"Does anyone watch the match?" I said, gesturing toward the tents, where most in the audience had their backs to the action, more intent on conversation than match play.

"Not many. Unfortunately, polo is merely a backdrop for social gatherings."

"Why are the horses' manes shaved?"

"That's the mark of a true polo pony. Most come off the racetracks at three or four, after which trainers spend two years training them with mallets."

"Polo sounds like an expensive hobby."

"That depends on what you consider expensive," Walter said, with a bemused smile. "Start-up costs would set you back about $250,000."

I whistled in amazement. "That much?"

He grinned at my shock. "You'd need a few ponies, a truck and trailer, feed, stabling, vet bills, and the ongoing expenses of membership and green fees."

"You need more than one horse?"

"Yes, indeed. It's customary to change horses at the end of each chukker," he said, before adding, "Period. Each match has six, with each chukker lasting seven minutes."

"Do you know most of the players?" I said casually.

"If I don't know them personally, I know someone who knows them. You can't avoid that in polo."

I pointed to the only man on the field with a ponytail. "That player looks familiar."

"He's new to the Centeria team. Richard something. I can't recall the last name, but I believe he joined midseason. Our team played them earlier in the year, but he wasn't in the match. He's not a member of the Federation, but I'm sure someone will twist his arm to join."

"Is he any good?" I said, as Richard's shot on goal missed by a wide margin.

"Fair to middling. Let's put it this way, he has a good horse."

I scratched my chin. "I swear I've seen him somewhere. Do you know what kind of work he does?"

"Real estate development, I believe. But don't quote me on that. Most of the fellas around here call themselves developers."

"What kind of work did you used to do?"

"Land development."

We both laughed, but he said seriously, "In the early seventies, I developed most of the land around Aspen. I had a good run at it. How about you? What's your line of work?"

"Real estate."

We laughed again. "You're pulling my leg!"

"I'm not! I've been a residential agent for twenty years."

"You don't say!"

I'd become so engrossed in my conversation with Walter Devonshire that I'd lost track of the crowd under the tents, which had grown considerably.

I decided to take a closer look. "I'm going to head toward the food. Thanks for the polo tutorial."

"Any time," Walter said amiably. "It was a pleasure meeting you."

"Likewise."

As I turned to leave, he grabbed my sleeve. "Richard DeWitt, that's the fella's name. I knew it would come to me."

I smiled wide and hugged him, which he didn't seem to mind.

Richard DeWitt.

How cozy.

Any relation to Kurt DeWitt, the appraiser who had given Jessica Stankowski's former house a valuation it didn't deserve, on behalf of Deidre Johnston, a woman who didn't exist?

Richard DeWitt. Kurt DeWitt.

I felt like skipping as I approached the tent.

I was about to break this case wide open!

CHAPTER 21

Maybe it was the excitement of galloping horses or the impending conclusion to my first major case, but I couldn't sleep Saturday night.

Not a wink, which was a rare occurrence for me.

I'd survived cancer, in large part because of the curative effects of slumber, always dreaming of better times and places, past or future. The brief respites had helped me cope with the pain of being awake.

This night, after three restless hours between the sheets, I decided to get up and go into the office, determined to finish up paperwork, a vow I'd made for at least two weeks.

When I arrived at the darkened building and crept down the dimly lit halls, I began to have second thoughts about working in the wee hours.

The office space—which in daylight now struck me as creepy, thanks to the facts that Sasha had pointed out in her sales pitch for new headquarters—seemed positively threatening in the middle of the night.

With trepidation, I unlocked the door to my office.

As I turned on the light, a movement in the corner of the room caused me to let out a startled cry.

Good thing I didn't carry a gun, or I would have pulled it on Sasha, who stirred on the couch.

She rubbed her eyes. "Hi," she said sleepily.

"What're you doing here?" I said sharply, my pulse still racing.

"Sleeping."

"All night? You can't do that. The Bidwells will file a missing person's report."

Sasha stretched. "No, they won't. You have to care about someone to report them missing."

I looked at the cocoon she'd created for herself out of my sweatshirts. "Have you done this before, slept in the office?"

She nodded as she yawned.

"How many times?"

"Just once. Yesterday, when I moved out."

"Moved out?" I cried. "Where's your stuff?"

"I hid it in the back of the closet, behind the rowing machine and exercise bike."

How had this escaped my attention? I could barely control my anger. "Why did you leave?"

"Because they told me I couldn't hang with my friend Molly anymore. She's my best friend, but she can't go out during the day. The sun burns her skin, so we do things at night. I tried to explain that to the witch and the warden, but they said she was too old for me and too weird. They called her a vampire. I don't know why Molly's mother called them in the first place. Why would she do that?"

I let the question slide. "Couldn't your friend's mother explain the situation to the Bidwells?"

"She tried, but they wouldn't listen. The fosters only hear what their little minds understand. They think we're in a cult. My friend designs video games, and the church tells them that those are evil. They're the ones who are evil. I'm not going back there, ever."

"Sasha," I said firmly. "You can't stay here indefinitely."

She shrugged. "I'll sleep in the streets."

"Under the viaducts? You want someone to stab you and toss you in a Dumpster?"

"Maybe. I don't care."

"I do," I said furiously. "You have to go back to the Bidwells."

"Why do I have to live with people who don't like me?"

"Because you're in their care."

Her whine intensified. "So?"

"Lots of kids don't get along with their parents, but they don't run away and sleep at their workplaces."

"That's because they work at McDonald's. It's greasy there, and most kids have acne already."

I took a deep breath and tried a different approach. "What about your biological family, could you live with them?"

Her jaw set. "They hate me."

"I'm sure they don't hate you," I said, trying to maintain reason in the sea of petulance.

Sasha nodded with a vehemence that would have broken a bone in a less flexible neck. "You don't know them."

I pushed her legs aside and sat on the edge of the couch. "Don't you miss them at all?" I said softly.

"Why should I? They gave me up because I didn't fit their plans."

"Maybe they've changed," I said hopefully.

Sasha threw off her makeshift covers and pounded her leg repeatedly. "You know what they said about my scar?"

When I didn't answer, she stormed on. "That it should serve as a reminder of my mistake, that I burned myself on purpose."

"You didn't, did you?"

She looked me in the eye, daring. "I wanted to be ugly, so no one would try to touch me."

"It didn't work," I said tenderly. "You're still pretty."

"No," she shrieked, her body convulsing. "He hurt my mother, but he won't come after me."

I reached to comfort her, but she slapped me away. "Who?"

"The man with the glasses," she said, in an immature whisper.

How did she know this? According to Rollie's sources at the police department, Sasha's mother hadn't seen her assailant.

I dropped my voice down to the level of hers. "A man hurt your mother?"

Sasha flinched and nodded. "It was my fault."

"What do you mean?"

"Daddy and my brothers went to the baseball game, but I didn't want to go. I made myself throw up so I could stay home, and Mommy had to stay with me."

I shivered. "What happened after your dad and brothers left?"

"The man came in and attacked Mommy. He hit her and made her do bad things. She cried a lot."

"Afterward."

Sasha's shaking subsided, and she became eerily still. "During."

I felt as if someone had kicked me in the stomach. "You saw it?"

She nodded, a subtle, almost undetectable movement. "I wanted him to disappear, but he wouldn't."

"Where were you?"

"In Mommy's closet. She told me to stay in my room, but I wanted to play with her shoes."

"Where did the man attack your mom?"

"On the bed, while she was napping. She liked to sleep when Daddy wasn't home. The bad man must have known that. He came in quietly, but I saw him."

"Did he see you?"

As Sasha chewed on the skin next to her thumbnail, she drew a drop of blood. I reached for her hand and held it in mine. She didn't resist.

"I was hidden behind Mommy's bathrobe," she said, in a dead tone. "He jumped on Mommy's back. He told her not to cry, but she couldn't stop. That's why he hit her with his fists."

"Sasha," I said quietly, trying to break the trance.

"They never caught the bad man. He's still out there, and I don't want him to come and get me."

"Did the police ask you what he looked like?"

She nodded.

"You never told them?"

She shook her head. "I would have gotten in trouble for playing with Mommy's shoes."

"Did you tell your parents?"

"No, they tried to get me to talk, but I wouldn't. They sent me to a doctor, and that's why I had to take pills."

"Antidepressants?"

"They were yellow. They made me sick."

Her chest heaved in dry sobs, and the faraway, glazed look in her eyes started to give me chills. I tried to get her attention by gently touching her on the arm, but she didn't notice.

"Sasha!" I said, at the top of my voice, trying to snap her out of the hypnotic pull of memories.

At last, she sat up and stared at me with clear eyes. "What?" she said, so ferociously I jumped.

"Have you ever told anyone that you saw the man who hurt your mom?"

The soft reply gave me goose bumps. "Not out loud."

• • •

The rest of Sasha's story came pouring out in the night.

She made us mochas that tasted sickeningly sweet, and over the drinks, she talked about the aftermath of one afternoon.

I could do little but listen.

After her mother's rapist left, Sasha spent hours in the closet, believing that her mother, in her paralyzed state, had died. When Sasha summoned the courage to check on her, her mother screamed at her touch.

Sasha fled, retreated to her bedroom, and waited for the rest of the family to return home from the Rockies game.

When her father arrived, he called the police, her mother went to the hospital, and Sasha played catch in the backyard with her brothers, as if nothing had happened.

Because the detective investigating the case had scared Sasha with his size and his glasses, she confided nothing.

In the days that followed, her mother never spoke to her about what happened; her father became withdrawn; and her brothers never knew what they'd missed.

Life in the Fuller home proceeded as usual.

Except that Sasha unraveled.

She became sick with an illness doctors couldn't identify. She ached, felt listless, and often stayed in bed with persistent, stabbing headaches.

School counselors sent her home repeatedly, before eventually advising against a return. Her mother took over her education, a duty she resented when it forced her to give up a career in nursing. As Sasha spiraled downward, a psychiatrist described her as the most depressed adolescent he'd ever encountered. Because the doctor never discovered the core of Sasha's problems, he took the easy way out with a prescription pad.

At ten, Sasha Fuller watched her mother's rape. At eleven, she lost touch with society. At twelve, she tried to kill herself with the same vodka her father consumed every night. At thirteen, she launched firecrackers from her nightstand. Shortly thereafter, she went into the foster care system.

She was placed with the Bidwell family almost immediately, but the transition hadn't been an easy one. Overnight, she went from an atheist household to an evangelical one. As she adjusted to intimate surroundings with girls her age, she missed her brothers desperately.

Those feelings deepened when she returned to school and ran into one of her brothers, only to be told he couldn't talk to her. After several more uncomfortable encounters, the Fullers transferred him to Mullen, a private, all-boys school.

The first Halloween Sasha spent with the Bidwells, she strolled through the neighborhood in her underwear, telling anyone who asked that she was dressed as a slut. The costume might have been clever, except for the blizzard that night.

It was a miracle that this girl sat next to me, with her pierced tongue, blue/yellow hair, and fingernails bitten to the quicks.

How she'd survived the wretched confluence of circumstances, I'd never know.

The mocha curdled in my stomach as I absorbed what she'd had to endure.

At the break of dawn, she broached the subject of the days after tomorrow.

"I could live with you," she said nonchalantly, but her eyes held a plea.

"That might not be such a good idea," I said quietly.

"Why?"

"The Bidwells would never go for it."

"They wouldn't care," she said earnestly. "Not as long as they got their check. I could live with you, and we wouldn't have to tell anyone. It's a big hassle to go through another placement. I'll bet the witch and the warden would give me up, if you agreed to let them keep the check."

"We couldn't do that."

"Why not? You don't need the state's money. You're loaded."

"How do you know?"

Sasha smiled bashfully. "I ran a credit check on you."

I stared at her, torn between pride in her investigative instincts and revulsion at the invasion of my privacy. I tried to keep the lecture out of my tone. "How did you manage that without my date of birth or social security number?"

"Rollie told me your birthday. I pretended that I wanted to buy you a present, which I will in October, I promise. Your social security number is written on a card in your Rolodex. At the back, the last one. You should be more careful."

"You should snoop less."

"Can you blame me?"

"No," I said, defeated. "It's a good quality in this line of work."

"Will you let me stay with you, just until I graduate from high school and can work full-time and afford a place of my own? That'll be less than a year."

"What about college?"

"College is for people who don't know what they want to do when they grow up, but I do. I want to be a private investigator, and you know everything. You can teach me."

"I'm not so sure about that," I said diffidently.

"I won't be any trouble," she implored. "You won't know I'm there. I make my bed every morning, I always ask before I eat food, and I pick up after myself—you've seen that."

"You're a lot neater than I am," I agreed.

"I can clean up after you, too, if you want."

My heart ached with her every persuasion, but I couldn't bear a commitment. "I haven't lived with anyone in a long time . . ."

"I could sleep on the couch," she said frantically. "I don't need my own bed."

"What about living with your friend Molly?"

Sasha's face fell. "I can't live there. They have the blinds closed all day. I'd feel like I was living in a cave with bats. Molly's too clingy. I like her as a friend and everything, but I need sunlight. I have to go out, and she stays inside. The house smells like cat pee, and they never buy good snacks."

She must have noticed my incredulity, because she stopped abruptly and employed a much kinder tone. "Not that I'd complain, not if I lived with you."

"I don't know, Sasha," I said, drawing out the words, waiting for my emotions to catch up. "I walk around the apartment at least six times a night."

"For what?"

"To pee. To get a drink of water. To make notes on a case. To adjust the air conditioner. To pee again."

"That wouldn't bother me. Not at all. Please, Lauren, please!"

"I'd have to talk to your foster mom," I said haltingly. "She might not go for this."

"She will," Sasha said, animated. "She's a money grubber. Her monthly subsidy for me is going to be cut in September by $100."

"How do you know?"

"I read the letter from the agency."

"Addressed to your mother?"

"Foster mother, and yeah, so what? The witch said I was too much trouble for only $800 a month."

I couldn't mask my shock. "You overheard that?"

"She told me to my face."

I winced. "Maybe you misinterpreted her remarks."

"She said I wasn't worth the lower rate of payment," Sasha said staunchly. "I understood her."

I let out a deep sigh. "You need to get out of there."

"Please say I can live with you," Sasha begged quietly, almost under her breath.

"I'll think about it," was all I could muster.

An ineffectual response to a circumstance I never dreamed I'd face.

My answer must have been less than what Sasha had wished for, but more than she'd expected, because it left her face covered with disappointment and hope.

Both of which distressed me.

CHAPTER 22

I spent all of Sunday in bed.

Alone.

Physically and emotionally exhausted, I slept most of the day.

Only minutes before sunset did I rise.

In the evening hours, I jotted down elaborate notes, playing out the next morning's scene in my mind, leaving nothing to chance.

I'd set the stage by asking Kurt DeWitt to meet me at 1206 Josephine Street, the house which Jessica Stankowski had sold to Denise Johnson, when she was posing as Deidre Johnston.

I considered the vacant house a fitting setting to expose the appraiser's fraud.

Under the guise of my Federal Housing Authority muscle, I told him I had a few more questions pursuant to the investigation.

Like a lemming, he agreed to meet me at the property.

Ten o'clock, Monday morning.

That's when it all would come to a head.

Despite massive amounts of daylight rest, I slept deeply that night.

• • •

I woke up excited that I would soon bring closure to Jessica Stankowski's family.

Yet, as my appointment with Kurt DeWitt drew closer, I felt pangs of depression that the journey would end, and that my reason for rising every morning would soon evaporate.

It had been too easy. Way easier than the SOB private eye instructor or Rollie Austin had led me to believe.

My first major case, solved.

Practically.

At ten o'clock, I arrived at the empty house on Josephine Street, the one Jessica Stankowski had sold to someone she knew as Deidre Johnston, in a transaction that had led to both of their deaths. I entered using the key I'd borrowed from Holly Stamos, Jessica's friend who couldn't let go.

As I walked through the house, I had the overwhelming sensation that time had arrested, a life had been interrupted.

The smallest details made me want to scream, recalling the stories Bev Stankowski had shared with me. I saw the curtains the mother and daughter had made together, the ceiling fan her father had installed the first summer she lived in the house, the mums a neighbor had given her as a housewarming present, the warm earth tones she'd chosen for the walls, and the welcome mat she'd left behind for the next owner.

As I battled to control my fury, Kurt DeWitt knocked on the front screen door and let himself in.

We toured the home—both agreeing that no renovations had been undertaken, much less completed—and returned to the living room, where I laid out an attractive option for an extremely unattractive situation.

Under the authority of the FHA, I assured Kurt DeWitt, I was authorized to absolve him of any wrongdoing in exchange for full cooperation and restitution. The Federal Housing Authority couldn't afford a scandal, I confessed, and it was more important to the "powers-that-be" that we trace the origin and sequence of fraud than that we file criminal charges.

I was on his side, I said, an assertion only an egotistical idiot would believe.

Kurt DeWitt believed.

Once he began talking, he wouldn't shut up.

"Everyone else in the real estate industry has made money," he said, pacing in the empty living room. "There's not an honest one in the bunch."

I leaned against the front windowsill, well out of his frantic path. "I agree."

"The goddamn agents and their fat-ass commissions." He waved his arms in the air. "They take a listing, push a sign in the ground, hold an open house, sign a few papers, and pocket ten thousand. You know how many appraisals I have to do for that?"

"Fifty or sixty," I said sweetly. "Did I mention that I'm a licensed broker with twenty years' experience?"

He paused and faced me squarely. "You know the score."

"I do. How about the amateurs with their weekend fix and flips?"

"They're the worst," he said vehemently. "Or the developers with their land grabs. Those bastards clear millions."

"I hate the mortgage brokers who sell three or four re-fi's to the same person in one year."

Kurt resumed his military march. "That should be illegal."

"Those crooks foist loans on people every day. No interest, no documentation, debt consolidation, knowing full well people can't manage the money."

"How about the home inspectors?" He tugged on his thick hair. "Why aren't they licensed? They don't take the time to do it right anymore."

"My favorites are the mold abatement specialists, the ones who couldn't find mold if it were growing in their noses."

He sniggered. "You've met those pricks, with their Internet certifications?"

"Two of them," I said sympathetically.

"I decided I'd lie for myself, instead of helping those other assholes."

"You were the only honest man left," I said, without a trace of sarcasm.

"Damn straight." Kurt squatted and slammed his right fist into his left palm. "For years, I turned away those cocksuckers who told me to hit a number when I did an appraisal for them. Then I said to hell with it, and I started playing their game."

"Until you invented your own," I commented idly.

"I wanted my share of the pie."

"I hear you."

"What I did was no worse than half of what goes on behind the scenes."

"It was a brilliant scheme," I said truthfully. "With the fake credit histories, you could do anything."

"It was pretty tight," he said smugly. "I was going to do a few in my own name, leverage the money, and pay it back before anyone noticed. But when my brother ran into that guy at the credit company, I couldn't stop thinking of the possibilities. We didn't even need seed money. We bought the houses with no-money-down loans. The mortgage brokers couldn't have made it easier for us."

"How did you find buyers who would accept no-money-down offers?"

Kurt stood again, rising to his full height, towering over me by at least a foot, outweighing me by a hundred pounds. Fortunately, he was several strides away. "By searching the MLS listings for zero-down programs or going after sellers with full-price contracts and making them chip in the down payments."

I hugged the wall. "You chose homes in neighborhoods where a jump in appreciation because of renovation wouldn't look unusual. That way, when you went for your hefty second loans, no one raised an eyebrow."

He nodded. "We did deals in Hilltop, Crestmoor, Park Hill, Congress Park, and Washington Park."

"Whose idea was it to bring Denise Johnson into the fold?"

"My brother's. Richard had been dating her for a few months. He knew he could talk her into anything, and we wanted to stay away from the closings. That kid at Colorado Credit Company created credit histories that looked good, and Denise was our front woman."

"Where did the social security numbers and the drivers' licenses come from? What about the work histories, all the information you had to put on Denise's credit applications?"

"We made up the work references and set up throwaway cell phones to verify employment and salary. The licenses were a piece of cake. One of my buddies knows a guy who specializes in identities. He hooked me up. This guy can get you anything you want."

"What about the tricky colors and the holograms on the licenses?"

"At first, we had the real deal. The guy had a connection at the DMV, until the authorities started investigating the Five Points branch. After that, he switched to forged ones, and those worked fine. Clerks at title companies make black and white copies of the licenses. They never look at them. No one does."

"Pretty soon, you had a house."

"I had seventy-three houses," he said boastfully. "Some weeks, Denise was going to five or ten closings. She started bitching about the workload."

"Was it hard to get the second mortgages?"

Kurt DeWitt laughed, a coarse sound. "Those were much easier. Most of them we did by phone."

"Because your fake credit identity still had good credit."

"The best. We made all the payments on the first mortgages, by money order, until the second loans came through."

"You applied for lines of credit and made sure the appraisals were at least as high as the first and second mortgages combined," I said, thinking aloud. "How did you manage to perform all the appraisals yourself?"

"Denise would suggest my name to her real estate agent or mortgage broker—"

I interrupted. "You switched up agents and brokers?"

"All the time. We followed the desperation. I'd hear about a guy who needed a quick commission or a gal who was new to the field, and Denise would start working with them. Denise suggested me for some jobs. Other times, I'd call the mortgage broker out of the blue and offer to do a few appraisals at no charge, as a way to introduce my services. The cheap dumbasses bit every time. They'd pass me the ones on their desks that day."

"One of which happened to be Denise's file."

"You catch on quick," Kurt said, with a twisted grin. "I didn't land all the appraisals, but I didn't need to. If the mortgage people used their own appraiser, no big deal. They'd find out Denise had been high in her estimation of her property's value, and there was no equity to loan against. They'd deny the line of credit. So what!"

I nodded knowingly. "That happens every day. There's nothing suspicious about it."

"Denise would switch to another lender, with the same property. If we were turned down twice, we walked away."

"Because you didn't want too many inquiries showing up on one identity's credit report."

"That didn't happen often," Kurt said, his smile complacent. "I'm telling you, it was too easy. As soon as those second loans were approved, bang, we converted them to cash."

"How?"

"The same way you would. If the bank provided a checkbook, we wrote checks. Namely, to me or my brother. Other times, we took a cashier's check at the closing, made out to Denise's identity of the day, and she'd endorse it over. Richard or I would deposit it in our accounts, no questions asked."

"Because the money was being drawn on a bank account, not an individual account?"

"You got it."

"None of the lenders came after you when you stopped making payments on the loans?"

"There was no one to go after. The lenders had phone numbers that went to the disposable cell phones Denise used. The rest, the kid at CCC made up. Fake addresses, fake references, fake employers, the works."

I shook my head in amazement. "You must have made millions. Where's the money now?"

"Wouldn't you like to know?" He moved several steps closer to me. "Forget about the FHA. Come with me to Belize, and you'll find out."

Sliding across the wall, I moved closer to the door. "Thanks, no. I'm rather fond of the United States."

His smile faded. "Suit yourself."

"I have to hand it to you, the plan was flawless. And it was almost victimless."

"You tell me, who did we hurt?" he said jovially. "Maybe a few multinational corporations and institutions, but they can afford the hit."

I clutched my purse with both hands. "What about Jessica Stankowski?"

"Who?"

"C'mon," I said impatiently. "You know, the girl who ran into Denise at the two closings."

"What about her?" he said cautiously, retreating.

"How do you rationalize your brother running her over with his Maxima? What do you call that?"

"I don't know what you're talking about, but if I did, I'd call it a necessary expense," he said flippantly. "The cost of doing business."

I stared at him hard. "You really believe that?"

Kurt didn't flinch. "I'm not saying Richard did anything, but if he did,

I wouldn't have blamed him. Why did that girl have to make a big deal of Denise buying two houses? She should have minded her own business. My brother's a generous guy. Too generous. He would have tried to buy her off. Maybe she had too many principles for her own good. Screw that! Time for Plan B."

"How could Richard have known that Jessica would be on Highlands Ranch Parkway that morning?"

"Maybe he knew where she worked. Maybe when she was at the closing with Denise, she couldn't keep her mouth shut, you know, chick talk."

"Sure," I said, encouraging Kurt DeWitt to dig a bigger hole.

"What if my brother went there one morning, to catch her before work, to try to persuade her to stay out of it. What if she pulled into the parking lot and took off jogging. Maybe that's when he came up with the idea, on the spur of the moment. Maybe he followed her until they reached a nice stretch of open road. Nothing to it! A split-second solution. An accident."

"Nothing?" I said, my anger rising.

Kurt DeWitt shrugged, his even tone belying the nastiness of his recollections. "Any bitch who did what she did got what she deserved. No one can prove anything. No one cares. The police dropped the case."

"True, but I haven't."

He squinted. "What are you talking about?"

"Remember when I told you that I was a private investigator hired by the FHA? I lied. I was hired by Jessica Stankowski's family. To care. Now I have the evidence I need to prove your brother killed her," I said, triumphantly yanking the micro-recorder out of my purse.

"You fucking cunt," Kurt DeWitt screamed, as he lunged at me.

"That wasn't very nice," I said, taking a step to the side and pulling something else out of my purse, the semiautomatic I'd lifted from Rollie's glove compartment. Sasha wasn't the only one who could borrow equipment without asking.

I aimed the gun at his chest, which stopped him in his tracks.

In that frozen pose, Kurt DeWitt looked every bit the killer. His eyes bulged, and a vein throbbed in his forehead. He clenched his fists and tightened his lips until they turned white. As his jaw trembled with rage, his eyes flitted from the gun to my lifeless eyes to the front door.

"Try it," I said calmly. "I can't tell you how much I'd love to shoot you."

He didn't move.

"Now we know who killed Jessica Stankowski, but I'm curious, who killed Denise Johnson?"

"Fuck you," he said, in a deadly whisper.

"You did, didn't you?"

"Think what you want."

"You know how I know?" I said icily. "Because your brother wouldn't have beat her like that. She wanted out. When she was broke and vulnerable, she agreed to your schemes, but she wasn't a murderer. When I came along and told her that Jessica Stankowski had been run down in the street, Denise had a change of heart. The easy money wasn't easy anymore, was it?"

"Go to hell."

"You know what, Kurt? The easy money never is easy."

With the gun aimed at his chest, I calmly pulled my cell phone out of my pocket and dialed my own version of 911.

CHAPTER 23

The next morning, Rollie Austin stopped by my office.

By her stern demeanor, I could tell I was in for a lecture.

She wasted no time. "You shouldn't have gone to that house without backup."

"I know. I screwed up," I said, exhibiting the proper amount of shame.

I'd learned from the master, Sasha, who thankfully wasn't there to witness my dressing-down. She'd left a few minutes earlier to restock supplies for the espresso machine.

"Rookie mistake. A word to the wise, don't lift my gun again unless you plan on using it, which you shouldn't. You can't kill them all, honey, or you'll get a reputation."

I cracked a thin smile. "Thanks for sending Carla."

"She's the only one I had available on short notice who's licensed to carry a gun," she said, emphasizing the words short and licensed.

"Did the cops hassle her?"

"No more than usual. She's a big girl. She handled it."

"Did it help that she turned over information on a Douglas County hit-and-run, a Denver County homicide, and a federal racketeering ring?"

"It certainly did. The Douglas County cops caught up with Richard DeWitt at a polo practice and took him into custody. But the detectives still want to talk to the mysterious lady they heard on the tape recording Carla gave them, the one who vanished before they arrived. You better stop down at the precinct."

"Will I be okay?" I said, my voice shaky.

"You'll be fine. I'll go with you. I have a friend or two in law enforcement."

"Douglas County, Denver, or the Feds?"

"All of those."

"You get around."

"You know it. You do, too, sugar, but we have to get you a license to pack, so you can stick around for the glory."

"That's not really my style."

"Change of subject," Rollie said with enthusiasm. "We're still on for Thursday?"

"You bet. You're going to love the Norman. This condo's for you. I swear you'll love it."

"Maybe I'll write a contract," she said coyly. "I have a good feeling this time."

That gave me hope for Rollie Austin.

• • •

I had hope for Sasha Fuller, too.

She had been correct about the Bidwells and their preference for cash over connection.

I checked with Gayle Bidwell, who consulted with her husband, and we all agreed that without notifying the foster care agency, on a trial basis, I'd be responsible for Sasha's care. Of course, they would continue to receive checks from the state.

The very thought of this teenager's dependence scared the hell out of me, but no more so than the alternatives. Without my intervention, undoubtedly she'd continue to rail against the Bidwells. If she landed back in the foster care pool, she might run away from the madness, prematurely tripping into adulthood.

I couldn't live with myself if I stood by while Sasha imploded.

How much worse could this be, she and I agreeing to roles neither of us would adapt to comfortably?

To improve our odds of still speaking in ninety days, I solved the "too much closeness, not enough privacy, whole life going to hell" dilemma by renting the studio apartment next to my one-bedroom.

I swore Sasha to secrecy about my ownership of the building, paid the guy next door a thousand bucks to move down the hall, and cosigned the lease after introducing Sasha to the manager as a family friend.

Sasha cried when she walked into her unit at the *Watchtower* and kissed me on the cheek, an impetuous move that flustered me.

Three weeks into it, the move had brought positive results.

She was much less moody at work, more easygoing and lighthearted. Something had changed in her.

On the inside and the outside.

One Friday morning, when I came into work, her self-conscious greeting amused me. "Aren't you going to say something?"

"You're not wearing any jewelry."

Sasha had taken all the posts, rods, and other assorted pieces of metal out of her piercings. Hopefully, the dime-size hole in her ear and the smaller pricks in her eyebrows, nose, lips, and tongue would heal completely, leaving no trace of prior mutilation.

"All gone," she said shyly. "What about my hair?"

After a temporary loss of words, I managed a faint reply. "It's glossy black, with patches of white."

"Do you like it?"

"It's interesting," I said, slightly dazed. "Why did you change from blue and yellow?"

"I wanted something more non—" Sasha faltered. "What was that word you used on my car?"

"Nondescript."

"That's it," she said eagerly. "If I'm going to do a good job on my next case, I have to be able to sneak around. That reminds me, Kip's wife said to tell you hello."

"Who?"

"Nancy Livingston. Your friend from high school."

"Oh, her," I said offhandedly.

"Kip said to thank you for the freebie. He owes you one."

"I don't know what he's talking about."

"The invoice you'll never send," Sasha needled. "He told me the hole-in-one case was your idea, to give me practice."

"Oh, really?" I said innocently.

"I can't believe you'd pay me when no one was paying you."

"You must be imagining things."

She looked at me sternly. "What's the matter with you, Lauren?"

I smiled faintly. "How much time do you have?"

"You really care, don't you?"

My smile broadened.

I hated to admit it, but I guess I did.

Care.

About something.

About someone.

It felt scary and unsettling.

I'd have to get used to it again, this idea of caring.

I put my arm around Sasha's shoulder, and we spent the next ten minutes arguing about whether she needed her own credit card for work-related expenses.

After she looked up the number, I called American Express.

About the Author

Jennifer L. Jordan, a two-time Lambda Literary Award Finalist, is the author of the Lauren Vellequette Mystery Series and the Kristin Ashe Mystery Series.

In 2008, she was awarded the Alice B. Readers Appreciation Award for her contributions to lesbian fiction.

Self-employed since the age of twenty-one, Jennifer has taught thousands of people how to start and run their own small businesses. She currently owns a marketing and consulting firm that specializes in search engine optimization (SEO).

As a teenager, Jennifer developed an interest in real estate, and over the years, she's participated in dozens of successful real estate investments and transactions.

Jennifer enjoys snowboarding, cross-country skiing, hiking, golfing, and collecting watches. She divides her time between homes in Winter Park and Denver, Colorado.

For more information or to read excerpts from her books,
visit her website, www.jenniferljordan.com.

Excerpt from Book 2 in the
Lauren Vellequette Mystery Series

UNDER CONTRACT

There was something spectacular about fire, almost spiritual.

I watched as streams of water arced toward the flames, colliding at the intersection of beauty and tragedy.

I never imagined that violence could feel so pleasurable, all but sensual.

I could have stayed for days.

Unfortunately, a shout from Dennis McBride brought me back to attention.

I turned, and he glared at me. "Meet me in my office at eight o'clock. You're getting a partner."

Partner.

I did not like the sound of that word.

What the hell had gone wrong?

CHAPTER 1

Eleven days earlier, Dennis McBride had hired me, on a Friday morning in the second week of September.

"Two houses gone. Do you mind?" He removed his sweatshirt, loosened his belt, and whipped down his zipper before I could reply. "I have a meeting with investors after we're finished here."

I steadfastly maintained eye contact.

He continued in a calmer voice. "Try to ignore the mess. The wife and I are between houses. We sold one in Cherry Hills, had to be out by the end of August, and we can't get into the new house until next week. Everything we own is in semi containers, and we're camped out at the Marriott. My Audi's so full of crap, I can barely squeeze in to drive. How's that for a sorry tale!"

He gestured in aggravation at the clutter that had spilled into his work environment.

The corporate offices for McBride Homes were located on the seventh floor of a mid-rise in the Denver Tech Center, off I-25 and Belleview Avenue. Dennis held down the southwest corner, and beyond two walls of floor-to-ceiling windows, he had a panoramic view of the Rocky Mountains, all the way to Pikes Peak.

The décor inside wasn't shabby either. The suburban office had wool carpet, cherry paneled wainscoting, crown molding, heavily textured walls in butter yellow, ceiling medallions, and antique iron sconces and light fixtures. The writing desk, hutch, bookshelf, filing cabinets, and banker's chair, all in cherry, added to the rich look.

Too bad disorder suffocated the design.

A duffel bag, a tennis racket, golf clubs, shoes, umbrellas, and a pull cart were tangled together in a corner by the door, while balls, bats, mitts, and baseball memorabilia were clumped on the couch. A fireproof safe sat on top of the desk, crumpling blueprints below it, and clothes were strewn across the room.

I tendered a faint smile. "Couldn't you move into one of your company's houses temporarily?"

Dennis yanked plastic wrapping off a lavender, long-sleeve shirt. "I don't have a vacant one. I don't break ground without a contract."

"That's good news, that the homes are selling," I said brightly.

"Tell my wife. She has room service and housekeeping, but can't stop complaining about the hotel closet. It's not big enough for her, not by a football field. Who knew? I've barely had time to get to know her, much less measure her wardrobe. Usually, when we're together, she isn't wearing much," he said, with a randy chuckle.

"You haven't been married long?"

He twisted his wedding ring, a titanium band with blue topaz and diamonds. "What's today? Friday. That makes it six days."

"Congratulations."

Dennis shook his head, mystified. "Damned if I know how it happened. I broke off a relationship in February. Marla and I met in March. I proposed in June. We tied the knot in September. I'm scared to think about what's next."

He was in no hurry to put on his shirt, all the while daring me to look away, which I did, happily.

Too much chest hair, too early in the morning.

A blonde-gray mat on the pecs of an offensive lineman who hadn't played in thirty years—not a pretty sight. He had the same color hair on his head, and he'd brushed it up and back, to where it fell just below the ears. His square head and jaw were proportional to his large frame, and a broken nose added to the hardy look. A distinctive birthmark covered his right cheekbone.

I had to look at something other than my client's half-naked body.

For the time being, I chose the mounted warthog head near my feet. Out of the corner of my eye, it seemed as if the animal's body were stowed below the carpet, a less unsettling visual than muscle turned to flab.

"Is this your first marriage?"

"One and only. Make yourself comfortable wherever you can."

I chose the only flat surface that would bear weight and sat, awkwardly. "What do you want me to do?"

"I want you to find out who's trying to ruin me."

"The police don't have any suspects?" I said, picking up a thread of conversation we'd begun on the phone the day earlier.

"*My* houses burned to the ground, and they're treating me like a suspect. I almost forgot to offer, you want something to drink?"

"What do you have?"

"You're sitting on it," he said, gesturing toward the red and white plastic cooler.

I opened the top of my "chair" to a stash of hard liquor, all at room temperature, no ice. "I'll pass. How about you?"

"Better not. I don't want the investors to smell booze on my breath."

I replaced the lid and repositioned myself. "You have to admit, two fires in three months is suspicious."

Dennis put on his shirt, buttoned it, and rolled up the sleeves. "Damn right it is. That's why I know someone's out to get me. One fire's bad luck. Two has to be intentional."

"Or worse luck."

"No chance. The first investigation, at Landry, everyone was nice and friendly. This time, at Southfield, they won't tell me anything, other than the cause of the fire is undetermined. A friend of mine who went through an arson investigation warned me that they'll be digging into my financials and interviewing anyone they can. Neighbors, partners, employees. I'd be a fool to sit by while they tear into my business and personal life."

"You made the right move, calling me."

"Why would anyone think I set those fires? How does losing two properties under contract benefit me?"

I pulled a notepad from my purse and began to scribble. "The fire at Southfield happened when?"

"Two nights ago. At dusk."

"And the one at Landry?"

He sauntered over to the revolving rack next to his wastebasket and selected a dark blue tie, which he knotted expertly. "About three months ago, on June 11. Two weeks before the house was supposed to close."

"Have you considered hiring a security guard? I could make a recommendation."

"What kind of image would that portray? I sell people on the idea of family-based communities. I can't have armed goons running around the neighborhood."

"They don't have to be armed, and usually they don't run unless they're chasing someone," I said evenly.

"Forget it," he said, in an end-of-discussion tone.

I sighed. "Okay. Let's start with details about the first fire, the one at Landry. Tell me everything you know."

Dennis sat, leaned back, and balanced his bare feet on the desk. "We were building one of our standard, two-story models in the northwest neighborhood at Landry. We're calling the collection Hunter's Field. At completion, we'll have seventy single-family homes. Price range: mid fours."

"What day of the week did the house catch fire?"

He laced his fingers and put his hands behind his head. "Sunday. One of my workers dropped by the job site around noon to pick up tools for a 'honey-do' project. He saw flames and called 911. Firefighters came in five minutes, but the structure was a total loss."

"What's the exact address?"

"1125 Trinidad Street."

I shifted uncomfortably on the cooler. Good thing I hadn't worn a short skirt, or I would have had impressions from the lid's bubbles on my thighs. My cropped-length, soft seersucker pants with artisan embroidery provided at least a little protection. "I'll go by the site after I leave here."

"Feel free, but there's not much to look at."

"What's the name of the worker who discovered the fire?"

"Glenn Warner."

"Do you have any reason to suspect him?"

"None. He's one of my best foremen. I've known him twenty years."

"Did fire investigators label the Landry fire suspicious?"

"Not at the time. They chalked it up to oily rags and sawdust left behind by a crew from Stan's Flooring Company, which ticked me off. Have you seen how much sawdust comes from hardwood floor installation? Bags and bags. Glenn told them not to toss anything into our Dumpsters because of the fire hazard. They were supposed to dispose of sawdust and rags off-site. So much for that plan. They admitted they left them in the house over the weekend. By Sunday, they'd caught fire."

"Did you agree with investigators, that the fire at Landry was accidental?"

Dennis sat upright and folded his hands in his lap. "At the time, I did. I've seen fires like that before, but someone always smelled something and caught them before they could do any damage. It's a miracle there aren't more fires at construction sites, with all the flammables and combustibles. You have to watch what you're doing, but I can't seem to drill that into my employees, much less subcontractors. They get sloppy, cut corners, you know how it is."

"Did the fire set off an alarm inside the house?"

"No. The hard-wired system wasn't connected."

"Two weeks before closing?" I said, unable to contain my surprise. "What about battery backups in the detectors?"

He rubbed his lips. "We hadn't installed them. We do now."

"Was the hardwood floor treatment finished at the time of the fire?"

"Just about. Stan's had installed the floors, stained them, and applied two coats of polyurethane. A spark from an electric outlet may have ignited wood dust, or the oily rags spontaneously combusted. Investigators couldn't say for sure."

"Had you hired Stan's before?"

"We've used them for years."

"Are you still using them?"

"For the time being. They do good work, on time, and they have a clean showroom where my buyers can make selections."

"Did Stan's lose equipment?"

"Quite a bit of it."

"Have they bought new equipment?"

"I don't know," he said irritably. "They have rotating crews. I can't tell who uses what."

"Could you find out?"

"I could get Glenn to look into it." He rummaged around on his desk until he located a Blackberry.

"Nothing struck you as unusual at the time of the Landry fire? Nothing before or after?"

Dennis propped his elbow on the desk, inserted his chin into his right hand, and stared ahead thoughtfully. After a moment, he spoke loudly. "Come to think of it, Glenn did mention something about cardboard."

I felt a surge. "Cardboard?"

"The Dumpster should have been full of it, from cabinets and appliances our guys unpacked on Friday. On Sunday, there was no cardboard in the trash."

"Maybe someone moved the cardboard into the house and used it as fuel for the fire."

Dennis emitted a snort of derision. "More likely, some bum took it for his shelter. They trespass on my property all the time."

I returned to my notes, slightly deflated. "Who had a contract on the Landry house?"

"Barry Christensen. Stand-up guy."

"Could Barry have torched the house to get out of the contract?"

Dennis shook his head. "Never. He loves Hunter's Field and Landry. We moved him into a house down the street. A contract fell through, and we had one available. Everything worked out."

"Has the insurance company settled with you on the first fire?"

"Not yet, but we're close."

"At fair value?"

His lips tightened. "It'll do. You know how it goes. They say a number. I say a number. We both piss and moan. Eventually we arrive at a figure."

"Okay, let's talk about the house in Southfield. What's the exact address of that one?"

"3022 Visalia Street."

"How far along was it when it burned?"

"We were finishing up plumbing, electric, and HVAC. Drywall installation was scheduled for next week."

"Who legally owns it?"

"McBride Homes until we turn over title, but we have a purchase agreement with Fritz Jubera. Now there's a piece of work. He tried to make a custom home out of one of our standard models. Sixty-two change orders. We moved walls, doors, windows, electric. I don't know what I got myself into."

"Why did you agree to the customization?"

"Do you know the markup on changes?" he said, flashing a greedy smile.

"But the hassle . . ."

Dennis retrieved a baseball from underneath a pile of papers on his desk. "Tell me about it! This guy's a real know-it-all. He's insulted every one of my employees who's had contact with him, cussed them out for no reason. My salesgirls won't deal with him anymore. They cry every time they see his Hummer pull up to the model. He's threatened me with lawsuits on three occasions, over minor glitches. I offered to let him out of his contract. Full refund of earnest money, option deposits, change order deposits, the works. Full escrow back, every cent. I've never done that in my life."

I stretched my neck, trying to earn relief for my sloping shoulders. "Fritz refused?"

Dennis nodded grimly, tossing the ball from hand to hand. "He estimates he has $30,000 in appreciation waiting for him at closing. I can't stand the son of a bitch. I was looking forward to his closing on September 21. I couldn't wait to get rid of him."

"It wouldn't have ended there. The closing's the middle of the relationship with a builder, not the end."

"You're probably right. Jubera would have had a twenty-page punch list and sued me if I didn't fix every little problem. I can't stand the thought of that jerk living in one of my properties. I'd almost rather have it burn to the ground than turn it over to him."

"Legally, you don't have to rebuild?"

Dennis set the ball on his desk with a decisive smack. "Not for him. In the purchase agreement, we promise substantial completion of the property six months after the start of framing. If it's delayed past that, either party can terminate the contract. I'm sending Fritz a notice of termination this week."

"You can't complete the house within the six-month time frame?"

He smiled slyly. "I can, but I won't. This is my chance to get rid of the jackass."

"Could Fritz Jubera have set fire to the Southfield house?"

Dennis McBride didn't hesitate. "To spite me? Damn right."

"Do you have any other people who hate you?"

He bellowed with laughter. "I couldn't begin to name them all."

"Try," I said pleasantly. "Any ex-employees?"

He stared at me as if I were brain dead. "This is the construction trade. We fire as many as we hire."

"Could I look over the employment records of every employee you've fired in the last six months?"

Dennis picked up a wooden letter opener and began to rub its handle. "Be my guest. I'll have my human resources gal make copies."

"Meanwhile, let's compile a list of other people who might wish you harm."

"How much time do you have?" he said, almost proudly.

Two minutes later, I had the names of nineteen people who had ongoing feuds with Dennis McBride.

Those were the ones he could remember off the top of his head, but he promised more.

"Do you have any suggestions about where to begin?" I said, disconcerted by the crowd.

He came around the desk, leaned over me, and flicked at the first name on the page. "Daphne Cartwright."

I looked up. "Any particular reason Daphne—"

Dennis McBride spoke over my words. "She thinks I tried to kill her family."

Clover Valley Press
publishes quality books written by women.

For more information about our books, go to
http://clovervalleypress.com

CPSIA information can be obtained
at www.ICGtesting.com
Printed in the USA
FFOW02n0724241114
8945FF